I0550172

Diversion Protocol

T. James LeDoux

Published by Alpha Group 3 LLC

Paperback book edition created 2018

ISBN 9780985226671

BISAC Classification: Fiction/Thrillers/Espionage - FIC006000

Cover picture: Graphic of a man and woman in the crosshairs as others are searching and aircraft are approaching their position.

Dedications

To my beautiful wife, Marilyn, whose patience, proofreading, attention to detail and advice did much to help make this book a reality.

Table of Contents

Chapter 1

Two Messages

"I send out intelligence and espionage teams to find out what threats there are to the United States. If the threat is great enough, we try to eliminate it by either direct contact or misinformation. Every time I send a team out, I know they are going into harm's way at great risk to themselves to keep the American citizen free to fulfill their dreams. I wish there was an easier way." – Rear Admiral Evan Roedl, US Navy Special Operations Group, ONI

It was a warm day in Washington, DC on July 11, 2017 as U.S. Navy Commander Elizabeth Norman sat down in Admiral Roedl's office in the Special Operations Section at the Office of Naval Intelligence (ONI) in the Kennedy Irregular Warfare Center. She turned toward the door that was the entrance to the office to look at the time. 10:05 AM in the morning and the Admiral said he wanted to meet her at 10:00 hours. It wasn't like him to be late.

She looked around the room, recognizing the very familiar layout had not changed much in the last two years. There was a desk in the center of the room that was heavy oak and very organized. On the desk was the obligatory phone, desk pad, a set of rubber stamps on a stand used for stamping documents and a nameplate reading 'E. Roedl, RADM' with a pen holder on one side with a gold pen in it. A computer monitor sat on his desk to the right side with the keyboard just in front of it. Behind the desk was a picture of a sea battle, obviously something out of World War II but, according to Lieutenant Lawson, was actually a high-resolution screen with a heavy wooden, very ornate frame around the screen. To her left was a wall with certificates, awards and trophies with a door at the end of the wall. On the right, another wall exhibited pictures of a guy that liked to play golf, go fishing and liked football. Below the pictures were a set of cabinets running the length of the wall. Behind her, above the door was the clock she had just checked and to the sides of the door was a calendar on one side (the typical three-month government calendar with last month at the top, the present month in the center and next month at the bottom) and a picture of the President of the United States on the other side.

A U. S. Navy Commander, Beth Norman was a rather attractive woman with an ability to remain unseen even in a small group. After graduating from the U.S. Naval Academy, she spent several years working as a liaison officer within the Defense Intelligence Agency (DIA). For the past two years, she worked closely with Admiral Roedl, head of Office of Naval Intelligence's Special Operations Group. Her personality allowed for her to not draw attention to herself which made her one of Admiral Roedl's best spies while also having the ability to speak both English and Farsi. She had brunette hair with a captivating smile and was five feet, six inches tall. Commander Norman had developed a good friendship with a coworker by the name of Lieutenant Lawson and, in the process, they developed a more intimate relationship. A relationship that Admiral Roedl kept a close eye on to ensure the interaction didn't interfere with operations. Lawson saw her as a paradox. He told Petty Officer Myers one time that she was like a cat, very caring and compassionate but could kill without hesitation if it meant not doing so would cause a mission to fail. They both respected each other's opinions and advice. Commander Norman was in charge of the most recent operation for the team identified as CAT205.

That operation was to break a cypher code that was found to contain a software program that could have started World War III.

Norman leaned back in the chair that faced the desk, unfolded a sheet of paper and looked at the message on the paper marked with a 'Classified' stamp. It was from Captain Wallace at the Pentagon by the direction of Admiral Johnson to activate 'Operation Shiny Object'. The activation of this operation sent chills across Commander Norman's body as she read the memo once more. Why was a worst-case scenario exercise agreed to by numerous military leaders around the world suddenly a reality? As she was thinking about the questions surrounding why the leadership would activate this operation, Admiral Roedl walked through the doorway and walked to his desk.

"Good morning, Commander," Admiral Roedl greeted as he turned to his chair and sat down.

"Good morning, Sir," Norman responded.

Rear Admiral Evan Roedl was a Rear Admiral Upper Half with two stars on his epaulettes. At six feet, one inch in height, he tended to loom over those he commanded. He was meticulous in his appearance, work area and expectations. At the same time, he was inclined to go rogue when the rules got in the way of his operations, which tended to irritate other officers in the Navy and Marine Corps. A graduate of Notre Dame with a Masters of Business Administration from Harvard, he started his career in the U. S. Navy later than most but moved up quickly to his present rank. As head of the Special Operations group at the Office of Naval Intelligence, he was known for getting things done. An operation in Iran initiated by Admiral Roedl a couple of years earlier put the U.S. into a situation that was of a questionable nature with the results impacting Admiral Roedl's reputation. Many of the officers familiar with the operation felt that his actions put the US on the edge of a major conflict. Tensions settled down but the opinions did not.

Looking down at the sheet of paper in Norman's lap, he commented, "I see you got the memo. I know there are a lot of questions so we need to get down to business."

"I have so many questions I don't know…," she started to say when the Admiral interrupted her.

"I understand," Roedl stated. "The 'Shiny Object' scenario was only to be initiated when we were able to identify a real international threat posed against multiple nations at the same time but had no way to determine what that threat was."

Norman looked down at the sheet once more. "But Sir," she protested, "for 'Shiny Object' to be activated there has to be a threat threshold met so high as to suspect that several first or second-level nations are in imminent risk. Has that threshold been met?"

"We feel it has been met," Roedl responded. "I'll give you the details once the rest of the team gets here. Now, as to your part in this mission, you'll be going to Volgograd, Russia as a part of the diplomatic mission to discuss the ISIS threats in the Middle East. You'll be meeting with a Captain Pavel Volkov of the Russian Diplomatic Corps. He will be your host. He also has background information on this perceived threat and, although your apparent function is to support the planning for the removal of ISIS, your primary function will be to find out what the Russians have on this threat."

Norman shifted in her chair as she began to realize that everyone was feeling around in the dark about the threat. She nodded her head exhibiting she understood the Admiral's comments. They continued their discussion with general topics on how the team was doing, what training they were getting and the condition of everyone's emotional status when the rest of the team came into the room.

U.S. Navy Lieutenant James Lawson was first to enter. Now a Navy Lieutenant, he was a U.S. Navy Second Class Petty Officer with a rating of Intelligence Specialist when he was selected for a mission to get documents from a research center in Iran. He was successful and, as a result, was promoted to Lieutenant after the mission and put in charge of the newly formed CAT205 team. Later, he and the CAT205 team, while under the direction of Commander Norman, was successful in preventing a Chinese Colonel by the name of Qiang Zhu from launching a nuclear attack on North Korea that would make it look like the U.S. was the attacker.

At five feet, nine inches in height, light brown hair, fair complexion and a good physical build, Lawson had no problems keeping up with the hectic demands of the Navy. He spoke English and Russian, having graduated from the Russian language training school at the Defense Language Institute in Monterrey, California a year earlier. Before entering the Navy, he attended Carnegie-Mellon University with a major in electrical engineering but had to leave in the last semester of his senior year due to lack of funds as he refused to indebt himself with a student loan. Once he left college, he joined the Navy and attended the U.S. Navy's 'Navy and Marine Corps Intelligence Training Center' at the Naval Air Station Oceana Dam Neck Annex in Virginia. He was sent on a short stint to Naval Station,

Rota, Spain then to the aircraft carrier USS Theodore Roosevelt. While on the Roosevelt, Lawson was instrumental in identifying threats to the Roosevelt while they were in the Persian Gulf after which he was selected for the mission in Iran. Known for his attention to detail and recognizing patterns in people's actions and events, he was sought for his opinions concerning motives and outcomes. He exhibited a sense of authority that kept other intelligence officers wondering what his real rank was.

The next person coming through the door was U.S. Navy Second Class Petty Officer Nicholas Myers. He was an MIT Graduate with a Master's degree in wave energy technology and, as a highly skilled electronics technician, had an ability to fix anything electronic with a minimum of tools. Besides being able to program at assembly-level and machine code on a computer and modifying it, he was also an expert at fixing communications and cryptographic equipment. With a normal physical build, his five feet, nine inch frame exhibited the wear of his thirty-four years of experience.

Being black and from East Boston, he had experience getting out of trouble by using logic, which worked most of the time. He revealed a level of brilliance at an early age which resulted in a four year scholarship to MIT in Massachusetts upon his graduation from high school at age 17. His grasp of advanced mathematics and technology was so extensive that several major corporations working on leading-edge automation got into a bidding war to get him. He chose the Navy instead. He spoke English, with a slight Bostonian accent, Russian and Farsi. He was a Christian that had planned to be a minister but events changed his plans. After he went up in rank in the Navy, he refused to be promoted to being a naval officer because as he explained, "Officers do nothing but paperwork and I only want to work on the newest technology." He was part of the team that worked with Lawson to get the Polevsky Papers at the Iranian research facility and, in a later mission, to break the code to stop a nuclear attack on North Korea by a rogue organization.

The final person coming in was U.S. Marine Master Gunnery Sergeant Arnoud 'Gunny' Glendenning. Whereas most Master Gunnery Sergeants would be called 'Master Gunny', Glendenning wanted to be called 'Gunny' because, according to him, calling him 'Master Gunny' took up too much time in a critical situation. A career Marine at six feet, one inch tall with dark brown hair, blue eyes and a moderately rugged build, he spoke English and Russian with an Irish accent. Going by the book, he was always impeccably dressed in uniform and held all enlisted personnel to the rules, no exceptions. Experienced in weapons, security and combat, he previously maintained security records and directed weapons maintenance for all personnel in the Kennedy Irregular Warfare facility. He was an expert with both rifle and pistol. A Marine Colonel on the shooting range commented one time that Gunny 'could shoot the eye off a fly at one-hundred yards'. His demeanor seemed to indicate that he was a typical Marine but his instincts and quiet character demonstrated a level of maturity and wisdom that helped keep those he worked with out of trouble. He was part of the team that worked with Lawson and Myers in the previous two missions.

"Gentlemen, please be seated," Admiral Roedl motioned with his hand as he picked up a folder that was obviously highly classified. Breaking the seal on the folder, he opened it up and pulled two sheets of paper from a divider in the folder. "Here are the two messages that caused us to activate 'Operation Shiny Object'." Everyone watched as he looked down at the pages in his hand.

"Who are these messages from," Lawson questioned. Roedl looked up at Lawson then back down at the sheets without answering.

"The first message is as follows," Roedl started. "It says 'Global shift won't happen without test run. We can't assume it will work coming out of the doors'. Now that message got us interested but not to any level of concern. This second message was the one that got our attention. It states 'The ability to assassinate can only be performed using swarm rather than relying on single entity. Five possibilities. End of July target'. Both of these messages were sent heavily encrypted and it took our guys four days to decrypt them. Now, as to Lawson's question, they both came from a person called 'Peacock' and one message is sent to someone named 'Ormack' and the second to 'Trechko'. One message was sent to an IP address in the Fergana valley in Uzbekistan near Osh, Kyrgyzstan. The other IP address was spoofed, we couldn't track it."

"Any idea what the messages relate to?" Lawson questioned as Roedl brought up the map of the area in question on the screen behind his desk.

"We feel it's something quite serious but not much to go on," Roedl answered while pointing to the screen. "You'll all be going to Osh, Kyrgyzstan, which is south of the Fergana Valley, but by different routes. Gunny and Myers will go together. I've arranged for Myers to meet with an Uzbekistani Professor by the name of Magnus Murodov at the Osh Technological University. According to contacts in Kyrgyzstan, he may have some knowledge of the activities in the area. Myers will be meeting him as a part of the technology sharing agreements we have with Kyrgyzstan. Gunny will go as Myers' aide. Norman will be going to Volgograd first then on to Osh. Lawson will be going to Crete then on to Osh. Any questions?"

"What am I seeing this Professor Murodov about?" Myers queried.

"It's in your itinerary," Roedl responded while handing each of them their tickets and itineraries. "You'll be discussing wave energy capture for electrical generation as the reason for the visit but your real goal is to see what he can tell you about what's going on in the area that makes these messages important."

Lawson was examining his travel documents as an expression of confusion began to show on his face. It was obvious to Roedl that Lawson was ready to hear his role.

"Lawson, you are to be the red herring," Roedl explained as he looked at Lawson's expression. "We feel that there are enough people that have seen the messages in both the analysis center and the Pentagon that the potential for a leak is significant and someone will be following the team so Lawson is to draw them off. If this situation is as impactful as we think it might be we want to take precautions to ensure we get to our destinations. By the way, an analyst from the Pentagon will be joining you in Osh thanks to Lawson's recommendation during your last mission. Joanne Benson will be joining you in Osh." Lawson smiled then grimaced as he heard the name.

"Sorry guys," Lawson lamented, "she was in a meeting with the Admiral and me and I couldn't let her get away with that elitist attitude of hers without challenging her to try to do our jobs."

"Great going," Gunny called out as he hit Lawson in the arm. Smiling, he continued, "We'll just have to put her to work." Everyone laughed as they got up to go.

"Now, as we have posed to each of you before each mission, does anyone have any reason or conscience-based reservations for carrying out this mission?" Roedl queried as he looked at each of them as the each nodded 'no'. "Myers, any concerns that conflict with your religious beliefs?"

"No, Sir," Myers answered, "as long as I'm not asked to take out an unarmed person, I'm good."

"Gunny has that responsibility if the occasion should ever occur. Lawson, stay behind," Roedl ordered as he stood up and wished them all well. Lawson sat down then continued to look at his travel documents.

Roedl sat back down as he looked at Lawson then the folder. "You'll be the person people will follow. You're the best known of the group seeing that your name is all over the orders at the Pentagon and, if someone has been tipped off to our breaking the code on the messages, you'll be the person they most likely will shadow. For that reason, you're going to Crete where you will take a ship from Crete to Volgograd. It'll take about four days to travel which, by that time, Myers should have some information. Norman should also have something by that time if the Russians know anything."

"So, what if I am followed?" Lawson questioned.

"The most likely place they will try to get to you is in Crete," Roedl replied. "If you are followed, there is a restaurant listed at the bottom of your itinerary that I added to the page after I received them. Go to that restaurant and you will meet a man there that will identify himself as 'Cory'. He will give you instructions and additional documents for you to get out of Crete. Be alert as it appears whoever is behind this threat has a lot of pull and may involve authorities in the attempt to stop you. We know they have a lot of pull by their ability to hide what they are doing at such a high level in numerous governments. Now get going. Your military flight leaves from Andrews in two hours and there's not another flight to Italy until tomorrow. You still need to be on your guard when you get to Italy but making your first appearance on a commercial flight in Rome to Crete should catch anyone by surprise that might want to follow. Still, I think Crete is where the threat should be. Remember to adapt and overcome if you run into problems."

Lawson stood up and smiled at Roedl. "Admiral, it's always an adventure doing business with you," he said while walking toward the door. "Joanne Benson, nice move, Sir." Roedl just grinned and sat down. The operation was active and the mission engaged, time to call the White House.

Lieutenant Lawson went out of Admiral Roedl's office, through the waiting room then through the security vault to get into the hallway. There he found Gunny Glendenning, Commander Norman and Petty Officer Myers waiting for him.

"Have you seen what your orders are, Jim?" Myers asked Lawson. Lawson pulled out the papers from the manila envelope and scanned them for anything that would stand out.

"What's Operation Shiny Object's objective?" he inquired as he looked over the orders. "It says here that we are to determine who and what the threat is that could bring down several key nations. Talk about looking for a needle in a haystack."

Norman explained to them what the 'Shiny Object' scenario was about. They all considered her words as they looked at their orders.

"So it seems that we have little to go on except for this Professor Murodov in Osh that Myers is supposed to meet, the Russian Captain in Volgograd that Norman is supposed to meet and the two messages that Roedl read to us," Lawson declared as he weighed the enormity of the task ahead of them. "What is the timeframe we have to get all this done? It doesn't give us that reference point except the mention of the end of July in one of the messages."

Norman thought over what Lawson had said. He was right. What urgency was attached to the operation? There were no real indicators of what the top brass thought was essential concerning the importance of getting an answer. She just looked at each of them then put her orders back in her envelope. She wondered how Lawson knew about the Russian Captain she was supposed to meet since Lawson was not in the room when Admiral Roedl told her about Captain Volkov.

"Well, we better get our civilian clothes on and turn our seabags into logistics for storage," Gunny advised. "We all have flights to catch and, Lawson, from what I see on your orders, your flight leaves in an hour and a half." Lawson agreed that they all had to get moving.

Lawson shook hands with Gunny and Myers and wished them a safe trip. Turning to Norman, he motioned toward the main entrance and started walking down the hall to exit the Kennedy Irregular Warfare facility.

"You be careful, Beth," Lawson stated as he took hold of her hand. "I don't want to hear that you've gotten sidelined due to some minor mistake." Norman pulled him to her. Looking around to be sure no one was watching, she kissed him and hugged him tightly.

"I'll be seeing you in Osh, Jim," she whispered. "You're the one that needs to be careful. You're the one everyone will be following. You know we work against people well trained and full of tricks so be on your guard." Lawson smiled at her as they walked out the door of the facility, took off their weapons and put them in their briefcases.

"See you later, Lady," Lawson stated as he and Norman went off in different directions.

Lawson changed his clothes, turned in his gear and went to Andrews Joint Base for a flight from Andrews to Aviano US Air Force Base in Aviano, Italy. He was surprised to find that he was taking a US Air Force F-15 Strike Eagle aircraft to Italy. The two-seater aircraft would get him there in four to five hours. From there, he would take a helicopter to Rome and get a commercial flight to the island of Crete.

Gunny and Myers went to Dulles for a flight to Amsterdam then Moscow and from there to Osh, Kyrgyzstan. Their travels would take them twenty-five hours to get to Osh.

Norman went back to her apartment, changed clothes and turned her gear into the Logistics Center. Getting a check number for her bags from the Logistics Center, she headed off to

Dulles International Airport for her flight to Paris. She would have to travel from Paris through Moscow to get to Volgograd, Russia scheduled for some eighteen hours after takeoff from Dulles.

Chapter 2

The Volgograd Incident

"The problem of being an espionage agent is that you don't know when you're seeing the truth and when you're being played. Either condition is fraught with dangers because where does the truth end and the lie begin?"
– Commander Elizabeth Norman, US Navy CAT205 Special Operations Group Team Coordinator, ONI

Commander Norman's flights were uneventful except for the long wait due to the weather in Moscow. Leaving from Dulles at 5:20 PM on July 11th, it took her twenty-four hours to get to Volgograd, Russia. She arrived at Volgograd at 2:30 AM, July 13th and took a taxi to the Volgograd Hotel, a twenty-five minute drive.

"You'll be at the Hotel entrance by 3:00 AM," the taxi driver informed her as they started from the airport. "Don't worry about your safety. We have a number of security people keeping an eye on anyone that may follow." Norman was surprised by the comment.

"Do you know who I am?" she questioned while looking at him in his rearview mirror.

"Yes," came his reply. "You're Commander Elizabeth Norman, sent here to meet Captain Pavel Volkov. He's waiting for you." Norman felt uncomfortable at the level of knowledge the taxi driver had concerning her visit. Did they watch everyone this closely? She just sat back in the seat wondering what other surprises they had in store for her.

As she arrived at the hotel, a man dressed in a Russian captain's uniform came out to the taxi and opened the door. "Good early morning to you, Mrs. Norman. I am Captain Pavel Volkov of the Russian Diplomatic Corps." Norman stepped out of the car and looked around.

Captain Pavel Volkov was a well-built, squared-jawed handsome man at age 38. Standing at five feet, eleven inches in his immaculately pressed and fitted uniform, he exhibited the epitome of order. The nine millimeter pistol on his belt rounded out the image of a man with a purpose. Captain Volkov had been in the Russian Diplomatic Corps for the past seven years. Prior to that time he had attended the Bauman Moscow Technical University getting a Masters in Electrical Engineering. After graduating, he was assigned to the Skoldovo Center in 2009. Skoldovo was a sort of Russian Silicon Valley of high-tech companies that Hillary Clinton tried to help to improve by encouraging companies like Google, Intel Corp and Cisco to engage with the center's operations. Volkov's ability to bring parties together in technical negotiations during this time led to his selection to the Diplomatic Corps.

"Why don't we go inside to talk," she suggested as she watched the driver get her bags from the trunk of the car and, intrinsic from her training, observed the surrounding area for the layout and for any threats. The main entrance consisted of several large archways made of highly-polished brick and stone with a glass rotary door in the center of the entrance. There were green plants and small trees around the entrance that had the strong fragrance of blossoms. They entered through the rotary door while the driver took the bags through a hinged door to the side of the rotary door.

Once the driver sat the bags down in front of the registration desk, he got the attention of the attendant and pointed toward Norman. The attendant at the counter nodded and proceeded to type some information on a keyboard at the counter. Norman noted all of the activity going on while Captain Volkov found a place for them to sit in the lobby. The lobby was well furnished with mahogany walls set between large windows that looked to the outside. There were large plants spread throughout the lobby with a large Maroon Persian rug covering the middle of the lobby's hardwood floor. Captain Volkov selected one of the 5 groups of tables, each having 5 large leather chairs around them, that were neatly organized throughout the lobby. Norman noted that, even at 3:00 AM, there were a number of people up and reading newspapers and magazines in different parts of the lobby. As she glanced around it struck her – they all were watching her and, from what she could see, they were all armed.

"I see you've fleshed out that these are not just travelers," Volkov observed as he watched her actions. "They are all members of my security team, ensuring that you will not be bothered." Norman was impressed by the Captain's use of the English language. It was perfect with no accent and had a full range of the nuances that are difficult for a person to acquire that has not been raised with the language. At that moment she wished that Lawson was here to give her a reading of what was really going on.

"I see you are concerned about the level of precautions we are taking," Volkov stated. "They think you are here for the ISIS talks. They don't know the real reason. Now, I have some pictures for you to look at. I know you are tired and want to get to bed but we have a couple of housekeeping things we need to do before you go to your room, so first, the pictures." Norman took the pictures from his hand and went through them one by one. After going through all eight of them, she handed them back to him.

"Anyone you recognized," Volkov posed as he held the pictures in his hand.

"No," Norman responded. "What else do we need to do?" Volkov started to put the pictures in his pocket when she stopped him. "Let me see those pictures again." Volkov handed her the pictures and, upon receiving them, she stopped at one picture that held her attention.

"Something catch your eye?" Volkov queried.

"This one, this Chinese guy," Norman responded.

"He may be Chinese as his name seems to reflect that but I think he's Kyrgyz," Volkov opined. "You see, the city of Osh is made up of two very dissimilar cultures. The Kyrgyz have very oriental, or as you would call, Chinese facial features. The Uzbeks have very European facial features. Both cultures have a tendency to clash in Osh. You see, the city is truly where east meets west."

Norman looked at the picture again, "What is this person's name?"

Volkov turned the picture over and looked at the back. "His name is Cho Ming but I think that the name is not real. He has many long-term contacts in the northern part of the Fergana Valley which is about forty miles north of Osh. I know he's been around for the past year and probably a lot longer as he was located up in the valley when Osh police took over patrol responsibilities from the Uzbekistani government last year in an agreement with them. The Fergana Valley is part of Uzbekistan but their police forces are focused around Tashkent so they have limited ability to monitor the border area near Osh. As such, the Kyrgyzstani government agreed to cover the area since some of the crime in Osh was from that northern area and the Uzbekistanis were doing nothing about it."

Norman looked at the picture once more and handed the picture back to Volkov as she continued to search the recesses of her memory, "I know I've seen him before but I don't know where."

"Well, if it comes to you, let me know," Volkov said as he reached into his pocket and pulled out a jump drive. "This drive has a number of documents and diagrams I want you to look at. All of the documents have been translated to English so that you can review them. You can look at them after you get some sleep."

"What languages were they translated from," Norman asked as she took the jump drive. A good question Volkov thought as he pondered his answer.

Looking down at a notebook, he flipped through the pages until he came to the page of interest. "Several of the documents were in Kyrgyz, several in Russian. Remember, a lot of people still speak Russian in Osh because Kyrgyzstan used to be a Russian satellite country. Diagrams were in Kyrgyz and Chinese." Norman realized that the Chinese were somehow involved as the comment on some of the diagrams being in Chinese caught Norman's attention.

"Chinese, you say," Norman commented. "Let me see those pictures again." Volkov handed her the pictures and she went to the one labeled 'Cho Ming'. "I need to verify it but I am sure this is a picture of Qiang Zhu, the rogue Chinese Colonel that disappeared last year after an attempt to launch a nuke missile attack against North Korea to start a war between the U.S. and China." Volkov sat up in his chair as a couple of the other people closest to Norman looked up from their newspapers. The name struck a nerve.

"We need to verify your observation," Volkov advised as he took the picture and put it back in his pocket. "You have a computer in your room. Once you get some sleep, check the documents on the jump drive. You need to be able to give your opinion on them after our ISIS rules of engagement meeting. The ISIS meeting is at 1:00 PM today. You'll have security people guarding the hallway where your room is located. We'll be meeting with Ivan Sergevich at the Volgograd Technical Institute later today at 6:00 PM. He may have some information on what this threat is about. If your hunch is true that the picture is that of Colonel Zhu, it's a game changer. Well, go to you room and get some sleep. Your bags are already there. The lady at the counter has your room key."

Norman got up and staggered as she realized how exhausted she was. Getting the key from the counter, she headed up to her room.

The room was a typical hotel room. The bed took up most of the room with a separate room for the bathroom. The main room had a set of drawers with a vintage color TV on it that required the person to change channels by turning the turner knob on the TV. A chair sat next to the dresser while a small percolator coffee pot sat on the dresser with a small can of coffee, dry coffee creamer, sugar and a coffee cup. A small table next to the room's only window had a laptop computer on it and a pad of paper with a chair in front of the table. There was one light on a table next to the head of the bed. A drape covered the window that could be opened to go out to a small balcony. Norman undressed and fell into bed.

It was 10:15 AM when Norman woke up. Setting up the coffee maker to get a cup of coffee, she looked at the desk with the laptop computer on it. Once she turned on the computer, she saw the request for a password and wondered if the Captain had forgotten something. Figuring the Captain was too thorough to miss the obvious need for a password, she looked first at her room key then the card that the key was presented with, still nothing. Frustrated at her dilemma, she took a shower and got dressed. She pulled out the jump drive from her pocket and wondered if there was another way to read it. As she turned the jump drive over, she saw the tape on the back of the drive with the characters 'sw8&21P'. It was obvious to her that this was the password. She entered the password, saw the familiar desktop appear on the screen and plugged the jump drive into the USB port. Satisfied that she was able to access the jump drive, she poured that first cup of ever essential coffee.

It was a couple of hours of reading and analyzing before she realized that the threat could be anything. The diagrams got most of her interest. One diagram was for some type of computer or controller circuitry while another diagram was of an aircraft. The aircraft one was most peculiar and had measurements too small for a normal aircraft. Since this drawing was originally Chinese, Norman remembered that the Chinese were famous for creating drawings that required additional individual formulas for vertical, horizontal and depth calculations to get to the correct measurements. Without those formulas, it was almost impossible to replicate the design.

There were also several documents that caught her attention. One was of a formula for fuel that Norman recognized would be used for getting the greatest efficiency from a combustion engine. There was another document that defined how the shape of an explosive charge had to be made to force the blast forward. A third document exhibited aircraft turn rates at high G's and where the stress points would be at on an aircraft. As she was reading the documents there was a knock on the door.

"Who is it?" she called out as she turned from the computer.

"It's Captain Volkov," came the reply. Norman went to the door and did a quick glance through the peep hole. Seeing it was the Captain, she opened the door and let him in.

"You're about an hour early," she said while walking back to the computer, all the time watching his reflection in the window to see his movements behind her. Her nature was always to take precautions if she didn't fully trust those she was in contact with and to use every advantage to know what was going on around her. Some might think this was being paranoid but, in her business, it was a key element of survival.

"So, have your come to any conclusions?" Volkov asked as he sat down in the chair next to the TV.

Norman pointed to the computer screen. "From the diagrams I've looked at, it appears that this is an aircraft that can be piloted by a human or by remote control. The dimensions don't look right so I suspect that you need additional formulas for get the proper dimensions. There also appears to be designs for a forward-blast shaped charge though, again, I don't know the amount of the explosive due to additional formulas being needed for measurements."

"So, from what you're saying, it definitely appears to be a Chinese design," Volkov opined as he pulled out a cigarette.

"Don't light that in my room," Norman exclaimed, "and yes it appears to be a Chinese design or a design by someone trained in Chinese methods,"

Volkov put the cigarette back in his case as he spoke, "So, based upon your analysis what do you think this aircraft is to be used for?"

Norman looked once more at the screen. "I think it is some form of a Kamikaze aircraft."

"In other words, a suicide attack aircraft like the Japanese created at the end of World War II," Volkov stated as he looked at the diagram on the screen.

"True," Norman acknowledged, "but this one can also be controlled by remote control which makes it another form of drone aircraft." Volkov nodded agreement as he got up to leave.

"1:00 PM, second floor conference room in the hotel. Don't be late," Volkov instructed as he walked out the door. Norman looked at her watch and realized that she had 15 minutes to get things shut down before she had to get to the conference room.

The meeting was short but heated at times. There were a number of interested parties in the room for the meeting. The Russian contingent of five officers was led by a Colonel Machinko of the Russian air combat wing in Syria. Colonel

Machinko was a heavy-set man that appeared to be somewhere in his forties. His face was full and exhibited years of hardship with a slight sagging of his mouth on one side that Norman felt was either from a minor stroke or a wound received many years ago. The intensity of his eyes and the forcefulness of his voice told Norman that this was a man that you didn't mess with. He was the most vocal of the Russian team and continuously pressing for the US air wings to stand down and not be involved in Syria. Commander Norman held her ground stating, that without the US air presence, Turkey and Russia would use the engagement as an excuse to wipe out the northern Kurdish tribes. An unacceptable condition. The meeting ended with both sides agreeing to honor the air spaces previously defined with one condition. The US forces would be able to go after the ISIS forces in eastern Syria to which Machinko agreed with reservations. Everyone shook hands and left the room except for Norman, Volkov and Machinko.

"Captain Volkov tells me that you think the Chinese aircraft designs are for a Kamikaze-type aircraft," Machinko stated as Norman looked up from her computer and realized that Machinko was also here mainly for the Shiny Object operation.

"Yes, that's the premise I'm working on," Norman responded as she brought up the design sheet.

"This is nothing new," Machinko lectured. "You Americans have a similar drone called 'Switchblade' made by a company called AeroVironment in California. The only problem with this design we see on this screen is that we don't know how big or small it is. I'm still curious why your government activated Shiny Object. These designs are not new so what is the major threat to our nations?"

"It's more than the design, Colonel," Norman answered, all the while wondering why she was defending the decision when she had the same concerns. "We also believe that there may be an assassination plan tied to these documents."

"I know. I read the two messages. They are somewhat cryptic," He replied back. "We will assist you any way we can but we are not going to be directly involved. It was good meeting you, Commander. Maybe someday we can sit in a nice restaurant in Moscow and drink some vodka to our peaceful relations." Machinko shook hands with Norman, nodded to Captain Volkov and opened the door. "Peaceful relations," he laughingly exclaimed as he walked out the door. "Either a dream or a nightmare. Depends on who is in control." Norman watched Machinko leave, looked at Volkov and realized Machinko was right. It does depend on who is in control.

Norman and Volkov met Dr. Ivan Sergevich at the Volgograd Technical Institute at 6:00 PM with all three going down to the cafeteria in the Engineering building on the campus. From Dr. Sergevich's appearance, Norman felt that he was the typical stereotype of the mad scientist. He had long, flowing dark brown hair, a beard that could use some trimming and a slender frame highlighted by a white lab coat with a badge that revealed he was in charge of the 'Automation and Control of Technological Processes and Productions' program. Norman smiled at the thought as she ordered a cheese sandwich from the cafeteria counter.

Volkov thought Dr. Sergevich's input might help get a better understanding of the diagrams Norman analyzed. After getting food and drink, they went to a table at the far end of the cafeteria away from any curious ears. Sergevich looked over the diagrams as he ate a beef and cheese sandwich. His brilliance became apparent almost immediately.

"There are several questions with this design," Sergevich said as he took a bite of food and proceeded to flip from one diagram to another. "First question, why do they have a combustion engine when a battery-powered pusher blade would suffice and be much lighter? Second, what's with the cockpit? This has all the trademarks of a drone so why would a cockpit be needed? Third, the fuel formula would burn out the engine after, maybe, twenty-five to thirty minutes of flight. The fuel is too high performance for a carburetor-based aircraft engine. Fourth, the dimensions don't add up. The present dimensions wouldn't provide enough lift for the weight I'm figuring the aircraft has."

"So you're saying this design won't fly," Norman concluded.

"Not so fast," Sergevich warned. "Just because it doesn't look like it would fly with the diagrams we have doesn't mean that these are all of the diagrams for the craft. A double tail with a rear wing across both of the tail sections would provide additional lift plus it would counter the forward weight that would cause the nose to keep going down. It's a really temperamental design but it will do well when it goes after a target from above. This thing is built for dive speed."

"So what are your conclusions," Volkov asked.

"This is a one-way mission craft," Sergevich answered. "Like Commander Norman explained, this is a Kamikaze drone. Having a cockpit is not needed and is out in left field and according to the diagram, there is no instrumentation, no communications hookups for a pilot and no seat, only a large circular plug with what looks to be some 90 connections inside the plug at the rear of the compartment. It's either a design modified from a present pilot-driven design or it is using some new technique we haven't thought of." Norman paced the end of the cafeteria while Sergevich talked, all the while listening to his comments. She noted he was using terms like 'trademarks' and 'out in left field' indicating that he had lived in the US for some long duration of time. Maybe not important but interesting to her.

"Where is the camera on the aircraft that the drone control person would need to use to see how to get on the target?" Norman questioned.

Her question triggered a change in viewpoint for Sergevich. "The cockpit is not for a person, it's for a control module," he mused. "This drone design can be used for many purposes. The type of mission can be defined by the type of control module put into the cockpit!" They all looked at each other realizing the significance of what Sergevich just proclaimed. The adaptable design means that the drone could target anything – a vehicle, another aircraft, a ship, a person or a high-value facility based upon the module inserted into the drone. The territory of their operation just got bigger.

Volkov and Norman went back to the Volgograd Hotel, both thinking of what the diagram was meant to be used for and wondering how far the designers were to making the aircraft operational.

Norman had a restless night of sleep. The next morning, she got up, made some coffee, got a shower and dressed. She had put everything away in her suitcase and proceeded to look once more at the design on the computer when the phone range. It was Volkov.

"Get out of there immediately," he shouted in the phone. "My security team was pulled off on a false call and I suspect someone is coming after you."

Norman slammed down the phone and looked around. Her training kicked in as she looked at what she could use to defend herself. Looking at the door, she jumped into action. Going to the lamp next to the bed, she looked down at the power cord going from the lamp to the wall. There was a voltage reducer plugged into the wall socket. It was then she realized that the hotel was operating on 220 volts and the reducer was used to bring the voltage down to 110 volts for the lamp. Unplugging the lamp's power cord from the reducer, she picked up the lamp and, with all her strength, pulled the power cord from the lamp, exposing two copper wires at the end of the cord. As she did so, she could hear the creaking of the floor as footsteps approached her door.

Norman stepped into the bathroom. The wall socket was close to the entrance to the bathroom which was situated right next to the entrance to the room. Norman separated the two wires farther apart from each other so she wouldn't shock herself, pulled the wires from the plug and shoved each wire into one of the wall socket contacts in the bathroom. Next, she took a couple of plastic tooth picks from the wastebasket and shoved them into the wall socket to hold the wires going into the socket in place.

Gently laying down the cord on the bathroom counter, she looked around the room for another item. The large welcome book showing the services for the hotel caught her eye. It had a dark leather cover; just what she needed. As she went to pick it up she could hear the familiar ratcheting sound of a weapon, most likely a shotgun.

There was a knock on the door. "I have a delivery for an Elizabeth Norman," came the voice.

"Just leave it at the door," she called out.

"I can't," was the reply, "you have to sign for it."

"Leave it at the front desk," she answered.

"That won't work. It's from Ben. You have to sign for it," the voice responded.

"Just a minute," she shouted.

Stepping into the bathroom with the welcome book in her hand, she jiggled the door handle and put the welcome book up against the peep hole in the door. The book was long enough for her to keep her hand away from the center of the door. Half a second later a loud blast created a large hole in the door where the peep hole had been which resulted in the welcome book being knocked out of her hand, flying across the room and slamming against the window. Stunned from the blast, she stepped back into the bathroom. Immediately regaining her composure, she grabbed the two separate leads of the cord, one lead in each hand careful not to touch the copper wires. Stepping back toward the door, she saw a man's face come up to the opening created by the shotgun blast. Immediately, she lunged forward and hit the man's head with both leads causing a buzzing sound to occur followed by a pop and the lights dimming. The man was kicked back against the opposite wall in the hallway. Unlocking and opening the door, she looked down to see the shotgun on the floor. Grabbing the shotgun and pumping another round into the chamber, she swung the shotgun barrel toward him as he groggily pulled a pistol from his belt.

Norman pulled the trigger with the kick of the weapon catching her off balance causing her to fall back into the room. Looking up from the floor, she could see he would no longer be a problem.

Norman got up from the floor and pumped another round into the shotgun. She figured that if there was one person there may be more. Stepping back into the doorway, she could hear more footsteps. She swung the shotgun around to face the new threat.

"Don't shoot, it's Pavel," came the Captain's voice. "We need to get you out of here. Whatever it is that's being planned, they see you as a threat." At that time two more men came into the corridor as Norman turned the gun their direction. "They're my people!" Captain Volkov shouted. Norman pointed the shotgun down then handed it to Volkov. Turning to the man she shot, she took the pistol lying next to him and searched his pockets. Pulling out his wallet and another clip of ammo for the pistol, she handed the wallet to Volkov and put the clip in her pocket.

"Wait a minute," she exclaimed as she ran back into the room. Grabbing the jump drive from the computer and unplugging her rigged up power cable from the wall in the bathroom, she grabbed her suitcase and raced out the door. "We need to get out of here now!" she shouted as she ran toward the end of the hallway. "There will likely be more people coming to get us."

Volkov smiled then shouted some orders to the two men as he ran after Norman. Catching her at the end of the hallway, he took the suitcase from her hand and suggested they use the stairwell to exit rather than take the elevator. She agreed then went down the stairway to the lobby. Once out in the parking lot, they got into

Volkov's car and raced to the airport. He gave her a courier bag once they arrived at the airport.

"But this is a Russian diplomatic bag and I'm an American," she protested.

"You'll have no problem getting this through customs," Volkov said as he handed her a Russian courier card. They can't open or x-ray the bag and this card gives you full authority to carry that bag even though you're an American. There is a Russian nine millimeter pistol and two clips in the bag for your protection. Now give me the pistol you took from the man in the hallway." Norman realized that she had the gun in her hand the whole trip to the airport as though it was a part of her. She grinned sheepishly as she handed the weapon and the spare clip to Volkov.

"You take care my golubushka," Volkov whispered as he kissed her on each cheek. "Maybe we can have a drink of vodka together in Moscow when you visit next time and tell Lieutenant Lawson 'hi' for me." Norman found herself blushing as she held his hand to thank him.

"What does golubushka mean?" Norman queried.

"It means 'little dove'," Volkov answered. "It's a term of endearment. Lawson is a blessed man to have such a woman as you." It appeared to Norman that Volkov knew more about her and Lawson than she had suspected. She began to suspect that Captain Volkov was in the intelligence branch of the military. She had to admit that he was a charismatic and charming gentleman. She felt a special attachment to him after the past couple of days. He truly was her protector.

As she got on the plane to Moscow to get her to Osh, Kyrgyzstan, a thought crossed her mind. "How did Captain Volkov know Lawson?" Something to ask about later.

Volkov left the airport feeling a little like he had made another friend. "She is special and one of a kind," Volkov thought to himself. "Pretty, smart and of good character. I would hate to cross swords with her, though," he thought as he drove and then laughed about the thought. The day was full of blue skies and green meadows and he felt good to be alive.

Chapter 3

The Crete Diversion

"I'm not sure why I got into the intelligence racket. There is so much deception and lying required that a person begins to wonder how that affects their character and future. I guess it's not any different than how the senior officers deal with each other in the military. There is so much politics at that level that you never know what people's agendas are or what can be believed. I hate military politics and I'm glad I have Admiral Roedl to act as a buffer." – Lieutenant James Lawson, US Navy CAT205 Special Operations Group Commander, ONI

James Lawson arrived at Aviano Air Force Base just past 10:00 PM Italian time. As the F-15 Strike Eagle came to a halt, the pilot told Lawson through the intercom to quickly take off his helmet and flight suit, get his gear and go to the waiting helicopter that was up and running to their left. Lawson did as directed and got ready to run to the helo. He was stopped by the F-15 pilot.

"I don't know what your mission is, son," the pilot started, "but I have a feeling that with all the priorities and attention you're getting it's something big. Be careful out there." Lawson nodded acknowledgement and ran to the helo. An hour later, the helo landed at the Rome Leonardo da Vinci-Fiumicino airport and he was directed by the helo pilot to the entrance into the main concourse. He showed his ID to the security officer at the entrance and was directed to a customs table where they examined his carryon and passport before stamping his passport with an entry stamp.

Lawson rushed to the Vueling Airlines counter for a nonstop flight from Rome to Heraklion, Crete. It was now 11:10 PM and the flight leaves at 11:30 PM. After getting his ticket, he ran to the gate just in time to board. It was a rather empty flight as he went to his seat. He looked around to see if anyone could possibly be a threat, put his carryon under the seat then sat down as the attendant started the instructions on the passenger rules. Leaning back in his seat he looked at his ticket. He'd be arriving in Crete at around 3:00 AM. As the plane taxied onto the runway, he fell asleep. Lawson was abruptly awakened when the plane made a hard landing. As the plane taxied to the terminal the attendant got on the intercom. She said something obviously in Greek then repeated the message in English.

"We are sorry for that harsh landing, ladies and gentlemen," she apologized. "Welcome to Heraklion, Crete. It is 3:05 AM. We had to set down rather quickly as there is nighttime maintenance going on at the other end of the runway so our landing strip is shorter than normal. Please have your passports out and ready for customs examination once you enter the airport."

Lawson went through customs then got on the reservation phone to a hotel near the port area and had a shuttle pick him up. He was checked in and in bed by 4:15 AM.

Inspector Bernardakis was sitting at his desk in the Heraklion main police station when Sergeant Giannis Doukakis entered the Inspector's office. Bernardakis looked up at the clock. It was 6:15 AM. He had been in his office a short 15 minutes and was already being interrupted.

Theodore Bernardakis was a veteran police officer with thirty-two years under his belt. He came up through the ranks to be one of five inspectors in the police department. He was no nonsense with an ability to see through the game-playing that was prevalent in the criminal circles. At five foot, five inches in height he was shorter than the typical Greek-Crete citizen. He was just hitting fifty years of age and his 210 pounds of weight tended to slow him down which was why he always sent one of his officers to chase down suspects when they ran. His black hair and mustache made him appear typical Greek along with his unbridled tendency to want to dance when he heard the sound of a Cretan Lyra; a pear-shaped, three-stringed bowed instrument that was, many times, plucked to play a tune rather than use a bow like that for a violin.

"What is it, Doukakis?" the Inspector whined as he sat his coffee cup down.

"Inspector, there's a guy here from Interpol to see you," the police sergeant responded.

"A guy from Interpol, the irritant sent to punish me for my sinfulness," Bernardakis whined. "Did you verify his ID was a blue Interpol card with his picture on it and a gold seal with a globe, sword and scales in the upper right hand corner?"

"Yes, Sir. He's waiting in the lobby," Doukakis answered.

"Great, just what I need to start my day. Send him in," the inspector reluctantly instructed.

Doukakis exited the squad room and came back in with a man that appeared to be in his thirties, well-built with blond hair and impeccably dressed in a suit and tie. After following Doukakis into the inspector's office, the man held out his right hand to shake Bernardakis' hand while extending his Interpol ID with the other hand. Bernardakis glanced at the ID while shaking the man's hand.

"I am Nils Hauptmann, Detective Inspector of Interpol and we need your assistance," the man said as he sat down.

"You mean you demand our assistance," Bernardakis protested. "You guys at Interpol don't request anything. You tell us what you need and we're supposed to jump to your demands. Isn't that the way it works, Mr. Hauptmann?"

Hauptmann adjusted his glasses and answered. "That is true but we normally don't come to you unless it's a significant situation on your turf."

"What is it you want?" Bernardakis questioned in a grumbling tone all the while wishing he could rid himself of what was about to come.

Hauptmann reached into his leather folder and pulled out a picture. "This is James Lawson. He is an American wanted for multiple murders in Europe and is on the run after committing a murder yesterday in Berlin. We believe he has stolen some nuclear codes from a courier in Berlin and has landed here in Heraklion early this morning."

Bernardakis took the picture from Hauptmann and handed it to Sergeant Doukakis. "Make about forty copies of this picture and bring them back to me," Bernardakis instructed then continued in a derisive voice, "Now is there anything else we can help you with?"

Hauptmann ignored Bernardakis' slap as he looked down at his notes, speaking as he did so. "Some additional information you may need. We believe that Lawson is to meet someone here then take a ship to Volgograd this afternoon. The ship is at the shipping port here at Heraklion at pier 6 and her name is 'Dove'. She's a general cargo ship and an unkempt rust bucket due to go from the port at 2:45 PM today. Our records show that Lawson is on the manifest to go on that ship today. That being said, we don't want him apprehended until he meets whoever is going to meet him at the 'Limani Skoupidia Frourio' restaurant on the hill above the port area. Once he meets whoever it is, we can apprehend the whole group. By the way, let your people know he is armed and dangerous. Don't take any chances. I'll be tracking your activity so you don't need to contact me." Upon Hauptmann completing his comments, Inspector Bernardakis thanked Hauptmann and had one of his officers escort Hauptmann out of the facility.

When Sergeant Doukakis came back in with the pictures, Bernardakis instructed him as he handed one of Lawson's pictures to him, "Tell officers Papadakis and Kourakis to go to the Limani Skoupidia Frourio restaurant in the port area and watch for this guy. Tell them not to apprehend him or anyone with him until they are all together in the restaurant. Also tell them to carry their weapons as the suspect, James Lawson, is armed and dangerous. Now go."

Jim Lawson woke up around 9:30 AM, cleaned up and got dressed. Once he was ready for the morning, he opened up his manila envelope and got down to the details on his instructions. According to his instructions, he was to eat at the hotel and let people see him there. Once he had done that, he was to go to the 'Limani Skoupidia Frourio' restaurant that was about four blocks from the hotel. He is to meet a person with the name 'Cory' from the US embassy around noon. Lawson is to follow Cory's instructions.

Lawson had his breakfast in the hotel, checked out of the hotel and proceeded to the restaurant at approximately 11:30 AM. He surveyed his surroundings as he walked, noting that there were several people loading a truck with fish. Except for a random passing car, no other people seemed to be around. He entered the restaurant and waited for his eyes to adjust to the dark room.

The restaurant seemed to come out of some Jack London or Mickey Spillane novel. There was the bar with overhead lights above the bar and an eating area occupied by six round tables with four wooden chairs around each table. The eating area had two dim lights overhead which made the whole restaurant appear dark and foreboding. The air was filled with a mix of sea, booze and tobacco fragrances that reminded Lawson of some of the Spanish bars he had gone into in Rota, Spain in his early navy days. There was a mustiness about the room that was typical of every bar he had been in. There were two men in suits at the far end of the bar and a couple of people being served some type of fish plates at one of the tables. Lawson walked to a table that was nearest the corner of the wall as far away as he could get from the people at the bar or the table. He set his carryon bag under the table and his manila envelope on the table. As he did so, a rather large man dressed in the typical wear of a Greek fisherman walked into the restaurant and went to a table behind the men at the far end of the bar. The man was dressed in brown pants, a dark green shirt with a brown leather vest and a knit cap. He shouted something in Greek to the bartender at which point the bartender brought him a pitcher of beer and a glass.

Lawson was reading some of his paperwork while watching the two men at the bar and the fisherman in quick glances when he saw that one of the two men at the bar had a weapon on him. The two men seemed particularly interested in him and that made him nervous. As he was thinking about leaving, three other people came into the restaurant and approached his table; two men and one woman.

"Cory?" Lawson asked as he stood up to face the first man to approach.

"Mr. Lawson, is it?" came the man's response. Lawson nodded 'yes'.

"I'm Cory Jacobs from the US embassy annex here in Heraklion. This other gentleman is Mike Christopher and this young woman is Barb Sanderson. We are all diplomatic staff members." As they sat down, Jacobs shoved a black leather courier pouch under the table next to Lawson's carryon bag. Next, he placed a thick manila envelope on top of the paperwork Lawson was looking at then pulled a sheet of paper from his pocket. Lawson took the sheet of paper and kept an expressionless face while he looked at it. It was a picture of him with a lot of Greek writing above and under his picture. Even though Lawson couldn't read Greek, the picture was obviously not a positive statement about him. He turned his gaze to Jacobs as he waited for an answer.

Barb Sanderson was first to respond. "It's a wanted poster for your arrest on murder and nuclear theft charges. Apparently Interpol has put a bounty out on your head. It appears that you have awakened someone important."

"That said, we have a way of getting you to your destination," Jacobs said while pointing to the envelope he placed on the table. "Some of the effort will require your creativity and some we have already put in place to run some interference for you. In the envelope are another passport, driver's license and credit cards for you as a British subject by the name of 'John Rochester'. There is also a small envelope inside that has four bolts and four nuts in it. Do not lose them. The courier pouch under the table is a diplomatic pouch with a seal on it that will allow you to go through any airport without the pouch having to be scanned. The pouch contains three Maxim 9 silenced pistols and six clips of ammo as well as a computer and burner phones, so it's heavy. The envelope on the table has a courier card for your new ID as well as one for your present ID. Follow me so far?"

"I understand," Lawson acknowledged then continued. "There are two guys behind you at the bar that have been watching us intently. Also a third, big guy behind them that I'm not sure about."

"The big guy is Hiram," Jacobs explained. "He's one of ours. The two guys at the bar, they're local police officers most likely here to arrest you. Not to worry, Hiram will detain them. Now where was I, oh yes. When you leave here go out the establishment door, turn right and head to the intersection. At the intersection turn left and go four blocks. You'll come to a building that has a large envelope sign above the door. That's the mail drop-off building for the port area. They send the mail down to the ships from that building after they scan the mail for weapons, drugs and other essentials. It's the only way mail gets to the ships. You'll have to go this route because they'll be watching for you at the ship terminal security checkpoint."

As Jacobs was giving instructions Lawson noticed Hiram's head disappear from view at the other end of the room. A couple moments later he reappeared back to where he was sitting.

Jacobs continued his instructions. "Once you get to the mail facility you will meet a man named 'Georgios'. Follow his instructions. You must get to a cargo ship called the 'Dove' before Inspector Bernardakis and his officers get to the port. Now get going, we'll take care of the two officers. They can't stop us because we have diplomatic immunity."

Lawson took the paperwork and envelopes off of the table and put them into his carryon bag. As he was doing so he watched Hiram get up and go out the door. Grabbing his carryon bag and the courier pouch, Lawson got up and immediately walked to the exit as Jacobs and his people got up from the table. As Lawson reached the door he could hear a loud crash and a lot of unintelligible swearing. Looking back, Lawson could see the two men at the end of the bar trying to move forward with their ankles handcuffed to the lower rungs of their barstools. He looked back at Jacobs to see him and his team laughing while Jacobs was motioning with his hand for Lawson to go. Hiram had done his job. Lawson quickly headed out of the exit to the intersection and turned left, going four blocks to the mail facility.

As Lawson opened the door to the mail facility he could see that the room was well lighted with windows going around the whole room. There was a counter extending half the length of the room with a woman standing behind the counter. At the end of the counter was a large bin with several mail pouches in it. Beyond the mail bin was a machine, obviously a scanner for scanning the mail bags for guns, drugs and other contraband. This was evident as a sign just before the scanner that showed pictures of a gun, drugs and other items each with a circle around them and a diagonal line that went through each circle. The room had a high ceiling with banks of fluorescent lights lighting up the off-white walls and a white tiled floor.

Lawson walked to the counter and set his bags on the floor. "Is Georgios here?" he asked while looking at the clock – it was 1:20 PM.

"He's in the back, I'll get him," the woman said in English with a heavy Greek accent. Picking up a phone on the counter she said something in Greek and set the phone receiver down. "He'll be out here in a moment."

Lawson was looking around the room when a door to left side of the counter opened and a man with dark complexion and black hair came out. "Mr. Lawson," he said as he extended his hand.

"You must be Georgios," Lawson assumed.

"One and the same," Georgios responded in near perfect English. "Grab your things and come back with me."

Lawson picked up his bags and followed Georgios through the door into a room that had one long table and a couple of chairs. This room had windows going all the way around it as well. Next to the table was a basket with some type of roller mechanism at the top end of four long metal extensions going up from a metal basket.

"You have the envelope with the nuts and bolts in it?" Georgios inquired which caused Lawson to dig into the manila envelope Jacobs had given him to get the smaller envelope with the parts in it. Handing the smaller envelope to Georgios, Lawson noted the sign on the side of the basket. It had something in Greek with '40 Kg' below the Greek lettering. Lawson figured this was the maximum weight the basket could carry. Quickly calculating the weight, he figured the basket was maxed out carrying 90 pounds. Georgios quickly removed four plastic nuts and bolts on the basket and replaced them with the four steel nuts and bolts Georgios had taken from the envelope Lawson had given him. It took him almost forty-five minutes to complete the task.

"The replacement of these parts will increase the basket's carrying capability from 40 kilograms to 110 kilograms. That's about 243 pounds. Now what's your weight?" Georgios questioned.

"173 pounds and luggage is about 30 pounds," Lawson returned.

"So, we can put a mail bag with about 40 pounds in with you when we run you down the hill to the causeway," stated Georgios.

"What's the plan?" Lawson asked as he walked over to the window overlooking the port area. As he looked he could see six piers extending out from the causeway. Two of the middle piers were shorter than the rest with the second pier from the right being very wide and able to support the offloading of a significant amount cargo. There was a marina off to the left of the port that appeared to have over 100 boats in it. Next to the marina was the leftmost pier in the harbor. Lawson could see the freighter 'Dove' tied at that pier. He realized that it would be a significant walk to go from the place where he would enter the causeway to get to the Dove. That left him exposed for what looked like almost half a mile. There were four other ships tied up to different piers. There was another cargo ship, a ship that looked like a ferry and a large yacht. There was also a helicopter on a float tied to the front of the pier closest to him that had some sort of sign that Lawson suspected was for aerial tours. A military patrol vessel was tied to the farthest right pier.

"The plan?" Georgios replied as he looked at Lawson. "The plan is simple. You are to put on this knit cap to make you look more like you belong on the wharf. With your jeans and plain shirt you should fit in with the rest of the dock workers." Lawson listened while he put on the knit cap. "I'll move the basket to the upper landing just outside of this door then I will lower you down to the causeway in the basket." Georgios said as he pointed to the door that went out to where a long metal cable went from the landing just outside the doorway, going down diagonally about 110 feet which would run the basket 40 feet lower from where the mail facility sat. "You'll ride in the basket with the mail bag in front of you so that, if anyone should look through the window from the shed down below, they will just see the mail bag. Once you get to the bottom, about ten feet before the basket reaches the end of the cable, get out quickly and move to the right side where there are barrels. The basket will continue to move until it reaches the end of the cable where it will hit a paddle that rings a bell inside the shed. Once the bell rings, a man will come out and get the mail bag. Once you get off of the basket, hide your bags between the barrels until after the guy in the shed comes out to get the mail. Once he's goes back in, you can go to your ship. Oh, and just before you go down, light up a cigarette so that by the time you're down it will look like you have been down there a while smoking by the barrels. With me so far?"

Lawson acknowledged he understood as he looked at the roller system on the basket then reached out the door to feel the size of the cable to see if he thought the cable could carry the load. He calculated that the size of the cable would support a couple thousand pounds of weight. The real question was how much weight would the supports that held the cable be able to withstand.

"How this all works is simple," said Georgios as he rolled the basket out the door to the landing. "This spool on this rod at the top of the landing holds a line that hooks to the basket. Once you are in the basket, I will lower you down on the cable by turning this crank that controls the spool. It will feed out the line allowing me to control the speed you are traveling down the cable."

Georgios hooked the line to the basket and set the basket's roller-pulley on the cable. Then, after moving the basket away from the landing so that is was hanging free, he motioned to Lawson to come forward. Lawson stepped into the basket with his bags. Based upon Lawson's calculations, Georgios put a fifteen kilogram mail bag in front of Lawson as Lawson put on the knit cap and pulled out a cigarette. Lighting the cigarette, Lawson waved to Georgios at which time Georgios turned the crank and the basket moved down the line.

As the basket neared the end of its travel, Lawson saw that the basket would hit the cement slab and bottom out before it got to the end. Something Lawson and Georgios had not expected. They had not considered how the extra weight in the basket would cause the basket to be lower because the cable tension was set to handle only ninety pounds. Lawson pulled his bags from the basket and rolled out just before the basket hit the pavement.

As he left the basket the sudden change in weight in the basket caused the basket to lurch up and he watched as the basket roller left the cable. Lawson jumped forward to catch the basket before it hit the ground but, much to his surprise, the roller landed back on the cable and continued toward the paddle. He quickly grabbed his bags, picked up his cigarette from the ground and glanced at the shed window, moving as he watched the basket hit the paddles. Seeing that no one was watching, he lunged to the barrels, swung his bags behind the barrels and proceeded to take a drag on his half-smoked cigarette. As he did so a woman came to the back of the shed, looked at him then pulled out the mail bag and carried it into the shed. Lawson just sat there smoking the last of his cigarette as he scanned the causeway and the port for anything unusual.

What first caught his attention were two men sitting on a plank bench across the causeway from the last pier at the end of the causeway where the Dove was tied up. There was a third man standing at the end of the causeway with some sort of beverage in his hand. The distance was too great for Lawson to determine what they were wearing but he noticed the man standing at the end of the pier wore some type of hat that gave off a bright silvery reflection at times when the man turned.

As Lawson was watching them, two police cars pulled up in front of the building he was sitting next to. He watched from the corner of the building as four men came out of the first car and three men out of the second. All except one of the men were dressed in police uniforms while the man without a uniform was dressed in a suit. They started talking to each other after they got out of the cars and Lawson didn't need a translator to tell him who they were looking for. He heard a lot of Greek conversation but within the conversation he distinctly heard 'James Lawson'.

At that moment, a worker from the building came around the corner to where Lawson was straining to look. As the man came around the corner, Lawson sat back up in his previous position as the man sat down. The man appeared to be Greek but seemed to have some other nationality mix in him. He had the sailor's knit cap covering his light brown hair that highlighted his youthful, square jaw and blue eyes. Lawson figured he had some Northern European blood in his bloodline. He spoke something in Greek as Lawson looked down. The man looked Lawson over then at his bags.

"You're who they are looking for," the man exclaimed as he leaned to look at Lawson's face. Lawson looked up at the man and wondered who he was.

"How did you know I speak English?" Lawson asked while turning once more to watch the policemen.

"Your courier case," the man explained. "I am Mark. I live in Athens and I crew the Dove, the freighter over there. I recognized your case as we have people come on our ship once in a while carrying cases similar to the one you've got. The American ones are easy to identify." Mark watched Lawson watching the policemen. "You want to know what they are saying?" Mark inquired, his head turning to better catch the conversation engaged on the causeway."

"It would help me. What time have you got?" Lawson responded.

"It's 2:20 PM. Now they say that they need to go down to the freighter and wait for Lawson," Mark described as he pulled out a cigarette. "The man in the suit says they must stay hidden until Lawson shows up. He's suggesting they all get into the building at the end of the causeway across from where my ship is tied up. The building is that one where those people are coming in and out of. He says that the building appears to have windows so they can watch from there. He's telling two of the officers to move the police cars to the other side of that same building so Lawson can't see they are there. Another officer just appeared." Mark listened for a moment then continued, "The new officer says that Lawson hasn't gone through terminal security yet so it appears he's not here yet. The man in the suit just told him to go back into the terminal area and watch for him. The rest are going to the building at the end of the causeway. I take it you're the James Lawson they're talking about." Lawson nodded 'yes'.

Lawson watched as the policemen went toward the end of the causeway as Mark lit up his cigarette. As he was watching, something unusual caught his attention. Turning to Mark, he asked, "Do you know these two men on the bench near your ship?"

Mark looked. "They are too far away to recognize but the colors they wear don't look like workers clothes, so they're not from my ship."

"That's interesting," Lawson observed, "because as the policemen started approaching their area the two men got up and sat down on the bench facing the opposite direction. The man at the end of the causeway also just turned facing away from the policemen."

Mark interrupted as he looked at the activity then back at Lawson. "Even at this distance I know one of the men. I know his hat, it has a silver band. He is Kyrgyz. His name is Guljigit Sukhrab and I know this because he has carried cases like yours aboard our ship on a couple occasions and I saw his name on the ship's manifest. I knew from the way he carried the cases that he was carrying something heavy, most likely guns. Look, James Lawson, I have to get to my ship as we leave in about 15 minutes. Good luck to you." Lawson shook Mark's hand and watched Mark leave. As Mark left, Lawson sensed he could trust this man he just met. Lawson saw that the policemen were getting close to the building where they planned to wait.

He realized that boarding or even getting near the ship was out and looked around for any other options. As he looked around he realized how much Mark stood out as he walked to his ship. Everyone working on the docks was wearing bright orange safety vests and white safety helmets. First, Lawson had to get the proper attire. Second, he had to find a way out. Looking into the manila folder he got from Jacobs he looked at the courier cards and secondary IDs. It struck him that the way out using any ship or boat was out of the question. However, the helicopter sitting on the float tied to the pier in front of him appeared to be a possibility.

As Lawson got up to move he realized that the building he was sitting next to was a working facility as people were going in and out from it. It stood to reason that a building of that size had extra safety gear hanging up. Stepping around the corner, Lawson gave a quick look at the inside of the building. Right near the entrance where he was standing was a bunch of helmets and vests hanging on hooks on the wall and a man standing about 20 feet inside the building writing something on a pad. With the man's back to him, Lawson stepped a couple of feet inside the entrance and quietly pulled a helmet and orange vest from the wall where they were hanging alongside eight more sets.

Stepping backwards, Lawson swung around the corner and put on the safety gear.

Picking up his bags and getting ready to cross to the helicopter, he noticed that everyone wore a badge either on their belt or around their neck. It appeared to him that those that were doing heavy work had it on their belts whereas the management and administrative people wore the badge hanging from their neck. Lawson noted that the badges were white and about the same size as his courier cards. Pulling one of the courier cards out of the envelope, he checked the color, shape and size. It had a hole in the narrow margin of the card, obviously for a person to put a neck strap on it. Next question was what to use for a neck strap. Lawson opened his carryon bag and took a shoe lace from one of his dress shoes. Using the lace for the neck strap, he took the present courier ID with his real name on it and hung it around his neck. Accomplishing that, he grabbed his bags and proceeded to walk across the causeway to the helicopter.

Inspector Bernardakis watched the whole causeway with his binoculars. Noting that a man was walking across the causeway carrying some bags, he turned to Sergeant Doukakis and questioned why a worker would carry someone's luggage to the pier.

"They do that quite often, Sir, for people taking the helicopter," Doukakis answered. "Many people will take the helicopter to go from here to Chania and they usually have their luggage taken by a port worker to the helicopter. If there's a lot of luggage, it's normally moved by forklift." Seeing the man apparently had a worker's badge on him, which Bernardakis assumed would be something Lawson wouldn't have, he just nodded to Doukakis as he continued to scan the causeway and piers.

"It's getting within 10 minutes of the Dove's scheduled departure," Bernardakis observed. "He's got to be coming soon."

While Bernardakis was observing the causeway, Lawson had gotten to the floating helo pad and introduced himself to the pilot who was lying on a lawn chair that was bolted to the pad. "How much to take me to Heraklion Airport," Lawson inquired. The pilot looked at him and then looked around to see if there were any other people. He was also curious why a man dressed in the port's working clothing would be asking him. He figured that the man in the port safety gear was asking for someone else.

"500 Euros per person, four persons minimum," the pilot quoted as he demonstrated his understanding of one of the four different languages in which he was proficient.

Lawson smiled then submitted, "I know there are times when you take VIP's to the airport. How much do you charge them?"

The pilot thought for a moment then offered, "2500 Euros to go to the airport."

"Will you take 3000 US dollars instead," Lawson asked as he held out the money.

The pilot's eyes lit up at the offer. "Get in, my name is Aristotle. Everyone calls me Stot." Lawson took off the helmet and vest then strapped himself in. Stot looked at the courier card around Lawson's neck then at the courier bag behind him as he started up the engines.

"How long is the flight?" asked Lawson.

"About 10 minutes," was Stot's reply. "By the way, you're the guy the police are looking for aren't you? Never mind, I'm not turning you in. In my experiences, when a man has a courier card that matches what he's carrying, it is probable that he's not running away from the law but rather from those that use the law for unlawful things. I'll get you safely to the airport."

"One thing," Lawson advised. "When you get back to the piers, the police will probably be visiting you. Be honest if the police pay you a visit, don't lie about anything. Tell them everything they want to know."

"That's usually the way I do it," Stot answered. "No lies means I don't have to remember anything I might have said."

Once they landed at the airport, Lawson entered the concourse door next to the first loading gate and showed the customs people that his passport had already been stamped for entry into Crete. The customs people waved him through.

The ticket counters were against the wall in a large open area that had the main entrance into the airport at the center opposite the ticket counters. There were the typical roped aisles leading to each counter with a baggage scale to the side of each airline counter. There was a large exit from the ticketing area in the center of the wall with a sign above it with the words 'Concourse' in several languages and an arrow pointing toward the food court area and the gates.

Leaving the customs area, Lawson passed through the concourse area, through the food court and then to the ticket counter area and proceeded to purchase tickets on four different airlines for four different flights.

Back at the seaport, Inspector Bernardakis began to realize Lawson had slipped through as he saw the crew of the Dove swing the gangway up and start her engines. He contemplated how Lawson could have gotten out then it struck him. The helicopter he had seen leaving about five minutes before was probably carrying Lawson.

"Sergeant, did you ever see the port worker return to the terminal building after he took those bags to the helicopter?" Bernardakis asked Doukakis.

"No, Sir, but I wasn't always looking that way," Doukakis replied.

Bernardakis shouted, "We've been had! He's gone to the airport. That's the only way left for him to get out. Get to the cars." All of the policemen raced around the corner of the building to the cars. Taking off at high speed with sirens going, Bernardakis figured it would take them about eight minutes to get to the airport. The other officers sitting in the car with him said nothing. They knew when he reached this fever pitch someone was going to pay.

They arrived at the airport and quickly entered the ticketing area. Bernardakis directed his officers to go to each of the different counters and quickly find out which flight he was on. Bernardakis went to the Lufthansa counter and showed the ticketing agent the picture of Jim Lawson. The attendant nodded 'no' when another ticketing agent came up and looked at the picture.

"Yes, I remember him," the ticketing agent said. He got a ticket for a flight to Paris that leaves in, let's see, 35 minutes at Gate 1." Bernardakis felt elated. He finally had him. As he walked toward the concourse to go to the gate, Doukakis walked up to him.

"I just talked to the people at the at the SAS counter. Lawson got a ticket to Amsterdam that leaves in an hour," Doukakis said while looking at Bernardakis' expression. Bernardakis just looked straight forward with a tired countenance. As they stood looking at each other, Officer Kourakis, one of the officers that was at the restaurant when Lawson was there, joined the group.

"I got his flight," Kourakis said as he smiled at the other two. "He's got a flight to Athens on Aegean Airlines. The flight leaves in ten minutes." Bernardakis was now beside himself. The guy played a perfect shell game on him.

"Well, let's go to the gate leaving the soonest," Bernardakis said as he started to turn toward the food court and the main concourse while wondering where Officer Dragasakis was at. As they entered the food court, Officer Dragasakis came running toward them. As Dragasakis came up to them he stopped to catch his breath.

"I checked Emirates Airline. They didn't have a James Lawson but, when I showed them the picture of Lawson, they remembered the man but he had checked in under the name 'John Rochester'," Dragasakis reported as he looked at his notes. "He's heading to Dubai and that's not all. He checked in with a passport in the name of John Rochester and paid for his ticket using a credit card under the same name and the transaction was approved. If this is the flight he is on, it just left at 2:45 PM." Looking at his watch and seeing that it was 2:55 PM, Bernardakis realized at that moment that something was horribly wrong. This Lawson guy was no amateur and wouldn't be the type of person to leave himself open for Interpol to track him. Red flags were up everywhere in Bernardakis' mind as Doukakis broke Bernardakis' thought.

"Herr Nils Hauptmann, the Interpol agent, is coming toward us," Doukakis declared as they all turned to see Hauptmann walking across the main ticketing area and through the concourse portal toward them.

"I will do all the talking," Bernardakis ordered as he began to put the pieces together. "No one, and that means no other person in this group, says a word or you're fired." They waited as Hauptmann approached them.

"Any success in apprehending Lawson?" Hauptmann questioned.

"We think he may be on a Lufthansa flight to Paris that leaves in about twenty minutes," Bernardakis responded. "You're free to join us to the gate."

"I'll catch you later," Hauptmann said as he got ready to turn around. "I'll catch you at the police station early this evening." Bernardakis nodded his approval and turned to go toward the gate.

As they watched Hauptmann walk out the concourse portal toward the ticketing area, Doukakis asked Bernardakis, "Why didn't you tell him about the other flights?" Bernardakis looked at Doukakis as he quickly went through the events of the day in his mind. Nothing fit. Everything appeared to be in chaos.

"Doukakis, I want you to call this Interpol number on my screen," Bernardakis requested. "Use my phone since they know who I am and ask the officer in charge for a picture of Detective

Inspector Nils Hauptmann to be sent to my phone. I need it immediately." Doukakis looked at Bernardakis while wondering what Bernardakis' concerns about Hauptmann were.

Bernardakis turned and spoke to his officers, "We're not making another move until I get some answers and feel comfortable that we are chasing the right person."

"But, Sir," Kourakis interjected, "Lawson's getting away."

"No, he's not," Bernardakis shot back. "He's most likely on one of those flights. If my questions are answered, we'll notify each of the airports to watch for him and give them the flight numbers and time of arrival for his capture." They waited almost fifteen minutes before Doukakis got back to Bernardakis on his call to Interpol.

"I've got the answer to one of your questions, Sir. The one from Interpol," Doukakis chimed in. "You're not going to like it."

"Ok, what have you got?"

"Well, Sir," Doukakis started. "After I sent the request for Hauptmann's picture, they responded back with 'why do you want it'. I explained that we were just talking to Hauptmann and we just wanted to verify him from his picture. They just came back with this text message – 'Hauptmann is dead, his body found last night in Berlin. The man you're dealing with is an imposter and is likely the one that killed him. Send us a picture of him if you can. If he is still with you apprehend him'. What do I tell them?"

Taking his phone from Doukakis, Bernardakis starting typing something on his phone. "I'll tell them he's already left. We'll try to get a picture of him," Bernardakis advised. "As for Lawson, he is of no interest to us. Contact all those we sent pictures to and tell them Lawson was misidentified for someone else and is not wanted.

"But, Sir," Doukakis protested, 'if we send that message out, Hauptmann or whoever he is, will get the same message and will know we're onto him."

Bernardakis smiled as he watched the main concourse. "Don't worry about Hauptmann. He's heading to Paris due to what I told him about Lawson's ticketing on Lufthansa. It's a full flight and Hauptmann will not have time to check all the passengers before takeoff. He also doesn't want to raise any suspicions that will cause the airport people to question his real identity. He'll ride the flight to Paris. I just told Interpol as much." They all laughed as they started toward the airport main entrance.

"Let's go find a nice bar where they are playing some nice, lively Lyra music," Bernardakis suggested as he was happy the work day was ending. "I wonder what Lawson was doing in Crete?" He thought while watching the faces of his men. "It sure made the day interesting, in a bad way."

Lawson's flight to Dubai rumbled down the runway and, once getting airborne, turned to the southeast as it gained elevation. Lawson sat back in his seat and closed his eyes. The first part of his mission was successfully completed.

Chapter 4

Discovery

"When I volunteered for my first mission as part of the CAT205 Team, I thought that my work would involve doing high-tech stuff. I didn't realize how much of the work involved self-defense and how many other people wanted to kill me which meant I had to kill them first, not what I signed up for. As a born-again Christian, this was opposite my values and desires. However, Lieutenant Lawson reminded me of how many lives we saved by the actions we took. Doing this work puts me in a real dilemma and tests the level of my sanity." – Second Class Petty Officer Nicholas Myers, US Navy CAT205 Special Operations Group Electronics Specialist, ONI

It was 6:35 AM on July 13th when Gunny Glendenning and Nick Myers arrived in Osh, Kyrgyzstan. They got their luggage and hailed a cab to go to their hotel, the 'Salam Hotel' on Masalieva Street. From what they could see, Osh was a very modern city with well-kept streets, mass transit, modern traffic control and many upscale stores and restaurants. It took them twenty-five minutes to get to the hotel and once they checked in, they went to bed.

They got up and went to the restaurant in the hotel around 1:30 PM. Gunny looked around at the hotel lobby. It was wide open with large windows and a lush lobby area with many green plants, a stone-tiled floor and thick leather chairs arranged in a fashion where people could sit and read or watch TV. As Gunny was looking around, the person at the lobby counter motioned to him. Walking over, he leaned against the counter as the man at the counter pointed to a woman sitting in one of the chairs.

"That woman has been waiting for you for the past 2 hours, Mr. Glendenning," the attendant said. Gunny looked to where the man was pointing then thanked him.

"You looking for me?" Gunny asked the woman that was sitting down. He noted her attention was fixed on the satellite phone in her hand.

The woman was about five feet, seven inches tall with blond hair and a thin build. Gunny could tell she was self-absorbed and totally out of her depth in the present situation. The only term Gunny could think of that matched from his experiences in the not-so recent past with women like this was 'Valley Girl'. He smiled at the thought.

"Hi, you must be Master Gunnery Sergeant Arnoud Glendenning," she said while leaning back in the chair. "I'm Pentagon Technical Analyst Joanne Benson." She could tell Gunny was instantly perturbed about something which made her immediately nervous.

"I take it you read your instructions before coming to the city," Gunny directed.

"Yes, I read them," Benson responded. About that time, Myers arrived to join in the conversation.

"This is Nick Myers, one of our team members," Gunny stated. "Now, let me see your phone." She handed him the phone while exhibiting a confused look. Gunny handed the phone to Myers which Myers took and noted Benson was reading a message that said 'Usb field 19'. She had been communicating on the phone when they took it from her so it was highly likely that they were already exposed to someone tracking them.

Clearing the message, he punched a number of times on the screen then took the back off of the phone. Once completing that task, he handed the phone back to Gunny.

"The phone has been erased and disabled," Myers declared as Benson looked on with horror.

"What did you do that to my phone for!" she shouted while others in the lobby looked up to see what was going on.

Gunny held his finger up to his lips and said, "Shush." After a pause while he looked around he proceeded to quietly instruct her. "First, your instructions said no phone, no computers and no trackable electronics. Did you not understand your instructions?"

"I did," Benson protested, "but my boss said to ignore the instructions. He said you guys are ultra-paranoid and you're just coming here to get information." Gunny face flushed and he was about to give her some physical education when Myers intervened.

"We are not being ultra-paranoid," Myers began. "First, you have probably exposed our location to those that are following us by your use of the phone. Second, you are now in as big a threat as we are. You don't seem to realize there are people out here that want us gone. We are looking at what your people call one of the biggest threats we've had to face since we started this organization called CAT205. Believe me, we have had some very serious threats that, if you had read the reports, resulted in us having to kill a lot of people to stay alive. Why do you think it was necessary for the powers that be to activate 'Shiny Object', one of the highest levels of threat activation? This is not an exercise."

"Stop trying to coddle her, Nick," Gunny interrupted. "Now, Miss Benson, you will do exactly what we tell you and when we tell you. This isn't the safety of the Pentagon. This is the real world where people die when they make one mistake. You were sent out here to learn what we do and you can't do it by following your rules. You will be dead within 24 hours if you do."

"Wait, Gunny," Myers stated. "Maybe that's what we need to do. We'll put the chip back into the phone and send her on her way throughout the city. They will be following her while we can carry out our mission." Benson began to show real fear on her face at Myers' suggestion.

"That might be a good thought if she were someone like Lawson," Gunny responded. "However, having her do that would be like sending a lamb to the slaughter."

"Wait, I will do what you want but I'm going to have to document my protest." She exclaimed as she pulled out a notebook and pen. Gunny pulled the notebook out of her hand and gave it to Myers.

"Nothing will be written except that which is essential for the completion of the mission," Gunny expressed. "We don't do anything in writing if we can avoid it. Everything's in our memory as we don't want what we are doing discovered. I know this is a shock to you but this is a different world you walked into. One more thing, outside of calling me 'Gunny' no one else identifies themselves by role or title. I'm Gunny," then pointing to Myers, Gunny continued, "this is Myers or also known as Nick. When the others get here it is Lawson also known as Jim and Norman also known as Beth. You will only go by Benson or by Joanne, just like in real life."

Benson was near tears as the impact of what she walked into became real. Gunny could see a breakdown coming and, in his typical Marine Corps way, removed any doubt of what was going to happen.

"Joanne, you will adapt. That being said, there is no going home and no pleading to be sent somewhere else. You are a part of this mission and will be until the mission is completed. We work as a team. We will look out for you and will chew you out when you do something stupid and protect you as best we can when you are threatened. Now, let's go to the restaurant and get something to eat." Benson got up slowly and picked up her purse as they headed to the entrance of the hotel restaurant, noting that her knees were having a difficult time holding her up.

After they had lunch they entered back into the lobby where the attendant at the counter motioned once more to Gunny. "I've got this message that is meant for Mr. Myers," the attendant said as he handed Gunny the sealed note. Gunny turned and handed it to Myers. All three of them walked over to some of the leather chairs and sat down in an arrangement where they could see each other.

"Whenever there are several of us together, we position ourselves so that we can see behind each other to ensure we are not being surprised from behind," Gunny instructed as Myers opened the note. Benson just nodded then looked at Myers.

"It's from Professor Magnus Murodov at the Osh Technological University," Myers said as Gunny saw the look in Benson's eyes. Jumping up, Gunny turned to face a man that was lunging toward Myers. Having no weapon on himself, Gunny blocked the man's knife thrust toward Myers using his arm, swung the man around and slammed the man's head against the floor. Myers jumped up and, grabbing Benson's purse, swung the purse around and caught a second man moving toward them, hitting the man across the side of the head with the full force of the edge of the purse. Benson sat stunned at all of the activity and how quickly it had happened.

With both men down and obviously unconscious, Myers looked into the purse to see what was creating all the weight. "Will you look at this," Myers exclaimed. "It's the new M17 nine millimeter military pistol. No wonder the purse was so heavy. She's got a loaded weapon and two extra clips in the purse."

Gunny checked on the two attackers then took the purse from Myers. "How in the world did you get an M17 pistol?" Gunny questioned as he looked at Benson. "They're not available in any unit yet."

"I was given the weapon by one of the guys in my department that does weapons tests for the Pentagon," Benson explained. "He felt that I might need it and, although I thought he was just being cautious, I took it anyway."

"How did you get it through airport security?" Myers inquired.

"I had military flights all the way," said Benson as she looked at Gunny and her purse. "Because I have Pentagon advisory certifications, I can travel on any space available aircraft that has an agreement with the US. Russia has such an agreement with certain restrictions and with the significance of this operation to the Russians, I met their conditions." As she was talking, local police came in to examine the situation. The police started treating all three of them as though they were suspects. Gunny showed them his courier card which one officer slapped away. The whole scene changed when Benson showed her Pentagon diplomat card. One officer took the card and handed it to another, more senior officer. They talked for a moment then handed her back the card and apologized, at which point, Myers asked why these men would attack them.

"We're just Americans that came to discuss improving the technology of Kyrgyzstan," Myers stated. "What would lead someone to attack us with knives?"

"They are probably Uzbeks that don't want our country getting advances in technology," the senior officer observed. Gunny was quick to correct the impression and give the officer an indication of how familiar the team was of the local culture.

"These people have the typical facial features I would expect to see in the Kyrgyz, not the Uzbeks," Gunny expounded as Myers and Benson both nodded agreement.

"You may be right," said the senior officer as he proceeded to put his handcuffs on one of the semiconscious suspects. "The area has had quite a mixing of both cultures over the past 20 years. Sometimes it's hard to tell." Gunny just nodded as the officers helped the two suspects to their feet and slowly walked them out the main entrance. The team watched as the officers left with their charges.

"Well, let's see what we can find out about our attackers," said Gunny while taking a wallet and cellphone from his pocket.

"What are those?" Benson queried.

"The wallet and cellphone from the second man that attacked us," Gunny replied. "The first man would not have been the leader of their effort to get us. Just like any other team, military or otherwise, the leader would send his underling first to take action then, if he failed, the leader would be the next to act. So I figured that the second man to attack was the leader and would have information on him or on his device that would tell us who sent him. You see, he would have to tell someone immediately if he was successful or not."

Benson was impressed by Gunny's explanation while Myers took the phone and proceeded to use a backdoor password to access the contents. While he was doing that, Gunny was going through the contents of the wallet.

"Don't you think that if they knew how to get to us they already know where we are and who we are," stated Benson as she began to see the logic of Gunny's actions concerning removing her cellphone from her when she first arrived.

"Can't be helped," Gunny responded. "We'll have to set up some sort of defense while we're here at the hotel. Well, look at this. From what I see in this guy's wallet, he's a senior attaché for the Kyrgyz government. They've got a deep state here too. Myers, go to the hotel desk and reserve two more rooms, one in the name of James Lawson and another in the name of Blanche Donovan. We are all going to stay in the new James Lawson room. And Myers, make sure one of the rooms is across the hall from our original room and one room adjacent to our new room." Myers nodded as he went to the check-in counter.

"You mean I have to sleep in the same room you guys are in?" Benson questioned as she realized she would have no privacy.

Gunny smiled at her then continued, "There is only one weapon between the three of us. That is the M17 pistol you brought. That means we have to stay together or one or more of us remains unprotected. Now that they know we are here, they are going to try again. That means no room service, phone calls or leaving the room once we are in it tonight. We will need one person to stand watch to ensure the others can sleep. Each watch will be two hours long. I'll take the first watch starting at 22:00 hours, that's 10:00 PM for you Miss Benson. Myers will have the second watch, then Miss Benson, you will have the third watch at 2:00 AM. Upon completing your watch, I will take the next watch at 4:00 AM. Here comes Myers." Myers came back after reserving the rooms and sat down.

"I guess it was my phone they tracked," Benson admitted. Both Gunny and Myers nodded agreement as they picked up their stuff and went to one of the new rooms.

"I made the reservation for both rooms under the names you gave me. Wasn't Blanche Donovan that girl you met at the Russian Language School?" Myers stated as they reached the elevator. Gunny just frowned and motioned Myers on. Getting to the room Myers opened the door and went in first. It was a typical hotel room with a queen-size bed, a lounge chair, TV, coffee-maker and reading table with a chair.

"Since we each have to stand watch, I suggest that one person sleeps in bed while the other person sleeps in the lounge chair," Gunny suggested. "The person standing watch will have the M17 pistol and the clips. When you are finished with your watch, you'll wake up the next person by shaking them awake, no talking and then transfer the weapon and clips to them. Is that understood? Both Myers and Benson agreed.

Myers was next to talk, "We need to get a taxi as it's about thirty minutes before we're supposed to meet Professor Magnus Murodov at the Osh Technological University. His text says that he's got another guy coming at the same time. He is Kyrgyzstani and his name is Nurlan Isakova."

"Kyrgyzstani?" Benson questioned. "From what I saw from the intel reports at the Pentagon, the Kyrgyzstanis are suspected to be part of this mysterious plot."

"I wouldn't paint them with a broad brush like that," Myers advised. "We don't know enough to know who is involved and I wouldn't want to set a preconceived notion of who is friendly and who is not."

"Although I agree with you, good buddy, I want to treat them all with caution until we know who we're dealing with," Gunny said as he stuck the M17 pistol inside his belt where it could not be seen. Handing the clips to Myers to put in his pocket, Gunny went out the door to get the taxi while the others followed behind him.

They arrived at the university around 6:00 PM and went to the main building that was five stories high and approximately a football field in length. Going to the fifth floor, they arrived at a set of double doors that went into a large lab area. When they entered the lab, Myers asked the first person he met where he could find Professor Magnus Murodov. The man in a white lab coat pointed to a set of test benches about halfway down the middle of the expansive room that looked more like a large warehouse.

As they walked down toward the middle of the room, Myers recognized the myriad of test instruments and monitors with cables going everywhere. There were instruments for measuring signal pulses and widths like oscilloscopes and data meters, other instruments that provided signals, instruments for temperature, pressure, volume, distance and energy levels with test benches and tables spread generously throughout the area. It reminded Myers of his college days at MIT.

They arrived at the test bench the assistant had pointed to. They noted a man sitting in a chair while talking to himself in his native language and hunched over a small chamber that had bright electrical arcs flashing from both sides. A loud pop followed by an ending of the arcing brought an obvious reaction and a flurry of obvious swear words no one could make out but sounded more obscene in his native language than it probably did in English. The man threw down his protective red glasses on the test bench and turned in anger. At that moment he saw the three visitors and quickly changed from anger to apology. As he started rattling off something in his own language Gunny stopped him by putting his hand on the man's shoulder.

"English, if you can," Gunny said quietly. The man looked at each of them for a moment then a flash of awareness came over his face.

"Is it six in the evening already?" he exclaimed in English as he sat down in his chair. "I am so sorry. I was completely entrenched in my experiment and lost all sense of time. I am Professor Magnus Murodov and you must be Mr. Myers," he said while shaking Gunny's hand. Gunny realized that this man was not a neophyte to the English language. He spoke it with fluency and richness.

"Actually, I am Gunny Glendenning. This is Nick Myers," Gunny stated while pointing to Myers. Murodov shook Myers hand then motioned for them to follow him.

Professor Magnus Murodov was short at five-feet, two inches tall. His weathered face told of years working in the fields and his stature was of a man that had spent too much time bending over. Looking at him, at first, one would have thought him to be frail but that impression was quickly lost when he picked up a forty pound chair with one hand that was blocking his path and set it aside in order to step past the bench. His quick step showed an indication of youthfulness not readily apparent.

"You speak English well," Gunny observed as they walked with him. Myers delayed for a moment, looking at the electronic setup that Murodov was previously swearing over. Smiling at the layout, Myers turned and went to the doorway the others were just going into.

"I speak six different languages, three of them fluently," was Murodov's response. "Now, I must get Nurlan Isakova to continue this discussion."

They entered a small side room where computers and screens were present in lines down one side of the room. Obviously, a college computer lab for students to do their programming exercises. The room had low lighting to reduce the light reflecting on the screens and the room smelled of cigarette smoke and beer while sandwich wrappers, empty soda cans and donut boxes littered the desktops. Both Myers and Gunny looked at each other and laughed at the scene. It was obvious programmers were the same worldwide.

Sitting at the end of the room at one of the computer stations was a burly, bearded man that Myers estimated could take down Gunny without much effort. As the man stood to see who came into the room, they all hesitated at the size of the man standing before them. Myers looked at Gunny then the man. The man was half a head taller than Gunny and built just as well.

"US Marine, I take it," the man said as he extended his hand toward Gunny. Gunny grinned and nodded 'yes'.

"I would like to introduce all of you to Nurlan Isakova," Murodov motioned with his hand toward Isakova. "We affectionately call him 'Izzy'." Everyone shook his hand as Murodov went to the door, locked it and hung a sign on the door.

"I figured you were a Marine from the tattoo on your arm," Isakova stated. Myers looked down at Gunny's arm tattooed with the US Marine logo of the eagle, globe and anchor and wondered why he had never noticed it before. "Just to let you know, I'm pretty good with the English language but I'm not yet good with some of the slang you use. I may say things sometimes that may not make sense. If that's the case, don't feel offended, just let me know your concern."

Murodov walked over to a small cabinet, unlocked it and pulled out 5 glasses and a bottle of vodka. After pouring each glass half full he handed the glasses to each of the men in the room, then to Benson and took a glass for himself. "To Mother Uzbekistan," he shouted then downed the glass.

"To Mother Kyrgyzstan," Izzy shouted as he drank his glassful. Myers just stood there holding the glass as he looked at Gunny. Gunny smiled as he raised the glass.

"To the United States Marine Corps," was his rendition of the toast as he proceeded to drink while everyone applauded. Everyone looked at Benson and Myers as they looked at their glass then at them.

"To world peace," Benson shouted then she drank the glass and coughed for a moment. It was clear to Lawson and Gunny that Benson seldom drank anything with alcohol in it. Murodov applauded her as she set the glass down.

It was now up to Myers. He was not normally into drinking alcohol but he knew this was more than a set of toasts. It was obviously a cultural tradition and he didn't want to create a sensitive situation. He stood thinking for a moment.

"To Mother….my mother," he shouted and downed the drink while everyone laughed. "So, just to be clear, how is it that you guys are able to work after taking a drink?" Myers questioned. "Do you do this all the time?

"My dear friend, Myers," Murodov answered, "We only do it when we have such esteemed guests."

"I'll bet you those guests don't get much done," Myers quipped as the others laughed.

"Izzy, why don't you bring the information up on the screen you showed me last week," Murodov suggested. "While he's doing that, I've locked down the room so that no one can see what we're doing."

While Murodov was talking, Isakova brought up a photograph of some computer code written in the Java programming language. Myers looked at the comment sections of the code but could not understand some of it because it was written in Kyrgyz and Russian. The Russian he could understand, the Kyrgyz not a chance.

"Anyway to convert this to English?" Myers inquired.

"That's the reason I had Izzy remain here, Kyrgyz is his language, my language is Uzbeki," Murodov explained. "Izzy usually goes home by this time. He works at a large software firm in the Fergana Valley north of Osh during the day and comes here from 4:00 to 6:00 PM to do his classes. He will translate the comments on the photographs for you so that you can see our concern."

As they looked they could see the first section had the title 'Code: аныктоо', the second section had the title 'Code: жайылтуу' and the third section had the title 'Code: мерген эркек / өлтүргүч аял'.

"This is a mix of Kyrgyz and Russian, probably because Kyrgyz may not have had an equivalent word," Isakova stated. "The first section of the code in English is 'Code: Identify', the second section of code is 'Code: Penetrate' or 'Penetration' and the third section of code is 'Code: Hunter/Killer'."

Myers looked down the page on the screen to see what the code consisted of. He could read some of the code that was in Russian. As he looked, he realized that this wasn't just one program but three programs embedded as one. He went to the top of the page where the data tables for the program were located. From the data tables, he could determine the data used to activate each of the three code sections. As he analyzed the code, he began to feel anxiety sweep over him as he began to realize what each of the sections represented. He turned to look at each of them then began to pace back and forth while talking to himself while Benson questioned if Myers had a stroke or something.

"I recognize that condition," Murodov observed. "It happens when you see something that is present but you know it can't be true. You're trying to make sense of something that has only a couple of possibilities and both of them lead to tragedy." As he was speaking Myers went back to the keyboard and moved the photo to see the code in the lower part of the photograph.

"Where did this photo come from?" Myers questioned.

"A friend of mine that does part time work at the firm I work for gave it to me," Isakova replied. "He was concerned that it was something ominous. After he gave the photo to me he hasn't been back to work. I got the photo a week ago and showed it to Professor Murodov at that time."

"What is bothering you, Myers?" Gunny asked while starting to sense an impending disaster was about to take place.

"The code is for three different and unique functions," Myers started. "I might not have thought much of it if it was three separate programs but this is one program with three different functions. What it means is that this program looks to be used for the same device but for different purposes. Maybe a military tank that can be used to identify the target, break down barriers to get to the target then search and destroy the target. In other words, from what I am seeing here, it can carry out all three functions without human intervention. From what I see here it's an artificially intelligent attack vehicle."

Gunny looked perplexed. "You do know that we have been developing something like this in the US for several years. What's the big leap here?"

Myers knew what Gunny was saying was true. This seemed to feel different and Myers didn't know why. His gut was telling him that this was a quantum leap in attack methods. He started pacing once more while considering the possibilities. He knew he needed to sleep on it. That would help him sort things out.

"Well, Professor," Myers began. "I've got enough here to consider. Please hide that photo from any prying eyes. I have a sense that, if they know you've got it, whoever owns it will come after you. Izzy, you need to be quiet about finding this and don't tell anyone else for your own safety. I feel that the person that gave you the photo may have already paid with his life."

"Thank you, Doctor Myers," Murodov said while shaking Myers' hand. "I've already told Izzy these things. It is good for him to hear it from you."

"Oh, Professor, one other thing," Myers advised as he walked toward the door. "On that experiment you were working on when we came in, put a one meg ohm resistor between your input power side of the anode and ground. That should keep the power supply from blowing out. By the way, I'm not a doctor." Murodov's eyes lit up as he realized what Myers had recommended.

"See you guys later," Murodov shouted as he ran out the door and back to the test bench in the middle of the lab. "You're a doctor to me!" came the fading shout from Murodov as he ran.

"He didn't even wish us goodbye," Gunny complained as they walked toward the exit with Isakova in tow. After saying goodbye to Isakova, they took the elevator down and a taxi back to the hotel.

After they stopped at three different restaurants just to find them closed, they went back to the hotel, arriving at 9:30 PM, and they were all tired. Gunny got the passkey for the room they registered in James Lawson's name and went to the room with the rest of them. Then Gunny headed downstairs after giving the weapon to Myers. After negotiating with the kitchen to make them a several sandwiches and some drinks, he headed back up to the room. The staff was more than willing to help provide the food when he offered each of them an extra five US dollars to complete the task. Apparently, American dollars were valued for their buying power in that part of the world.

After each of them ate and got ready for bed, Gunny flipped a coin to see who got the bed and who got the chair. Myers was willing to take the chair but Benson said that, as she was part of the team, she was to be treated no differently, thus the coin-toss. Once everyone was settled, Gunny began the first watch.

Chapter 5

Rasulov

"I've been a US Marine for 23 years. In that time, I've helped a lot of men and women to develop character and discipline using a defined set of rules. Now, here I am working with a team that is teaching me about working in chaos with no rules. It's nothing I would have signed up for had it not been this team. These team members don't know when to quit and don't let anyone else dictate the rules. They work seamlessly and with respect. The ultimate result of what I was looking for when I joined the Marines." – Master Gunnery Sergeant Arnoud 'Gunny' Glendenning, US Navy CAT205 Special Operations Group Weapons and Tactics Specialist, ONI

It was 4:10 AM on July 14th when the doorknob rattled. Gunny was on watch and immediately moved to quietly wake Myers and Benson. He quickly held his hand over Benson's mouth when she began to speak. Through the darkness, Benson could see it was Gunny and immediately got up. All three moved to the corner of the room along the wall that would require a person to step into the room before the intruder could see them.

The sound of a key going into the lock caused them to crouch lower as Gunny held the pistol pointed toward the short hall that made up the entryway. The door opened and a luggage bag on rollers came in first followed by the form a person, obviously male. As he turned on the light, he jumped backward then laughed. It was Lieutenant James Lawson. He stepped toward them and gave each a handshake as the door slammed behind him.

"Glad you could make it, Joanne," he said as he saw Benson and shook her hand.

"It's not what I expected," came her reply.

"Well, welcome to the team anyway," Lawson said while he broke the seal and undid the latches on the courier pouch. "Boy, this case is heavy. I got these from the US embassy in Crete." He pulled out three Maxim 9 pistols with built-in silencers and six clips.

"Well, that solves one problem," Gunny said as he examined the weapons. "We can now have everyone armed."

"It sounds like you've had trouble," Lawson discerned. Gunny explained the events that took place.

"I've also got five burner cellphones and a laptop computer with a power cord," Lawson continued as he handed out the items. "Myers, you take the laptop. You can leave the power cord in the room when we're out of the room but the laptop must always be with us."

"Ok, Jim," Myers acknowledged.

"Why don't we go through this in more detail in the morning," Lawson suggested. Everyone agreed. Once they got the weapons rules set up, Gunny checked the other room reserved under the name Blanche Donovon. It was adjoining to their room and he wanted to make sure that they could easily get to the room from their room without going into the hallway should something require them to evacuate the room they were in.

"Put a chair against the door so that it will take an intruder some time to enter," Gunny advised. "We do not use room service and we'll keep the phones and computer off for right now."

"Agreed, nothing electronic is to be on," Lawson replied. "By the way, you might want to take that exercise watch off of Benson. It's got tracking capability active within it." Gunny jumped up at the comment. What he thought was a regular digital watch was, in fact a trackable exercise watch. As Benson turned, Gunny grabbed her hand and took the watch off. Benson looked startled at the move.

"Do you realize that it's possible we've been tracked all day because of this," Gunny shouted. Benson pulled back in fear as she saw his anger.

"I'll take care of this, Gunny," Lawson offered as he took the watch.

"Good, do so," Gunny shot back. "Just think of this, she wore the watch to the university today and the tracking can put her right in the same lab as our professor. If they find him, he's as good as dead." At that moment Myers stepped in. Taking the watch, he went out the door and down the hallway while both Gunny and Lawson looked out the door, questioning what Myers was up to. Ten minutes later, Myers came back to the room. Knocking on the door and identifying himself, they let him in while Gunny held a weapon on him to make sure someone wasn't behind him.

"I used the computer at the reservation desk to read the watch," Myers said. "It was accessed at 6:20 PM yesterday according to the log. I've cleared the data on the watch. I couldn't change the ID tracker number on the watch so I did the next best thing. It's attached to the rear bumper of a taxi that's taking a couple of armed businessmen from Osh to Andijan, Uzbekistan. That's 48 miles. They were speaking Russian so it was easy to figure out where they were going." They all laughed at Myers' creativity and then laid down to get some sleep while Gunny continued his security watch duty.

It was 10:45 AM when Gunny came out of the bathroom, dressed and ready to go. He shook Benson awake and directed her to get ready in the bathroom while Gunny began to make coffee. Lawson and Myers both sat up, Myers from the lounge chair with Lawson rising from the floor.

After they all got ready, they headed down to the restaurant to get some breakfast. Gunny ensured everyone had their weapons on them. Gunny, Myers and Lawson put their Maxim 9 pistols in their pants pockets as they were too large to put inside their belts. Benson put the M17 pistol inside her purse while Myers put the laptop computer and power cord inside the courier pouch once he removed the diplomatic seal from the pouch flap. His Maxim 9 pistol was also in his pocket.

Once they entered the restaurant, they sat down with Gunny on one end of the table, Myers and Benson with their backs to the wall at the back side of the table and Lawson at the other end of the table. They had just finished their breakfast and were getting ready to leave but still sitting when a man with a heavy build, slight oriental features and a thick Fu Manchu mustache walked up to them and sat down. Each of the team members went for their weapons but did not pull them out.

"I am Ansar Rasulov, the local Assistant Police Chief," the man explained. "I received word from Bishkek, our capital, that you are here on some very important matter. In the past few days, a number of people have arrived in our city from many parts of the world and a review of those entries show us they are people that have extensive experience in both scientific and diplomatic circles. Your names were on that list. You were also involved in an altercation yesterday here in the hotel lounge. Now, before you go anywhere, I would like to know what you are doing here and what your intentions are." He looked from one team member to the next as Lawson noticed two men standing in the doorway to the restaurant. They appeared to be watching the team and Rasulov.

"Are these men with you, Chief?" Lawson asked as he looked toward the doorway. Rasulov turned to look and, from Lawson's angle, could see Rasulov's expression change to one of fear.

"No one make any quick movements," Rasulov advised as he turned toward the team then back to the two men at the door. He slowly got up and proceeded to approach the men. Lawson and Gunny already had their weapons out of their pockets and ready to fire from their sides of the table. Myers reached his hand back to an outlet next to the table. Pulling a plug out of the wall that provided light to their table, he took a paperclip that was attached to the zipper on the courier pouch and slid the paperclip over the prongs of the plug. While watching the conversation going on between the two men and Rasulov, he slipped the plug to the entrance of the electrical outlet but did not push it in. They all waited as the conversation continued to get more heated.

Lawson looked at Gunny as Gunny slowly nodded at Lawson. As they both looked back at Rasulov, Gunny could see one of the men pull a weapon from his belt. Both Lawson and Gunny jumped up at the same time. At that moment, the overhead lights flickered and went dark as Myers pushed the plug into the wall. The restaurant still had light from the windows but the room had lost its bright lighting. Gunny reached the man that had pulled the weapon while Lawson was one step behind, shoving his weapon into the second man's neck. Both men froze.

Speaking in perfect Russian, Lawson ordered, "Move and I'll pull the trigger." Rasulov turned to look at Gunny, then at Lawson and then turned to see both Myers and Benson had their pistols pointed at the surprised group of men standing frozen at the entrance.

"My superiors did say that you were capable," Rasulov observed as the result of the confrontation became obvious. "However, this display of protecting me was unnecessary. He was merely showing me that he had brought his weapon in case I was to experience any trouble. Now, how did you get the lights to go out and how did you get those guns into my country?"

"I saw fear on your face when you turned to look at them," Lawson explained as he wondered about Rasulov's comment about his superiors knowing about their capabilities. If that was the case, then Rasulov's superiors knew who the team was before he came to the restaurant, a thought that disturbed Lawson.

"That was not fear, that was disappointment," Rasulov stated as he went back to his seat. "They were supposed to stay out of sight. Now, as to the weapons."

Benson pulled out her diplomatic card as Gunny and Lawson pulled their courier cards.

"We are carrying highly classified information and, as official diplomatic couriers, we are authorized to carry weapons in your country based upon prior diplomatic agreements," Benson clarified.

Rasulov looked at each of the courier cards then turned to Myers, "What about him and his weapon?"

Lawson smiled and answered, "He's the highly classified information. We always have a weapon in the courier pouch as well as on ourselves. He happens to be the courier pouch and, just so happens, he's able to use the weapon that is with him." At that moment, Gunny turned away from the rest of them to pick up a piece of toast from the table. What he was doing, in fact, was turning so they couldn't see him grinning at Lawson's explanation. The two men and Rasulov just looked at each other as Myers went and unplugged the cord he had put in the outlet and took the somewhat charred and distorted paperclip off of the plug.

"I don't know if that is the way the agreement is concerning the item you're protecting as having a weapon should be interpreted but I guess it could be seen that way," Rasulov expounded as he leaned back in the chair. "I'm not going to raise an issue with it as I can see you all went out of your way to protect me even though you may have thought I was interfering with your project."

"You wanted us to tell you what we are all doing here and why so many suspicious people are coming into your country at this time," Lawson commented.

"That would be helpful," said Rasulov.

"We have no idea yet why we're here," Lawson expounded. "The reason we are here is because there is some threat and we are trying to find out what that threat is. Your help would be greatly appreciated." Gunny winced as Benson wondered why Lawson would tell Rasulov their intentions.

Rasulov leaned forward in his chair as Lawson and Gunny sat back down. "Why would you need my help?'

"It's simple," Lawson started as he glanced at Gunny then back to Rasulov, "You have a need to know what all the activity is about and we need to find out what this threat is. You have resources and knowledge we need and you have knowledge of the culture and the terrain that makes up the Osh Oblast. Something major is about to happen and it may mean serious consequences for your community. We can be eyes and ears for you to determine what is developing. Your support may help us nip this problem before it gets out of control." Rasulov sat up and rubbed his face with his left hand as he contemplated Lawson's words.

"How do I know I can trust you or your intentions?" Rasulov asked as he pulled on the suspender under his suit jacket. Lawson noted that Rasulov was left-handed as every move he made with his hand was with his left and he barely moved his right hand. Lawson played a hunch.

"I know you sacrificed a lot for your people as a policeman as you moved up the ranks," Lawson detailed. "You have wounds that stay with you, ones that require you to adjust your daily routines to continue in your work. This is much the same. Adjustments are required to stay on top of the issues that face you but you're not a novice in doing that. We have the same issue. We are not familiar with the environment we are walking into and, like you, there is a question of trust as to whether we can expose our intentions to you. So we're both in the same boat."

Rasulov rubbed his right arm as he listened to Lawson. The pain in the arm didn't bother him as much as the constant nagging of the dead weight it created as he would make quick turns and movements. "You are very observant," Rasulov responded. "I appreciate your understanding of my physical situation and I do think that we might be able to help each other. I am concerned that there are parties coming into my city that intend great harm. The quality of the characters arriving recently matches with the ability for much mischief. I would like to know who you are. Looking at your appearance and how you carry yourselves, I would conclude that you three men are military. As for the woman I'm not so sure." Lawson figured at that moment it was time to let the whole cat out of the bag.

"I'm Lieutenant Lawson of the US Navy," he said. Pointing to Gunny, Myers and Benson in that order, "This is Master Gunnery Sergeant Gunny Glendenning of the United States Marine Corps, US Navy Petty Officer Nick Myers and US Diplomat Joanne Benson."

Rasulov looked at each one then said, "I feel I can trust you and I think that I can help you. Wait a minute." Rasulov reached into his left pocket with his left hand and pulled out a small notebook. Flipping through the pages using his left thumb he stopped and looked up at Myers. "Are you the same Myers that is supposed to meet with Professor Magnus Murodov at the Technical Institute?" Myers nodded yes.

"So you knew we were coming?" Lawson inquired.

"Yes," Rasulov answered. "Your visit was important to us because our electrical system in the city is getting old and we need more efficient energy resources to deal with the ever increasing demand on our electrical utilities. Our leadership read some of Doctor Myers papers on energy wave generation and wanted Professor Murodov to draw some knowledge from Doctor Myers' efforts. Doctor Myers is a US Navy Petty Officer? How does that work? Never mind, now I know I can trust you since we invited you. This other effort you are engaged in wouldn't be 'Shiny Object', would it?"

Lawson smiled as Rasulov reached across his body with his left hand, picked up a fly swatter from the next table over, swatted a fly on their table then used the swatter to brush the fly off the table. "Dirty little beasts," Rasulov cursed at the annoying insect.

"So you know about 'Shiny Object'," Lawson probed.

"Yes," Rasulov confirmed. "We got a secret memo from Bishkek, our country's capital yesterday. Does your group know who those two men were or who they were associated with that were apprehended yesterday in this hotel?"

Gunny slapped his hand down on the table, "We were attacked by those two men with knives yesterday and we think they are somehow associated with the Kyrgyzstani government." Looking at Gunny and weighing his remark, Rasulov suddenly realized that this was much more serious and disconcerting than he had previously assumed.

"I had a man by the name of Nurlan Isakova come to see me yesterday," Rasulov stated as he looked at his notebook. "He works for a company called 'Propheta Nostri' in the northern part of the Fergana Valley north of here. He's also one of Professor Murodov's technical aides. He claimed that a friend of his disappeared about a week ago and he has not heard from him. This friend also worked at the Propheta Nostri Company."

Lawson looked at Gunny as both he and Gunny exhibited a startled look on their faces. Rasulov looked at both of them and figured something was just triggered that had significance.

"We know of this guy's disappearance from Nurlan Isakova. We met Isakova yesterday," Lawson commenced. "What caught Gunny and my attention is the name 'Propheta Nostri'. You see, Gunny and I both studied this in our Latin histories training between projects. It's Latin meaning 'Our Prophet'. It's from a set of writings by Richard Hakluyt called 'Navigations, Voyages, Traffics…' and something or other written in 1594. The writings cover stories of political activity and warfare that went from 1190 AD to 1594 AD and involves the Masters of the Order of the Dutch knights, commonly called the Hospitaliers of Jerusalem. Gunny and I had to use this document to see how Latin was translated to Old English."

"So what does that have to do with the name of the company?" Rasulov inquired.

"The writings had much to do with the warfare and intrigues that went on that allowed certain countries to gain control over other countries," Lawson explained. The name of the company seems unique in that the name has come to represent conquest, complete conquest." At that remark, Rasulov's eyes widened as he saw the focus of Lawson's comments.

"In other words," Gunny added, "the name may have a potential association with this unknown threat we are looking at. Add to that, we saw some computer code yesterday that indicates that the company in question is working on some type of artificially intelligent weapons system."

Rasulov put his notebook on the table and proceeded to write in it. Once finished, he put the notebook in his suit jacket pocket and smiled as he got up. "I will take you to the location of the company tomorrow. You will all dress in police officers' uniforms so that it will look like a normal safety inspection. Miss Benson, you will be a mute officer and talk by writing only. I suspect that you can't speak Russian and you don't know Kyrgyz. As for you Gunny, speak as little as possible. Your Russian sounds like you're strangling a cat."

Everyone laughed at Rasulov's comment.

"We'll meet tomorrow afternoon at 1:00 PM here in the restaurant," Rasulov instructed. "We'll have you change into uniforms in your rooms before we leave. I want to get to the company by 2:30 PM as that's the time they have their shift changes and that is the optimum time to do an inspection. Any questions?"

"Yea," Gunny called out. "Who made you boss?"

"It's OK, Gunny," Lawson interjected. "He knows the territory and the players. Let's follow his lead. I'm sorry, Mr. Rasulov, Gunny is just showing his US Marineship courtesies." Gunny just nodded as Rasulov smiled, then laughed and left with his two cohorts while the team went back to their hotel room.

When they got back to the room, Myers sat down and began to do research on the Osh area. While he did so, Gunny began cleaning and checking the weapons as Lawson continued to look through the paperwork that was in the courier pouch.

"So, can we use our phones?" Lawson asked of Myers.

Myers turned and responded, "According to an encrypted message I got this morning, you can use the phones without fear of being tracked because you are identified as local citizens on the phones. Each of us has a Kyrgyzi, Russian or Uzbeki name as our caller ID. The first letter of the first name matches up with the first letter of our last names. So, my phone has the caller ID name 'Mushin Amaritov'. The first letter of the first name is 'M' which is my name 'Myers'. It's the same for each of you. So if Lawson is calling me I will know because the caller ID shows 'Leonid Korvoskov' with the letter 'L' being the identifier for Lawson. Everyone understand? By the way, Admiral Roedl has the list of names for our phones so if we call him, he'll know who it is."

After a few hours of conversation and brain-storming, they finally decided to get some sleep. Benson figured that she was safe enough to get some sleep using the adjoining room and Gunny agreed as long as she left the door between the adjoining rooms open. Lawson said he's take the first watch as everyone began to get settled. Lawson informed Benson that each person on watch would be going into her room as well as into the room the men were in as a security check. She agreed, at which point, Lawson reminded her not to shoot him when he came in.

As they were getting ready for bed there was a knock at the door. Lawson moved toward the door as the others found their positions and had their weapons pointed toward the door. Lawson opened the door with his pistol in his hand to find a police officer with a number of suit carriers over his shoulder. Looking rather shocked at the reception, the officer looked once more at the door to the room and the number on the door. It was the right room number.

"I've brought uniforms from Chief Rasulov. He says they will fit unless you have gained weight or changed in stature. He's got good records on all of you except for Miss Benson. For her he had to guess on the size of the uniform. Is my English OK?"

Everyone started laughing as Lawson responded, "You're English is perfect," then took the uniforms from the officer and handed them to Gunny. The others put their weapons away as the officer stood in the doorway.

"So what did Rasulov do to determine Benson's size needs?" Lawson probed as his curiosity peaked.

"The Assistant Chief grabbed one of the women from the documents room that he thought matched Benson's features," the officer said. "He took her to the uniform room and had her try on women's uniforms until she found one that fit. She said later that she didn't want to be a police officer as the uniforms are too hot and itch too much." Everyone laughed at the officer's explanation.

"Anything else we need to know?" Gunny asked as he took the uniforms.

"I just want you to know that all the leather stuff for the uniforms is there but Chief says you have to use your own weapons in the holsters," the officer informed the group as he turned to leave. Lawson closed the door and they set up their security as they went to bed.

Chapter 6

The Russian Connection

"CAT205. That team has been an irritating pain to me for the last two years. Where do the American's get such people? They appear to have no rules, no methods, no plans, just goals and they don't seem to fail. I'd love to have just one team able to do what they do. They don't seem to understand that there has to be some predictability in their methods to keep other countries from assuming the worse about their intentions. Until they came along I slept reasonably well at night. Not so much anymore." – General Mikhal Vikovny, GRU Intelligence Group Operations Directorate

It was 6:00 AM on July 15th when Captain Pavel Volkov arrived at the Russian embassy in Osh. After going through security checks and verification of who he is, an aide led him into the main conference room of the embassy.

The conference room reminded Captain Volkov of the conference rooms at the Kremlin in Moscow. As he opened the double doors of the conference room, he could see the doors were heavy mahogany with engravings of working people on both doors, reminiscent of the Soviet Union era. Opening the doors, he stepped into the room where two generals sat. The room's walls were covered in mahogany with pillars evenly spaced out going down the length of each wall. The pillars had exquisite carvings of groups of people that were workers holding flags. Again, something of a throwback from the communist era. At the center of the room was a heavy mahogany table with heavy mahogany chairs covered in red velvet fabric on the back and seat of each chair.

"Good morning, Captain," came the voice from one of the generals. "This building used to be the Central Committee's building for this oblast during the Soviet period so the decorations are reminiscent of such. We felt it would be a waste of such beautiful wood to change it so we decided to leave it the way it was. I'm General Smolask and this is General Vikovny. We have been sent by the President to give you orders and instructions. Do you care for something to drink?"

"Thank you General," Volkov remarked. "I could use a good cup of expresso." Volkov knew in his diplomatic circles that if someone offers you something to eat or drink, you don't refuse it even if you don't want it.

General Smolask was in his late sixties and heavyset with a short, military haircut and a uniform that had seen better days. Volkov could see that he smoked a lot as the cigarettes in the ashtray could attest to. He wore the insignia of an intelligence officer, though Volkov assessed that he was just in the business of directing traffic for the activation of different operations. His spying days were way in the past. However, Volkov knew not to underestimate the man. Something in his expressions told Volkov that Smolask was a survivor and was very good at it.

General Vikovny was a different story. He was well built, in his mid-thirties with an impeccably tailored uniform. His face had a determined look about it and he was always watching all the movements and expressions of each person in the conversation. If there was one flaw Volkov picked up almost immediately, it was that Vikovny was overconfident with his skills. Something Volkov picked up observing people during his negotiating days. It was a similar trait Lieutenant Lawson exhibited from what Volkov had seen of Lawson, except in Lawson's case, the confidence matched the skill.

"Expresso for the Captain," General Smolask shouted. "Now Captain, you have been acquainted with an operation called 'Shiny Object'. Is that true?"

"Yes, Sir," Volkov confirmed.

"And you met a young US Navy Commander by the name of Elizabeth Norman, did you not?" Smolask asked as he drank from his coffee cup.

"I did, Sir," Volkov admitted as he watched a young woman walk across the floor and place a tray with a small cup, cream, sugar and a small pot filled with expresso coffee. "She was quite an accomplished woman, that Norman. She took out the assassin 'Dominici', which was no small task."

"Very accomplished she is and you have done very well yourself," Smolask responded. "General Vikovny, he's all yours. You both have a good day." With that, General Smolask got up and proceeded to walk to the big doors to exit. "Don't drink too much of that expresso. It'll put your heart into hyper-speed," he said as he pushed the door and exited the room. Volkov sat perplexed as to what this was all about. He was about to get that question answered.

"Are you familiar with a US team called CAT205?" Vikovny began.

"Yes. Commander Norman is one of the prime team members of that team," Volkov stated.

"And I understand that as a language exchange candidate to the US, you trained one of their key team members, Lieutenant James Lawson in the Russian language?" Vikovny posed as

Volkov began to get concerned about the direction the questioning was going.

"The answer is yes and why don't you get to the core of your concern," Volkov protested.

"Don't get all torn over the questions I have, Captain," Vikovny asserted. "I'm merely asking these questions to confirm what was reported as to your experience with the CAT205 Team. You have the rare value of actually working with the team indirectly and we are desperately trying to understand how they operate and what their methods are. They made fools of us in Iran and they appear to be getting the upper hand on this Colonel Zhu situation. We don't want them being able to confiscate the weapon system Zhu has developed and we feel they are extremely capable of moving and hiding whatever weapon system Zhu has in his possession. CAT205 is quite advanced for such a small team and we need to know the upper boundaries of their capabilities, which we don't right now."

Volkov began to understand and was willing to continue. "Very well, Sir, what do you need to know?"

Vikovny was perplexed by Volkov's reactions. They were quite abrupt for one serving in the Army's diplomatic branch. He began to realize that Volkov's reaction was out of character because he didn't like the interrogation methods of the GRU and here he was talking to a General in the GRU. "It can be forgiven," Vikovny thought to himself.

"First, let me finish," Vikovny requested. "We lost 87 good Russian soldiers and a key, prominent Russian scientist by the name of Polevsky in Iran. This was due to the actions on July 31st of 2015 when US Navy Lieutenant James Lawson, US

Marine Master Gunnery Sergeant Arnoud Glendenning and US Navy Petty Officer Nicholas Myers with help of a Colonel Edward Draper of the US Army's 25th Ranger Regiment destroyed a good portion of an Iranian army base, our research facility in western Iran, took out a battalion of Iranian soldiers, destroyed two years of laser weapons research including all the documentation and, as an after action, took out one of our key European spies named 'Tripoli'."

"They're the ones that took out Tripoli?" inquired Volkov. "Now I am impressed." Vikovny just rolled his eyes at the focus of the action that impressed Volkov. "The kids today," Vikovny thought to himself as he prepared to give Volkov his instructions.

"Here is what you are to do then I will give you the information we have," Vikovny declared as he prepared to lay out the plan. "I want you to watch the CAT205 Team without them knowing you're watching them. If something comes up that will give the CAT205 Team an advantage to make the mission a success for them, I want you to approach only Lieutenant Lawson with what they need to make that happen. We need for you to observe the team's methods, how they operate and, most importantly, how they get themselves out of difficult situations. Do you understand?"

"Yes, Sir, but what about keeping them from getting the weapons or whatever Zhu is developing?" Volkov asked.

"That's important and, if you keep your eyes on them, we should know the time to come in to grab the weapons," Vikovny advised. "If we feel the CAT205 Team is too far ahead of us in getting the weapons, we may have to take them out to keep them from confiscating the weapons. We feel that the action to take them out, if necessary, will be right after Zhu's test demo, which we think can be any day now. That's when the CAT205 people will be going for Zhu's weapons and designs and will be the most vulnerable. Do you understand?"

"I understand," Volkov commented while thinking about destroying the lives of such capable people. This spy business was not to his liking and, once this was finished, he wanted nothing more to do with these GRU intelligence people. He also realized that the GRU had more information on the threat than they were giving out to teams involved in finding the threat.

"Now as to the information we have so far and how to get new information to you," Vikovny directed. "We know that Assistant Chief Ansar Rasulov has been assisting the CAT205 Team based upon information from our spy in the Osh Police Department. We also know that Chief Rasulov is taking some members of the CAT205 Team out to a facility in the northern part of the Fergana Valley. The facility is known as the Propheta Nostri Corporation and the CEO of that company is a guy named Cho Ming who we suspect may be Zhu but are not sure."

"Wait! That matches with what we got when Commander Norman looked at a picture I showed her in Volgograd," Volkov interrupted. "The picture was labeled Cho Ming but Norman said it was a picture of Colonel Qiang Zhu."

"Why weren't we told this? We needed that confirmation!" Vikovny shouted.

"I provided that information to the intelligence people yesterday," Volkov responded. "It may still be going through the channels."

"That should have been stamped 'Essential' and sent to us directly," Vikovny demanded.

"That may be the way you work within your agency but I'm an outsider. I work for the Diplomatic Offices," Volkov countered. "So don't put something on me where I'm not doing my job. If you wanted to have immediate response, you should have given me a direct line to someone in your agency that had the ability to expedite discoveries."

"Ok, calm down," Vikovny responded. "Your objections are convincing. I'll be providing you a direct number to call. It'll be the same number we will use to provide updates to you as we get them. I will send confirmation from what you just told me to the President that Zhu is verified and the weapons are being developed at the Propheta Nostri facility. I'll also pass that on to our analysis and planning people. Now to go on with our present information."

"Ok," Volkov acknowledged as he prepared to continue writing. "So this also matches with your belief that it is Colonel Zhu we are interested in. I won't ask you how you linked Zhu up with this threat.

"Next item," Vikovny continued as he ignored Volkov's comment, "is the presence of an American warehouse somewhere up in the same area as Zhu's facility. There's also the rumor flying around that the US brought in 5 nuclear artillery shells but it's just a rumor. We also know that a woman that's not part of the CAT205 Team was sent from the Pentagon in Washington, DC to be with the team. We don't have her name yet but we think she's part of their analysis group. There's another person involved in all this by the name of Guljigit

Sukhrab. He is a senior member of an organization called 'Rogue World'. He has somehow become connected to Colonel Zhu but we don't know in what capacity. He was seen in Crete along the docks at the same time Lieutenant Lawson was seen in the vicinity. We don't know if Lawson had some exchange of information going with Sukhrab but is seems very coincidental that they both were there at the same time. As to your report..."

"This is in my report but, since you haven't seen the report yet, I feel I should update you on it," Volkov interrupted as Vikovny glared at him then nodded for Volkov to speak. "Commander Norman did some initial analysis of the diagrams your office sent to us. You know, the aircraft diagrams."

"The aircraft diagrams?" Vikovny questioned. "Oh, yes, the diagrams of the aircraft without a tail section. I remember our people thought the dimensions were inaccurate."

"That's the same thing she mentioned," Volkov remarked. "She said the Chinese will often show diagrams that require a set of algorithms to get the real dimensions. However, what really caught her attention was that the cockpit of the aircraft had no seat for the pilot and no mounts showing the installation for a seat. The dashboard was completely void of any instrumentation."

"That is very unusual," Vikovny pondered as he thought about Volkov's assessment. "Did Commander Norman give you any indication of what it might be used for?"

"That's what I'm getting to, Sir," Volkov stated as he continued his report. "Commander Norman and I met with a Doctor Ivan Sergevich at the Volgograd Technical Institute. Dr. Sergevich thinks that the cockpit is actually designed to hold a control module. He thinks that the design is for a Kamikaze-type drone that can be used for targeting different types of targets, be they be buildings, people or vehicles. He says the load size of the aircraft and the size of the engine indicates the aircraft could fly for 15 to 20 minutes before the engine overheats and burns up."

"Ok, I got that," Vikovny cut Volkov short. "We can deal with the issue of the aircraft later. I need for you to get prepared to surveil the CAT205 Team. That's your first priority. I'll put another person on determining what these aircraft are for. Now where were we?"

"Sukhrab was on the docks at the same time Lawson was," Volkov reminded Vikovny.

"Oh, yes, Lawson," Vikovny recollected. "Our intelligence people believe that there is a CIA agent, maybe two in Osh at the present time. We've heard of a large shipment of military-type cases being delivered somewhere in the Fergana Valley. What caught the attention of the people in Moscow was that there were two large trucks that were loaded at the river port in Termez, Uzbekistan and delivered to someplace in the Fergana Valley. One of our agents watching the docks in Termez says that many of the crates had NATO markings on them."

As he was talking an embassy clerk walked into the conference room with a folder and placed it on the table in front of Vikovny. The clerk turned and left as Vikovny picked up the folder and opened it. He read through one page then turned to another as he frowned then started to smile.

"It's messages from our intelligence listening post in Balashov, Russia," Vikovny apprised Volkov. "The first message informs us that the analyst the Pentagon assigned to the CAT205

Team is Joanne Benson. Our information on her is that she is a Senior Analyst in East Asian Affairs for the US Defense Intelligence Agency. She's been there for nine years and has some links with some questionable people in the global new world order effort. It doesn't appear that she's a part of it but has had many meetings with some of them. Probably part of the job."

"She's not someone I had been informed about," Volkov observed.

"The second message is more interesting," said Vikovny as he picked up the page. "It says Michael Blanding from the CIA has come to Osh. It says that he has contacted Professor Magnus Murodov at the Osh Technical Institute several weeks ago and has since disappeared. They think he may have been involved in that shipment of military-type materials to Osh we talked about earlier. It's possible he dropped the shipment off in Osh and left the country. However, I'm wondering what he had to talk to Professor Murodov about."

"Michael Blanding," Volkov reminisced. "I seem to be running into him a lot lately since I got into the diplomatic arm of the Army. He's like a ghost, there one day and gone the next. By the way, General, it would make sense for him to see Professor Murodov in order to set a link-up between Murodov and Petty Officer Nicholas Myers. You know Myers is the MIT graduate that's on the CAT205 Team. We approved the meeting between Myers and Murodov as a part of me getting involved with the 'Shiny Object' operation. Someone had to set up the meeting between Myers and Murodov and Blanding seems to be the most likely candidate, so I suspect Blanding left immediately so as not to draw attention to the CAT205 Team. Since Blanding is such a high profile agent, his continued presence in the area would draw attention to something important happening here in Osh, not a good situation for a team that's working undercover."

"I agree. There's something else here," Vikovny said as he pulled out a small piece of paper. "It's directed to you, Captain. It says, 'Tashkent upset over storage of 5 NATO nuclear artillery shells in warehouse'. It's directed to you to find out what this is all about. What are we doing storing NATO rounds of any type outside of our military or analysis labs?"

"I don't know, Sir, I'll check it out," Volkov replied as he made more notes in his notebook. "Do I have any backup on this effort? Any people supporting me?"

"No one officially," Vikovny answered as he pulled a cellphone from a box. "However, this is a satellite cellphone so you can talk anywhere even if there's no cell tower. The one number in the contacts list will take you directly to the person taking your reports and it will be the same one sending you the instant updates. If you get into serious trouble come to the Russian embassy or call the embassy if you're arrested. Any other questions?"

"Not immediately, Sir, no questions," replied Volkov as he placed his notebook and the phone in his briefcase.

Vikovny looked down once more at the folder on the table. "Thank you, Captain, for coming to Osh and coming in on such short notice. Remember, the only person you're to talk to on the CAT205 Team is Lieutenant Lawson. Communicate only by text. Here is the number for the burner phone he got from Cory Jacobs from the US embassy annex in Heraklion, Crete. Jacobs provided me with the number when he verified I was with 'Shiny Object'. Take this number and don't let anyone else see it or know you've got it," Vikovny instructed as he handed the piece of paper to Volkov.

Once Volkov got the piece of paper and put it in his briefcase, Vikovny got up from his chair, collected his items and walked to the door. "You're in God's hands now," Vikovny called back as he opened the door. "I hope you're a praying man," he said then smiled as the door closed. Volkov just sat at the table for five minutes as he gathered his thoughts before leaving the embassy.

Chapter 7

Assembling the Pieces

"I thought this was going to be a simple collection of information, record it and report back to command with some additional responsibilities. So far it's been anything but that. I feel like I'm battling ghosts - people we never see, names we don't know and threats we can't identify. This is a totally different world but I have to admit that I haven't felt as much alive in the past few years as I do now. Still, it's way outside my comfort zone and my orders." – Senior Analyst Joanne Benson, Defense Intelligence Agency, The Pentagon – On loan to the CAT205 Special Operations Team

Gunny was making coffee as Lawson got up, showered and changed clothes. Looking at his watch, Gunny could see it was 6:30 AM on July 15th. Maybe they would be able to get some traction today on what this threat was all about. Gunny was a Marine and he liked to get a plan, go in and execute the plan. Not all this spinning around with limited information and without any goals. It drove him crazy. As he was standing and thinking about the lack of progress, Benson walked into the room from the adjoining room.

"Where's Lawson?" She demanded. "He walked into my room at 2:30 this morning and proceeded to go crashing across my bed and onto the floor. Scared the hell out of me!"

"Well, at least you'll start the day knowing that hell has left you," Myers quipped as he got up. Gunny laughed at that remark then handed Benson a cup of coffee.

"Maybe I wouldn't have fallen over the bed if you hadn't moved it!" came a shout by Lawson from the bathroom. Stepping through the doorway from the bathroom into the room, Lawson buttoned his shirt and gave Benson a cold stare which she responded in like manner.

Gunny laughed then admonished them, "Now children, let's get civil and, if everyone gets up fast enough, we can go downstairs to eat." Benson looked at Gunny then Lawson and smiled.

"They do serve excellent food here," Benson observed. "I'm hungry, let's go."

"Let's let Myers get a shower and get dressed first," Lawson advised as Lawson and Gunny checked their weapons and put them in their pockets. Myers grabbed his clothes and went into the bathroom. Ten minutes later he came out and had a perplexed look on his face. Moving the slide of his gun to load a cartridge, he noticed the round did not seem to go into the weapon as loosely as he expected. As he pulled the round out of the chamber he felt the weight of the round in his hand. Something was wrong. He looked once more at the weapon then realized he had picked up the wrong weapon by mistake. He had Benson's M17 pistol but something else registered as wrong as he held the round in his hand. He had handled 9mm rounds before and this one seemed odd.

Lawson came over to see what the problem was while Gunny took the round from Myers. Holding the round in his hand, Gunny instantly knew what was wrong. The bullet moved too freely inside the brass component of the cartridge. After pulling the bullet from the brass cartridge, Gunny could see the bullet had been previously removed and the powder had been previously emptied out. The cartridge was useless. He took the clip from Myers and removed all of the cartridges from the clip. Selectively pulling five rounds from the clips, he found the other cartridges were in the same condition and assumed that all of the cartridges had been tampered with. Forty-five rounds of useless ammo that had been professionally modified and he knew it didn't happen after Benson had arrived in Osh.

"Joanne, can you give me the name of the person that gave you the weapon at the Pentagon?" Gunny requested as he began to wonder how deep this charade was taking them.

Benson thought for a moment. "It was Louis McMasters that gave me the gun but the clips were handed to me by Lenny Kover."

"Was there a clip in the weapon when you got it?"

"No, I had to put the first clip in after I got them from Lenny."

Gunny pulled the clip from his own weapon. After removing a round, he shook it and listened to the powder moving in the cartridge. His rounds were good. Meanwhile, Lawson had taken one of the rounds that Gunny had examined from Benson's weapon. Playing on a hunch, Lawson pulled a toothpick he had gotten from the restaurant from his shirt pocket and put it into the cartridge. He pulled out some brown waxy material and handed the toothpick with the material from the cartridge to Gunny. Gunny looked at the material, smelled it and, setting toothpick down on the ashtray on the table, he motioned for Lawson's cigarette lighter. Gunny ignited the material which resulted in a very hot fire where the waxy material was situated.

"These rounds have been loaded with plastic explosives, looks to be Semtex 10," Gunny explained as he watched the fire burn down. "Had we fired one of the rounds, the pistol would have blown up and, if the explosion of the round being fired was significant enough, it would have set off all of the other rounds in the clip. Also, because the bullet in the cartridge has an expandable backend and each of the openings of the brass portions of the cartridges were slightly expanded which made the bullets sit loose in the cartridge, when the pistol was fired, the quick expansion of the rear of the bullet in the chamber would cause the bullet to jam in the chamber which would guarantee the weapon would explode in the person's hand. This pistol wasn't meant for defense, it was meant to kill its user." Benson just stood there as her face became beet-red. At that moment, she realized someone intended for her to be on a one-way trip. They all took a moment to think about what they had just found then put it out of their minds as they had more immediate concerns to deal with.

"Let's go down and get some breakfast," Lawson recommended as he picked up the courier pouch with the computer and power cable and handed it to Myers.

Gunny unzipped the garment bag with his name on it that was delivered earlier by the local policeman. "You guys go ahead. I'm going to try on my police uniform before I come down." They left Gunny in the room as they went to the elevator and down to the restaurant.

While this was going on, Professor Magnus Murodov and Nurlan 'Izzy' Isakova were experimenting with the high voltage generator they had modified after Myers recommended adding a resistor to the design. As they were working on the device on

Murodov's test bench, Izzy looked up to see two men enter at the far end of the main lab. Immediately recognizing that the men were a threat and were looking for them, Izzy got Murodov's attention and whispered, "big trouble." Murodov looked up and realized the significance of the threat. He pushed a metal grate under the area of the bench where a person would stand while working at the bench.

"What are you doing?" Izzy asked as Murodov connected one of the leads from his high-voltage generator to the grate.

"One of them has a gun and we can't compete with that," Murodov whispered as he saw the men moving closer while they looked at the nameplates identifying the persons responsible for each bench. "I'm giving them a welcome. Don't touch the bench and don't step on the grate. Do you have a copy of the picture you took of that first page of computer code?"

"Yes, here in my briefcase," Izzy responded as he opened the briefcase and handed Murodov the picture.

"Where's the 178 page printout of the computer code you got from the company?" Murodov questioned as he attached the second lead of the high-voltage generator to the test bench then took a bottle of alcohol and poured it on the floor over the grate. "The test bench is sitting on insulators so it's not grounded so doing this is safe until someone steps on the grate and touches the bench." He took the picture of the computer code and laid it on top of the running generator, hiding it from someone looking at the bench.

"The printout is with my case in the computer lab," Izzy answered as he and Murodov ducked down and moved to the computer lab. Closing the computer lab door, Murodov watched through a small separation in the blinds as the two men moved toward his bench.

"What if this doesn't work?" Izzy mouthed as they both looked through the blind.

"I guess we'll both be dead," was Murodov's response. They watched as the men approached the bench. One of the men saw the picture and went to reach for it. As he placed his hand on the bench surface, there was a flash and an immediate fire. The man that put his hand on the bench was thrown approximately 50 feet through the air while engulfed in flames. The second man ran from the lab with his clothes on fire.

"I think it's time we leave," Murodov exclaimed. "The sprinklers will put out the fire and I don't think we're coming back." They both headed out of the main lab while watching for where the second man had gone. They didn't see him and didn't stick around to find out what happened to him.

Back at the hotel, the team was just sitting down in the restaurant when Lawson looked through the doorway toward the front desk and saw Beth Norman. He immediately texted Gunny then headed for the front desk.

"Norman is here," he said to the others while he got up to go to the desk. Walking up to her, he put his hand on her shoulder which caused her to jump forward and turn around. An immediate smile erupted across her face as she saw Lawson and immediately hugged him.

"It's so good to see you, my love," she exclaimed as he held her and gave her a quick kiss. Benson stood wondering if this is how all the team members relate to on another when a voice from behind her grabbed her attention.

"They have been quite an item for the past year," Gunny said as he approached from the elevator area and smiled at Lawson and Norman. "Their affection for each other is a constant reminder to all of us that our job is more than just getting the job done. It's also about respecting and caring for each other. As Gunny was talking, everyone had turned their attention toward him and started laughing.

"What's with the police uniform?" Norman inquired as she continued to laugh.

"It's what we are going to wear this afternoon and I had to try it on," Gunny answered as he realized that other people in the hotel lobby were looking at him.

As he was looking around, a woman came up to him and spoke in perfect English, "Young man, would keep an eye on my bags at the front door until my limo gets here. They are very valuable and, since you're an officer of the law, I would expect you to be kind enough to watch them until the limo arrives. Oh, and once the limo arrives, I want you to come into the restaurant to get me so that I can make sure everything is handled properly." At that point she walked away as Gunny was getting ready to follow her and protest about her request. It was Norman that stopped him as she grabbed Gunny's sleeve. Gunny turned to see why Norman was interrupting him.

"Guys, I saw that woman's face in a bunch of pictures shown to me by Captain Volkov of the Russian Diplomatic Corps while I was in Volgograd," Norman said as she looked toward the restaurant entrance. It's the same group of pictures that had

Colonel Qiang Zhu's picture in it. They were all pictures of people the Russians think are somehow involved in the threat we are trying to assess." Lawson looked at Norman then at the luggage near the front door of the hotel.

"Qiang Zhu, huh? We need to see what's in those bags," Lawson stated as he realized the woman was most likely American and she appeared to be a link to the threat. "Myers, see what you can do about getting into the bags. I'm going to check on her passport at the front desk. Benson, you're with me. Have your diplomatic ID ready to show the front desk attendant."

Myers and Norman went over to the luggage while Lawson and Benson went to the front desk. Gunny sat down in a chair near the restaurant entrance where he could see the woman in question. Gunny pulled his weapon out of its holster and placed it next to his leg where it could not be easily seen.

Myers took a look at the luggage. One piece of luggage immediately caught his attention – a makeup kit that had built in locks on both of its latches. He figured he could open the latches with a paperclip. He walked to the front desk and picked up a paperclip from a small turntable that had pens, paperclips and rubber bands on it. Going back to the makeup kit Myers opened each of the locks and freed the latches. What he saw caused him to motion to Lawson. Lawson finished taking pictures of the woman's passport then came over to see what Myers had found.

"It's a tiny gas engine, the smallest one I've ever seen," Myers observed as he pulled the tiny engine from the case. "It looks to be very high tech and professionally made. Look at the detail and the quality of the machine. It feels like it weighs less than a pound but sports fuel injection to four cylinders. This is quite an advancement in engineering." Lawson took the engine from Myers and turned it over in his hand. It was about the size of his hand and appeared to be made of materials that were not cheap and very capable of stress.

Lawson gave his opinion. "In my last year at Carnegie-Mellon, we attempted to build a battery-powered motor that was about this large and had the ability to lift 40 pounds, not including the weight of the battery. We couldn't meet the parameters of what was needed. This engine appears to have been designed to be able to accomplish what we could not and appears to be designed for use in either a small but powerful ground attack vehicle or in a small aircraft that must be able to travel at high speeds. By small, I mean possibly a very small drone-sized aircraft. Also, there are some markings on the bottom of the engine which says 'Dolotecque Corp, SN 01020' which I suspect is the company that made this device and it is probably the 1020th copy of this engine built."

While Lawson was talking, Norman had moved her attention to the second piece of luggage of the three pieces on the floor. It was an aluminum briefcase with built-in combination locks for each of the two latches. As she was doing so, Myers noted that there was also a credit card in the case from where he took the engine. Wondering what the credit card would be doing in the case, he took a picture of the front and back of it and placed it back inside the case while, at the same time, Lawson was taking numerous pictures of the tiny engine. Lawson handed the engine back to Myers which Myers placed back into the case.

Norman turned the briefcase over to Myers and as she did so, she watched out the window to see if the limo had arrived, no limo yet. Myers looked at the two three-digit rotary combination locks on the briefcase and then at Lawson. Going back to the combination locks, he noted what each lock was set to.

"You took pictures of her passport," Myers posed to Lawson. "Could you tell me her birthdate on the passport?"

Lawson read off the date which Myers tried in the left-hand combination lock. It was no good. He then tried the right-hand combination lock which resulted in the latch opening. "Now we've got to figure what the other lock has for a combination," Myers instructed as he looked at the passport picture to see what other number combinations might work. Meanwhile, Lawson walked back and forth between the entrance of the hotel and the luggage. He could see a limo off in the distance coming up the street.

"Limo coming," Lawson reported as he stopped and looked at the makeup kit. "Did you lock the case yet?"

"No," Myers responded.

Lawson opened the case and pulled out the credit card. Realizing the number would have to be three digits, he looked at the back of the credit card to see the three digit verification number. "Try '185'." Myers selected the numbers which resulted in the second latch opening. Myers opened the briefcase to see several drawings. Lawson immediately took his camera and proceeded to take pictures of each of the drawings as the limo was pulling into the entrance of the hotel. Once Lawson finished, Myers immediately closed the briefcase and set the combination numbers back to their original settings. Completing that action, Myers took the paperclip and proceeded to relock the makeup case as Lawson nodded to Gunny. Gunny holstered his weapon and went into the restaurant to tell the woman that the limo had arrived. Lawson stacked the luggage back into the original layout as the limo driver was nearing the door of the hotel. They all moved quickly to chairs in the lobby as the entrance doors opened. Moments later Gunny came back into the lobby and stood by the luggage until the woman came into the lobby from the restaurant as Gunny was not allowing the limo driver to pick up the luggage.

"Thank you for watching over these for me," the woman said to Gunny as she picked up the briefcase and looked at the combination locks. Satisfied that no one had tampered with her possessions, she motioned for the limo driver to take the luggage, gave Gunny a twenty-dollar tip in US currency and they both left. Once they left, the team went back up to the room to decompress.

Once in the room, Lawson looked at the pictures they had taken in the lobby of the documents and small engine. "What are you going to do with the twenty dollars that lady tipped you?" Lawson questioned as he saw Gunny waving the twenty dollar bill in the air.

"Maybe get some pizza," Gunny replied. "You know something, Lawson, I was only in the police uniform for 30 minutes and I've already earned money with it. This could have some potential for some additional income." Everyone laughed at Gunny's observations as Gunny went into the next room to change clothes.

Norman took the jump drive she had received in Volgograd and put it in the computer Myers was managing. She pulled up the pictures on the jump drive of the aircraft drawings and proceeded to discuss the drawings with the rest of the team.

"These pictures appear to be of some type of aircraft but I'm not sure of the dimensions since the Chinese are known to do drawings where you have to have specific formulas to determine the final measurements," she explained as she went from drawing to drawing. "According to an analyst in Volgograd, the drawings are incomplete as the tail section drawings of the aircraft appear to be missing. There are also formulas for some type of fuel combination that the analyst said would cause a carburetor-controlled engine to overheat in 15 to 20 minutes of constant use. However, that engine we saw today is a fuel-injection engine which would probably work well with that fuel mixture." Everyone looked at the pictures as Myers and Gunny began to realize that the software code they had seen a couple of days before tied into the drawings and the drawings tied into the engine they just saw.

"Maybe this is what that tiny engine is for," Lawson suggested. The comment brought them all to the realization that the woman with the luggage may well be a part of this whole mystery. As they were evaluating the drawings, a knock was heard at the door. Lawson pulled his weapon as he called out asking who it was.

"It's Professor Murodov and Izzy. We need help," came the voice from the other side of the door. Everyone pulled their weapons and waited for Lawson to open the door at the pronouncement. Lawson looked at Myers for confirmation that it was Murodov's voice and it was safe to open the door. Once Myers nodded 'yes', the door was opened, then Lawson pulled Murodov and Izzy into the room and checked the hallway for anyone else. Everyone put their weapons away once they were satisfied that there was no threat.

Myers made the introductions to everyone and explained who Professor Magnus Murodov and Nurlan 'Izzy' Isakova were. Murodov explained the situation at the lab that caused them to leave. "It's like they knew right where to find us," Murodov exclaimed while Gunny and Myers turned to look at Benson.

"That's because, when Myers, Benson and I went to visit you at the lab, Benson had an exercise watch on her that can be accessed from the outside and Myers said someone accessed the watch at 18:20 hours, the same time we were there, "Gunny explained.

"We were there from 6:00 PM until 7:35 PM that day so the 6:20 PM access on the watch by some outside party was probably the reason those men came after you," Myers instructed. "Benson was given instructions to not carry anything electronic on this operation but she was told by her boss that the instructions were not that important."

"Benson, you almost got us killed!" Izzy exclaimed. "That boss of yours needs to be fired. If this is the quality of leadership you've got back in Washington, your field teams have got some serious problems!"

Lawson leaned and whispered to Gunny, "Any foreigner talking about Washington, DC would call it Washington, DC. So why did Izzy call it Washington?"

"Maybe he's used to dealing with enough Americans in his work as a scientist that maybe he has picked up the language," Gunny advised. "Lawson, sometimes you're too paranoid."

Once the tempers died down, Izzy pulled out the 178 page computer printout and proceeded to explain.

"I brought this along with us when we were forced to leave the lab," Izzy started. "I printed this out yesterday. After some analysis I found that they're making a set of attack vehicles that can be fielded in short notice. I also found that they made changes sometime in the last month that requires a redesign of a propulsion system, most likely a gas-powered engine. One other thing that has me puzzled. They have measurements for heights that don't make sense. At first I thought that it was for clearances to not get stuck in openings in buildings but the translation from Kyrgyz to English may also represent altitude or.."

"That makes sense about the redesign of an engine," Norman interrupted. "We saw a tiny engine this morning and got pictures of drawings of the engine that may match what you're seeing. As for the use of the engine relating to your code, I don't think it's for a ground-based vehicle. I think it's for an aerial drone or series of aerial drones. I brought copies of aircraft diagrams that appear to match the potential of the threat and in looking at the pictures Lawson took of the engine we saw this morning, the size of the engine seems to match the space shown in the drawings for the aircraft. In other words, the dimensions shown on the drawings are the real ones. Also, one of the drawings shows the weight and shape of explosive charges that are destined to be installed into the nose of the aircraft. There are three different charges, each a quarter pound in weight and each shaped differently."

"A quarter pound shaped charge would be perfect to annihilate a person or even a group of people that are close together," Gunny instructed as he looked at the team's expressions. "It's the same as setting off a hand grenade." When Gunny said that both Lawson and Myers looked at each other and came to the same conclusion at the same time – this was a setup for an assassination attempt as the original message in the Admiral's office alluded to. But who?

Lawson looked at the people in the room and determined the next process. He pulled Norman aside and began discussing the steps going forward. "Beth, we have a lot of additional information that needs to be screened and analyzed," Lawson started as he watched Myers and Izzy looking at some computer code in the listings Izzy brought. "I suggest that I take Gunny and Benson with me while you work with Myers, the Professor and his aide on determining what the technological side of the picture looks like. I also want to ask if you could send the picture of the woman's passport we took this morning to see if anyone at ONI can come up with who she is and why she is here. I have a pretty good idea of why she's here but it would be good to see where she's been and who she's been talking to."

Norman thought about Lawson's suggestion then replied, "Jim, you need to be careful when you go out this afternoon. If the facility you're going into is the source of this threat, you may be identified by someone in the facility. Stay alert. I agree with your approach with one minor change. Benson is the only one Qiang Zhu doesn't know, a least that is what I'm assuming. But she's a neophyte and, as such, she can get you all in trouble. I personally would like you to take someone else but I know that's not possible so please keep her near the front door of the facility so she can't expose you or Gunny. You and Gunny read situations real well but, from what I've seen from her actions so far, I am not sure she would be able to respond adequately or quickly in a real action."

"Your suggestion is my concern as well," Lawson agreed as he picked up his garment bag with the police uniform and turned to go into the other hotel room adjacent to the room they were in. Turning back to Norman he said, "Have you ever given thought to the possibility that all the drawings and code we're looking at could be fake and just a diversion?" Norman thought about Lawson's comment as she realized she had been so focused on finding out what the diagrams and code represented she had never given a thought that it all might be a ruse. Moments later she watched as Lawson, Gunny and Benson left in their police uniforms as she looked at the clock on the nightstand – it was 1:00 PM and they had a lot of information to go through. She typed out a message on her cellphone, attached a picture of the woman's passport that the team got that morning and sent the message off to Admiral Roedl at ONI in Washington, DC.

Chapter 8

The Propheta Nostri Facility

"I've seen some real threats in my time as a police officer and police commander. As an Assistant Police Chief, I have had my share of major operations with significant impacts to the greater Soviet and Russian sphere of influence. The Chechen situation, the chaos of the change from communism to an open government and the 2010 uprisings in Osh were ones that come to mind. This situation that appears to be developing with all of the foreign agents, questionable characters, cryptic messages and even more unusual information from Bishkek like the 'Shiny Object' operation seems to be something that may make all these other operations pale by comparison." – Chief Ansar Rasulov, the Osh Assistant Police Chief

Lawson, Benson and Gunny met Chief Rasulov in the main lobby of the hotel at 1:05 PM. Once they greeted each other, they went to two police cars in front of the hotel where two more policemen were standing. Lawson checked his weapon in his holster before getting into the car.

The cars traveled down highway A373, taking a road east of the town of Andijan to highway P-135. Turning north at the town of Kashkar, they went a short distance to the village of Barrazh.

The drive from Osh was through many small towns with field after field of various crops. Having grown up on a large farm, Lawson was struck by the vast sizes of the fields of different grains, vegetables, fruit trees and grassy areas for grazing, all of which seemed to go on as far as the eye could see. It also struck Lawson how abruptly the rich fields abutted against dry and barren hills that were scattered about the valley. It also interested him on how many small streams that, even in July, still had water running through the valley. A perfect place for farming and good crop yields.

They traveled down a paved road at the northern part of the Fergana Valley entering the village of Barrazh, Uzbekistan. On the left side of the road, there were farm houses, small stores and large fields. On the right side of the road there were eleven large buildings that appeared to be warehouses, businesses and processing facilities for cleaning produce before shipping. Behind the buildings were hills gradually rising above the valley and were covered in dry grass. This appeared to be the northern edge of the Fergana Valley that was some 80 miles long and 50 miles wide.

They arrived at one of the buildings toward the end of the group of large buildings, the Propheta Nostri facility, at 2:35 PM. Parking the cars in a large parking lot in front of the facility, they got out and looked at the building. It had a large entrance for an inside loading dock with smaller doors going down the front of the building and no windows. The building had been constructed from large, pre-formed cement slabs that made the building stand approximately 30 feet high. Lawson estimated that the front of the building was approximately 350 feet wide.

Rasulov and his uniformed officers went to the first of the smaller doors next to the large entrance. He entered the facility, pulled out his ID and explained in Russian that, as part of the Uzbekistan/Kyrgyzstan health and safety enforcement agreement, he and his police force had the responsibility to do cursory safety checks of industrial facilities in the area.

As the group was escorted from the small waiting room into the main facility, Lawson looked around and took inventory of the layout. There was a large smoke-glass windowed room to his left with a matching smoked-glass sliding glass door that was continually opening and closing as people went in and out. The people inside the room were all dressed in white lab coats and pock-clipped ID cards. Lawson noted that the people inside the room appeared to be working on some sort of laser device that appeared to be a scanner of some type.

Looking to the right side of the facility, Lawson saw a side door going to the loading dock and a large number of wooden crates and pallets loaded with machinery against the right wall. Looking forward from where he entered was a long hallway with many double doors on each side that opened up into different areas. He also noted a group of people far down the hallway coming toward them that were obviously management of some sort as they were all dressed in suits. Lawson continued to look around as he wrote notes into the notebook Rasulov had given him. What caught Lawson's attention was that, unlike other corporations he had gone into, there were no posters on the walls as well as no charts, diagrams, advertising, notices or anything else. The walls around the areas he could see were deficient of anything, totally bare.

As he was looking up while make notes about the hallway area, he saw what looked like a man carrying a small metal object crossing the hall from one room to another. He was close enough for Lawson to recognize that the item the man was carrying appeared to be a wing of a model airplane. Lawson knew that he would be grabbed immediately and a major situation would develop if he took out his phone to take a picture so, realizing that restriction, he drew what he saw into the notebook. As he was doing so, he looked down the hallway once more to see the group getting much closer.

Three things immediately caught Lawson's attention. First, a man walking with the group but to one side was wearing a very definitive hat, a dark gray fedora with a silver band, the same hat he saw that the man at the end of docks in Crete was wearing. The second observation that caught his attention. The man at the front of the group was Colonel Qiang Zhu, the rogue Chinese colonel that was the core problem of his team's previous operation. Then the third observation. The woman walking next to Colonel was the same woman he saw that morning in the lobby with the small engine. Lawson immediately turned so that Zhu or the man in the hat would not see his face. As he turned, he looked directly into the face of Chief Rasulov.

"There are two men coming in that group that will likely recognize me," Lawson informed Rasulov. "They may also be able to recognize Gunny too."

Rasulov looked over Lawson's shoulder down the hallway. "Get out of here and go to the police car. Sit in the car with the door of the car open so that you can respond to help us if things get out of hand. Act like you're writing out your report. I'll get Gunny and get him out of here."

Lawson looked back to where the men were still approaching in the hall. They were close enough that he could hear their voices. "Benson has no experience in this stuff," Lawson instructed as he turned to face Rasulov once more. "If things get hot, she'll have no idea how to respond." Rasulov nodded agreement as he motioned Lawson to leave.

Lawson went out to the car and sat down in the rear passenger seat facing the facility with the car door open. Gunny came out a few moments later and walked up to the car Lawson was sitting in.

"I ran face to face with our old nemesis Colonel Qiang Zhu," Gunny said as he watched what Lawson was writing. "I don't know if he recognized me but he gave a facial hint that he thought something about my face looked familiar."

"We have to assume he has made us," Lawson replied. "They have cameras both inside and outside and you know what Zhu's response will be. That he somehow knows he has seen you somewhere which means he will look at the videos made of the camera shots of us. He will see you and me in the videos and the realization of who we are will come to him. I figure that he already knows we're here based upon what you told me about the attack against you and Myers in the lobby the first day you were here and the fact they put one of those guys I saw in there on me on the docks in Crete."

"Based upon what you just said, that means that they probably came out in force once they saw us enter the facility," Gunny surmised as he watched toward the entrance. "I sure wish Benson would get out here." At that comment from Gunny, Lawson took out his weapon and chambered a round. As he did so he could see Benson, Rasulov and the two other officers exit the building and walk toward them.

"I cited them for safety violations," Rasulov said. "I told them they have no safety notices or emergency exit signs and they have 30 days to get them installed or get fined." Lawson smiled at Rasulov at which point Rasulov exclaimed, "I hope you realize that if these guys succeed at whatever you people think and I think what they will do, I'll be one of those they will retaliate against. You'll be happily back in the US and I'll be unhappily in prison."

"The Uzbeki's wouldn't put up with that," Lawson said with a smile knowing that Rasulov was Kyrgyz. The smile irritated Rasulov even more than the possibilities that he could be outed by this series of events. He then realized that irritating people at the most opportune time was one of Lawson's skills that made him very effective. Rasulov just smiled back and motioned for everyone to get in the cars. As they did so, Lawson realized that Rasulov was beginning to read him much better than he had anticipated which Lawson felt was a good thing.

The hour and a half drive back to the hotel was a quiet one with no one speaking. Gunny was about to speak when Rasulov put his finger up and said 'Shush." Gunny looked at Rasulov for a moment then turned his head and looked out the side window at the passing view.

While Lawson's team was returning from the trip, Myers, Norman, Professor Murodov and Izzy were analyzing the computer programs and applying the information on what they knew about the aircraft design. They knew that the program was meant to control three different modules from one program by identifying the type of module from an ID number built into some readable code on the module. Myers came to the conclusion that the code was designed to control an aircraft drone with three different capabilities based upon the type of control module installed into the drone.

They were also able to determine that a new section of code was put in to control the injector valves on the engine. The engine was previously controlled by a carburetor. With the replacement of the carburetor with fuel injection, the injectors were controlled by the program which determined the flow of the fuel and the speed the engine thereby allowing greater control of the engine against overheating. This would allow for the drone to be able to fly for much longer periods of time. They were also able to determine the highest number of drones that could be controlled at one time. Myers calculated the total to be approximately 1000 drones. Finally, they were able to determine that each drone had a unique address and could be reprogrammed in flight. The same communication link used for one drone to talk to another could also be used to program a drone from the ground.

Once the team from the facility arrived at the hotel they found the others in the restaurant arguing over flight dynamics and g-force turn ratios. Rasulov motioned without speaking to everyone to go up to the room. When they all entered the room, Rasulov put his index finger once more to his lips. Everyone immediately understood not to speak as Rasulov wrote a note on a notepad and showed it to everyone. It said, "We've been bugged. Everyone with uniforms go into the other room one by one and take off your uniform and get dressed in your regular clothes. Make sure to remove your shoes too."

Everyone that was with Rasulov did as they were told. Once they completed the task, Rasulov went into the next room with one of the bathrobes provided by the hotel. Moments later they could hear the radio in the next room playing music as Rasulov came out of the room dressed in the robe and closed the door to the adjacent room.

As Rasulov was getting the robe and going into the room, Myers showed Lawson his findings by pointing to Myer's written comments. Seeing the results of Myers' and Norman's analysis and weighing what he had seen, Lawson paced the floor thinking about the possibilities of what these people in the facility were up to.

"Now we can talk," Rasulov advised. "I am pretty sure one of us had a bug put on us when we were in the facility. The reason I know this is that I saw one man in a white lab coat with an earbud in his ear respond and turn to look at me when I said 'what a bunch of jerks' in Uzbeki. He was about, let's see what's that in feet since you guys don't like metrics, oh yes, 45 feet from me. He would not have been able to hear me without some type of aid since I said it so softly. As Lawson and Benson were near me at that time I figured he could have picked it up from any one of us. Now, I would suggest that you, Mister Myers, go into that room with your computer and your skill and find out where that bug or bugs are located." Myers looked at Rasulov then the others as Norman nodded 'yes' to him.

As Myers walked toward the door with the computer, everyone could hear him say to himself, "Ok, it could be a cellphone frequency or it could be a 900 MHz signal. I'll try the cellphone frequency first," and he continued talking as he closed the door.

It was 45 minutes later when Myers came out. "There were two bugs. One in the sleeve of Chief Rasulov's suit jacket and one on the leather strap that would be on located on back of Lawson's uniform when he has on his leather holster belt and shoulder strap. Both bugs are continuous transmitting and link to cellphone towers. By hacking into the bugs I was able to see the phone numbers they are transmitting to and found that, if that receiving phone hangs up, the bug will try the number again in two minutes then continue sending the conversation. Even though I disabled the ability of the bugs to pick up voices, the bugs are still in the other room with the radio on."

"So we have no doubt that they are on to us," Lawson observed. "However, what I was able to see and document shows that they are definitely doing something with a small aircraft design. I saw one wing a lab guy was carrying that appeared to be a foot wide at the widest point tapering down to six inches at the wing tip. The wing was two feet long and was a right wing for a miniature aircraft. Also, one more thing. People in the lab at the left of the entrance into the facility were testing a scanning laser. I know it was a scanning one since I've used scanning lasers to scan surfaces of metal for anomalies. This one appeared to be pointed toward a bust of a head."

Gunny and Myers looked at Lawson then at each other as Myers was about to speak. Norman spoke first with the same conclusion the other two had come to. "I think what you saw was a facial recognition experiment using laser. When I was in weapons training, the instructor recommended not using a laser sight at night; you know the one that puts a red dot on the target. He stated that the target can immediately see where the origination of the laser dot is at which exposes the location of the shooter. I think a facial recognition method would have the same problem in that it would alert the target that they are being scanned, so why would they use laser for facial recognition?"

"It would seem that a laser scanner confirming a facial recognition either day or night would be seen by the target but that might not be a bad thing," Gunny stated. "From what we've seen so far, it appears that the device used to disable or kill would be something moving fast that can change course. That being said, a person panicking and trying to avoid the attacking device still can be hit because of the quick ability of the device to change to the target's movement."

Lawson walked back and forth a couple of times while stopping to look out the window while making a strange expression. Rubbing his head, he asked Norman if she had a pain pill for a headache then turning back to them he gave his assessment. "What Gunny and Norman just told us gives us the logic to say that, with a high level of confidence, someone or some target is to be attacked by an aircraft drone. Now bear with me. The small engine, the wing I saw, the shaped charges shown in the diagram, the dimensions of the aircraft in the diagrams, the modified fuel, Myers stating the coding shows three different capabilities for three different module functions for the aircraft, the testing that seemed to show facial recognition, the artificial intelligence communicated to other devices and the ability to communication to up to 1000 different devices says they have to be drones and they are probably designed to work as a swarm." Lawson stopped to catch his breath from the long description.

Everyone's eyes opened wider as Lawson's last part of the analysis hit home – a drone swarm? Norman sat down in the desk chair while Myers sat down in the lounge chair and Gunny sat on the edge of the bed. No one said a word for about 30 seconds then Rasulov spoke, "Well, isn't that what you came to find out? Lawson is probably as close to the truth as any one of us could be. Seeing his logic, I think it's probably the only real conclusion you can come up with. Remember the rule of 'Occam's Razor', the simplest explanation or the most obvious one is probably the right one. The more assumptions you have to make, the less likely you have the answer. You all have your answer, now what are you going to do about it?" Lawson looked at the others while he thought through the possible options.

"I think I have an answer," Lawson suggested while everyone sat up to listen. "Let's get some dinner."

"That's it?" Myers shouted as everyone laughed.

"Sir," Lawson stated while facing Rasulov, "you and your men are probably hungry. Why don't you all join us for dinner? We're buying but it won't violate your meals rule because this is a diplomatic dinner compliments of Diplomat Joanne Benson."

"Lawson?" Benson exclaimed then paused. "Well, I guess this is ok because they helped us get the information we needed." Then turning to Lawson, Benson remarked, "Jim, you can be a jerk at times." Lawson smiled and saw Norman doing the same thing. It was their chance to get their digs into the DIA and the Pentagon. They were both enjoying it and Benson knew it.

They all went to dinner except for Myers. He arrived about 15 minutes later and handed a small object to Lawson. Norman remembered that Lawson had a headache and she was supposed to have gotten a pill for him. It was 6:35 PM when they finished dinner and exited the restaurant. Everyone, except for Benson, Rasulov and his two officers, left to go back up to the room while Lawson and Norman went out the front door of the hotel and started walking together in the parking lot.

"Well, Jim," Norman started, "we haven't had time to talk to each other since I got here, How are you doing?"

"I'm doing well, Beth, just a little tired, and you?" Lawson replied.

"Ok. How's the headache? I'm sorry I forgot to get you a pill," Norman said as her hand went across Lawson's forehead. About that time Benson came up behind them. Lawson said something to Benson which caused her to go back inside.

Once Benson was back inside the hotel she fumed about the exchange between Lawson and her. "Lawson can be a real creep sometimes," Benson said to Rasulov as she looked out the hotel door toward Lawson and Norman. "He told me to get lost."

"Yes, sometimes he's a little caustic but not this time," Rasulov answered back. "Just watch and learn."

Lawson took Norman's hand and pulled her toward him. "Is the guy still watching?" he asked as Norman looked toward a car with a man in it in the parking lot.

"Yes," Norman replied. "Why don't we show him the love we have for each other."

Lawson laughed as he took Norman into his arms and gave her a passionate kiss. As he kissed her, Lawson was beginning to understand how women talked with their eyes and it was a response he was not expecting. From the look in her eyes during the kiss he could tell she was up for a fight and wanted to take the man in the car apart. "So much for my male charm" he thought to himself as they both turned and continued to walk hand in hand in the general direction of the car that got their interest.

As they approached the front of the car, the man in the car looked down, Lawson sidestepped and tapped on the driver's window which caused the man to look up and roll down his window. At that moment, Rasulov motioned to his two officers to follow him while motioning for Benson not to follow. She stood watching the policemen walk out of the entrance of the hotel.

"You seem to be paying special and particular attention to us," Lawson said to the man in the car. "I wouldn't necessarily be concerned since we are two lovebirds just taking a walk but the video camera on the car seat next to you tells me I should be concerned."

As the man moved his right hand down to the seat he turned his head back at the sound of a click as Lawson ratcheted a round into the chamber of his weapon and pointed the weapon at the man's head. The man was about to move when he saw Norman standing in front of the car with her weapon pointed at his head. He decided that any further movement would be detrimental to his health. About that time, Rasulov came up to the car with his two policemen.

"These two assaulted me," the man said as Rasulov and the two policemen looked on. After a moment the man continued, "What are you going to do about it?" Rasulov looked at Lawson and Norman then at the man and said nothing.

"Bring your right hand up and your left hand and put them on the window frame of the car door," Lawson instructed. "Oh, and don't even think about moving either hand down to the gun you have in the door drink holder. You listen to what I tell you and you will live to see tomorrow."

The man put both hands on the door window frame while Lawson opened the door. As he pulled the man out, he could see a revolver in a holster in the door cup holder. Lawson pushed him against the side of the car as Norman moved over and removed the revolver from the door. Then Norman stepped behind the man while Lawson reached in and retrieved another pistol lodged between the driver seat and the console. Next, he pulled out a video camera, cellphone and microphone amplifier. Taking the revolver from Norman, he handed the weapons and devices to Rasulov then pushed the man back into the car.

"If you want these items back you will have to come to the main police office in Osh to pick them up in the morning," Rasulov stated as he held out the items. "I'm not going to arrest you as I don't see yet where you have created a crime but I do see you as a threat and can take this action. Do you understand?" The man nodded his head affirmative, started up his engine and left.

"I understand you not arresting him but couldn't you have held him overnight?" Norman queried as Rasulov smiled.

"Did you do it?" Rasulov asked while looking at Lawson.

"Yes," Lawson responded. "It's attached to his belt. They'll figure it out after a few calls. He'll be thinking we're following him and almost always on top of him. By the way, he's the guy that wears that black fedora hat with the silver band on it."

"What are you two talking about and what does a man with a hat and a silver band have to do with anything?" Norman exclaimed.

"First, the man with the hat and silver band that was following me in Crete, was at the facility this afternoon and was the one we just sent off," Lawson explained. "Second, Myers modified one of the listening devices to show its location about 40 feet away from where it's really located, that's why he was late for dinner. He also fixed it so that it wouldn't go active again until I pulled the tape off on one side and attached it to the man. One minute after the tape was removed the bug goes active. They can see where the bug is located but they can't hear anything so it will take them some time to figure that he's carrying the bug and we're not following him. It will be a very exciting night for the man."

Norman smiled at Lawson's deviousness and realized that he couldn't tell her what he was doing without Benson hearing the plan. It also became apparent to Norman that Lawson didn't trust Benson. Norman thought it might have something to do with what Lawson told her about the M17 pistol and the sabotaged bullets. Norman assessed that Benson would have known that the team wasn't scheduled to bring weapons with them. Norman figured that Lawson suspected Benson could have seen to it that the cartridges were modified since she would have known that it was more likely that Lawson or Gunny would have taken possession of the weapon. She would have known that, in using the weapon, one of them would have been killed and the mission would have been scrubbed. As Norman thought through the issue she understood Lawson's wariness and her own concerns about Benson's real objectives or orders. Her next concern was how she was to ascertain what Benson's intentions were and could she be trusted.

"You realize I've gone as far as I can to help you," Rasulov told Lawson and Norman. "Any further help without direct orders and I might be violating our country's neutrality in this matter, you do understand?"

"You've been a great help, Chief," Norman said as she shook his hand. "We have made great leaps in getting an idea of the threat, something we could not have done without your help."

Rasulov smiled then gave her a kiss on each cheek then looked at Lawson and back to her. "You marry this man. He is good and smart and he loves you, my friend." Then, turning to Lawson, Rasulov smiled and grabbed his hand, "You are a friend forever. You honor me and my country by coming here to stop evil. My good friend Bahram Khaliqi said that you are a good man. I would agree. Goodbye to both of you." Rasulov left out of the entrance while Lawson and Norman looked at each other while Norman gave Lawson a questioning look.

"You remember Bahram Khaliqi?" Lawson posed to Norman. She nodded 'no' then he explained. "He was our Kurdish protector when Myers, Gunny and I were in Iran on that mission to stop the Russian development of the antiaircraft laser weapon."

"Oh, yes, I remember you talking about him," Norman exclaimed. "He was Ed Draper's Kurdish militia leader in Iran. So, how is it that Chief Rasulov would know Khaliqi?" Lawson didn't answer but he wondered that as well.

Leaving Rasulov and his men, Lawson and Norman walked back into the hotel, got some drinks and sat and talked for the next two hours while Rasulov and his officers left for the day. Lawson sat thinking for a moment as they wound down their discussion

"Beth, I think we've been had," Lawson assessed. "My guess is that the Admiral let Rasulov know we were coming and what we were looking for long before we got here. It would be like the

Admiral to fly cover for us." Norman smiled at Lawson's assessment and pulled him close to her as they walked down the hall to the elevator.

"Let's call it a night," she said as they entered the elevator then to their floor with Lawson going into the room where the men were sleeping while Norman went into the adjoining room where Benson was fast asleep. Norman checked her weapon and got ready for bed after she jammed a chair under the door knob. Once she was satisfied all precautions were completed she went to sleep.

Chapter 9

Cho Ming aka Qiang Zhu

"I've worked with many good scientists and engineers in my time. I've helped develop new technologies that have moved the world forward and have some pride in that progress. There is, however, a developing fear that I, like many other technologists, have. We seemed to have designed our way into ever more threatening devices and technology that appears to be spiraling towards our destruction. It's not the nuclear threat I fear, it's the artificial intelligence advances that could create an enemy void of morals, empathy or humanity. We appear to be approaching that abyss." – Professor Magnus Murodov, Osh Technological University

It was the morning of July 16th at 7:22 AM when one of the scientists at the Propheta Nostri facility came into a large, exquisitely decorated office in a far corner of the facility. The solid oak door to the entrance to the office had a gold metal plate in the center of the door with the words 'Propheta Nostri Corporation' in large letters and below that inscription was the words 'Cho Ming, CEO'.

The room had mahogany walls with 17th and 18th century artwork hanging on them. The floor was covered in a massive exotic Persian rug with an equally massive mahogany desk in the center of the room. Across the back of the room were numerous video screens neatly arranged to show camera shots of different areas of the facility, views from different satellites around the world, maps showing international communications links and news feeds from around the world. There were several wireless keyboards on the desk with a nameplate on the desk that said 'Cho Ming, Chief Executive Officer'. A man with obvious

Chinese features sat behind the desk watching as the scientist entered his office.

"Colonel Zhu, we've got a problem," the scientist in a white lab coat stated as he watched for Cho Ming's reaction.

"Aziz, you must lose this desire of calling me by my real name," Zhu said while he glared at the man facing him. "My name is now Cho Ming. Please remember that as I can't have anyone else outside of you and Mr. Sukhrab knowing who I am. You and he are my most trusted friends and I do not want to endanger that friendship. Now what has you so excited?"

"Well, Sir, we've had someone from the American team following Mr. Sukhrab all night," Aziz began as he knew Zhu did not like bad news and Aziz was already on thin ice. "Mr. Sukhrab was in contact with us a number of times last night and we found that one of the American team members has been following him throughout the night. Every time Sukhrab contacted us, one of the Americans was near the area Sukhrab was at based upon out GPS reading of the location of one of the trackers we put on the Americans."

Zhu or Ming, as he was now called, thought for a moment then instructed Aziz. "Have Sukhrab come to the building then to my office. Before he comes to my office check around him to make sure no one is following him. This American CAT205 team is very creative and may have found ways to watch us without us detecting them. I don't want to risk having one of them somehow being able to get through our security. Before Sukhrab comes in, have security surround him and watch for anyone that seems out of place." Aziz nodded he understood and carried out Ming's directions.

Sukhrab arrived about thirty minutes later and was stopped at the entrance to the facility. Aziz noted that it appeared Sukhrab had someone following him that was out in the parking lot. The security team, armed with AK-47 rifles, streamed out into the parking but couldn't find anything. Aziz thought this was unusual and played a hunch. Having Sukhrab follow him into the building, Aziz realized that, wherever Sukhrab moved, the GPS reading showed someone following him about 40 feet away. Aziz took Sukhrab's hat off and looked into it, nothing. Next, he felt around Sukhrab's shirt and pants finally finding the tracker on the inside of Sukhrab's belt around his waist. Aziz took the bug from Sukhrab's belt and analyzed it. It was one of their bugs that had been modified later on to give them false readings. Further analysis showed that it was one of the bugs they had put on one of the Americans the day before. Having answers to what was going on, Aziz had Sukhrab follow him to Ming's office.

Upon entering Ming's office, Aziz walked up to his desk and dropped the tracking device on the desk. "This is what we've been tracking all night while thinking the American's were following Sukhrab," Aziz said as Ming looked at the bug. "It kept telling us that it was 40 feet from where is actually was located."

"Wait," Ming exclaimed, "this is one of our devices. How is it that it suddenly shows itself 40 feet from where it actually is and how is it we are not picking up any audio?"

"It's been modified, Sir," Aziz explained. "The Americans apparently know how to reprogram our devices." Ming sat looking at Aziz then Sukhrab.

"Take that silly hat off, Sukhrab," Ming shouted as his frustration built.

"It's a fedora hat, Sir," Sukhrab responded as he took off the wool felt fedora hat with the silver band. "I wear this because it allows my people to know where I am at when we're in the field."

"That's great," Ming shot back. "Aziz thinks that so many people have seen you with that hat on that they can recognize you from a distance. I've had complaints from our people in Crete that you've worn it so many times on the docks there that the merchantmen know that when they see it, it's time to get off the docks because there will be trouble. Can you be a little more discrete in the field?" Sukhrab just held the hat in his hand as he blushed at Ming's comment.

"So, what do we do now?" Aziz asked.

Ming thought for a moment then answered, "It's obvious the American CAT205 team knows where we are and might even know what we're doing. I saw several of them in the facility yesterday. I know there are several other countries with their teams here in this country trying to find out who we are and what we're doing but CAT205 is our biggest threat. The other teams operate within rules that we can anticipate. The CAT205 team is a rogue operation and has no rules, which makes them a major threat to our operations. We have no choice but to eliminate them. I've already crossed swords with them once before and I underestimated them, not so this time. I'm sending out strike teams to take them out and we must also accelerate our timetable for this project. I'll notify 'Ormack' and 'Trechko' of the need to do the test run within the next couple of days. The bleachers and bunker are done and the test range is almost completed. We just need to get enough of the new fuel processed to do the test run. Aziz, you're in charge of getting the fuel completed on time for two days from now. Sukhrab, you go out to the test range and make sure the video mount installations for the cameras are finished by tomorrow and tested." Both men acknowledged their orders then left.

Once they left, Ming pushed a button on his desk then shouted, "Ergashev, get in here." A large man entered the office a few moments later and stood waiting for instructions. "Ergashev, I want you to get two teams together of three men each. You are to eradicate the American CAT205 team. They are located at the Salam Hotel on Masalieva Street. I want it done by the end of the day tomorrow, now go!" Ergashev turned and left the office.

As Ergashev was leaving, Ming sent messages using his codename to operatives with codenames 'Ormack' and 'Trechko' through another person with the codename 'Peacock'. The message sent was 'confirmed same date as sent to you before'. Ming completed his activities and turned his focus to readying the drones for the test run.

Chapter 10

The CIA and Evacuation

"Lawson is playing a very dangerous game. I know he is trying to get us to expose ourselves by reacting to what he did by finding and modifying our trackers then making sure we knew he did so. But there is a gnawing feeling within me that I don't see the whole picture of what his game plan is. He is devious and I underestimated the breadth of his abilities last time. Is it possible I'm missing something and he is merely diverting my attention from something else? I think he's about to change his tactics. He is a capable adversary and plays a good game." – Colonel Qiang Zhu (aka Cho Ming), Chinese Army Intelligence Officer until he went rogue

July 16th was a warm day and the hotel's air conditioning had failed sometime during the night. Lawson was sitting in the hotel room with Myers, Gunny and Norman at 9:45 AM. Looking for a cooler location, the others had gone down to the restaurant against Lawson's objections due to the concern for their safety. However, Norman wanted to know what Lawson's plan was now that he and Chief Rasulov had exposed the team by letting the opposition know that the team knew who they were. This left Norman uncomfortable and Gunny wondering what was the end game.

"I understand you not telling me about your plan concerning the guy in the parking lot last night, I mean with Benson being around, but you caught me by surprise," Norman exclaimed. "You realize that we are in the wide open with Colonel Zhu and his team and he has a lot more firepower and knowledge of the terrain than we do."

Lawson looked at the other three then began, "When we were at the facility yesterday and saw what was going on, I knew we had to do something to get Zhu to react. He already knows we're here. Yes, he's in his home field but we are able to be much more adaptable than he is. He is anchored to his location, we're not. We've gotten too settled here and that has already put us in jeopardy of having any chance of moving forward. At some point, we're going to be a 'kill or be killed' target. I'd rather set the stage for that so that we don't get surprised. I'd rather know they're coming after me then think I've got some room to play,"

Norman shook her head in disbelief as Gunny spoke up, "I was opposed to your move, Lawson, until just a few moments ago." At that moment, Norman looked at Gunny as she wondered where he was going with his comment. Gunny continued, "One of the basic rules of combat is that in order to win you must come off of playing defense and go to offense. You may be able to wear the enemy down in numbers on defense but sooner or later they will find a way of taking you down. In order to obtain a victory, you have to leave your safe zone and engage the enemy in his safe area. From what I've heard from Lawson's explanation, it makes sense. He's right. Zhu knows we're here, of that I'm sure. Lawson just set the stage to put us on offense and, I have no doubt, Zhu realizes that as well. It's actually a brilliant move since we know we're going to lock horns and I'd rather do that on a field of our choosing."

"I understand our need to get some action but we need to discuss the options and agree together," Norman protested as she looked at Lawson.

"Not so fast, Commander," Myers interrupted. "Lawson is in command of this operation and, as such, he has some freedom to act. He couldn't tell you what was being planned because there was no time. We had people here that we didn't know and haven't worked with. Rasulov passed by Lawson when we were talking last night and said only one word to Lawson, which was 'window'. Lawson went to the window and saw the car and the man sitting in the parking lot. When we were getting ready to go down Lawson said to me, 'the trackers, can you disable them and set the GPS for 40 to 50 feet from where it actually is'. I told him 'yes' which is one of the reasons I was late to dinner last night and, when I arrived at the dinner table, I didn't give him a pain pill, it was the tracker I handed to him."

Norman realized at that moment that everything was happening so fast there had not been time to plan much of anything. "Since we have a few minutes together, can we at least lay out a basic plan so that we can move as a team?" They all agreed to Norman's question.

"The basic plan is simple," Gunny started. "We must get out of the hotel, get our gear on to start field ops and proceed to scout out the areas north of here that are in question. If they're going to have a test run and they're testing drones, they will have to have some large area set up as I feel it will be for a formal demonstration for interested parties. That being said, there will have to be prepared sitting areas, refreshments and something to demonstrate as a target for the drones." Lawson was impressed at how quick and thorough Gunny had laid out the conditions.

"We have one other problem," Norman observed. "We have three players that are not a part of our team and will need to be put some place where they can be obscure and protected. Murodov and Izzy are locals and are easier to hide. Benson is a greater problem as she wouldn't be able to see a threat as readily as the other two." Lawson realized that Norman was right but there may be other concerns.

"I agree, Beth," Lawson stated. "However, I'm not sure that one of the other two is who they say…"

"I just got this message," Norman interrupted. "It says, message intercepted and decrypted from Fort Gordon. The message reads 'From Peacock: Discovered. Target - President of the United States, President of Russia, Prime Minister of Great Britain, President of China, President of France or Chancellor of Germany'."

"Well, I guess we've smoked the wasps from the nest," Lawson assessed. "Now we have some idea that they are reacting to our actions. From what I hear, they know they've been discovered."

"They also have narrowed down the field of targets," Myers added. "If I recall the second message Admiral Roedl read in his office when we started this thing, it was something like 'The ability to assassinate can only be performed using swarm', which confirms what Lawson surmised about them using a drone swarm and it also confirms that it's going to be an assassination attempt on one of those six targets."

Norman looked down at the notes in her briefcase. "It looks like they increased the number of possible targets to six. The original message that the Admiral read to us says 'Five possibilities'." Lawson thought about Norman's observations. They were missing something.

"We need to get out of the hotel within the next two hours," Lawson advised. "We will leave the rooms checked in so that our adversaries will think we're still staying here. Meanwhile, Gunny, you need to get some food and supplies based upon that list you made. We'll need enough for two more people."

"But I thought we would put up the other three into another hotel under assumed names," Gunny responded.

"Yes, we plan to but we may need to extract them and keep them with us if things go wrong," Lawson replied. A knock at the door stopped them in their discussion as they all drew their weapons.

"Who is it," Norman called out.

"It's us," came Benson's answer. Norman carefully opened the door as those inside held their weapons pointed toward the door, ready to act. Norman could see they were alone and let them in.

"Welcome back," Gunny said as he grinned.

"I'm sorry, we're just finishing up a meeting and I think I interrupted Lawson before he had a chance to finish his comment," Norman offered. "Jim, you said something about someone isn't who they are what?" Lawson placed his weapon in his lap with his finger on the trigger while he pointed the pistol in the general direction of those that just came into the room.

"Izzy, why don't you step away from the door," Lawson advised as he directed the weapon's barrel toward Izzy. "Why don't you tell us who you really are? You see, Izzy, when you, Gunny and Myers were at the lab before I arrived in town you were interpreting stuff shown on photo in the lab from a computer printout and, according to Myers, you had a problem translating the Kyrgyz word for 'penetrate'. Now someone who has lived his whole life in this area and claiming to be Kyrgyz would not have had any problem with the word."

Izzy stood for a moment looking at each of them and was about to protest the accusation when Professor Murodov spoke up. "You know, Lawson's right. There are some other mistakes you made that convinces me that you are not from this area."

"All right, put the gun away," Izzy answered. "You've got me. My name is Michael Blanding and I work for the CIA. My ID is sewn into my belt and, if someone has a knife, I can remove it from my belt and have you call my director in Langley. He will give you a code. When he does, call the number he'll give you and the code will bring up a picture of my ID and details. Here's the number."

"Thanks but no thanks," Myers stated. "I will call the CIA officer in Langley with the number I know and go through the process. After all, giving us the number does nothing more than potentially tie us to a false front that will appear to give us the right information. My way reduces the potential for error." Myers dialed the number while Lawson wondered how many more numbers Myers had in his head. It was always a surprise.

Everyone else had taken their duffle bags to the car while Lawson waited for verification of Izzy being Blanding. It took Myers almost an hour to complete the confirmation and get a downloaded picture of Blanding. Lawson wondered about the wisdom of Myers using the computer to get the picture as there was a risk that it could expose Blanding's true identity. Myers saw Lawson's expression and slid over to him while sitting in the chair.

"The question I sent by phone was to send a picture of their agent in Osh," Myers explained. "That was sent via a text. The picture I got back was on my email with the picture attached to a message that said 'This man would make a good candidate for scientific research'. Also, I will have a much more secure connection than the hotel Wi-Fi once we get to your room. I will install a satellite uplink dish that I asked Blanding to provide me which I can use since your room is facing to the south."

"What room are you talking about?" Lawson interjected.

"The room you registered under the name 'John Rochester'," Myers replied.

"How did you know about that room and that I was considering moving the team there? I was considering that move as no one outside of the person that stamped my passport at the airport knows I've come in under that name?" Lawson expounded.

"I know because there were five rooms registered by this team and we're only using four," Myers responded. "I got up at 3:00 AM this morning and looked at the cubby holes with the mail in them down at the main desk. There were only two slots that had mail in them with a name above each slot. The mail would only be put into the slot once a person checked in. As I was talking to the attendant at the desk, I could make out that the return address on the top envelope had the Energy Consultants 'EC' logo on it. As I know they won't do business in Central Asia, I figured it was you and the name above the slot was 'John Rochester'. I figured that Admiral Roedl would send you something with that logo and not the ONI logo so that you knew it came from him but no one else would. There was also the fact that it had no stamps on it so it had to be an envelope brought in by embassy courier. So what I see is using that room is really the only option we have at the present that allows for us to get sleep and get cleaned up. Besides, it is one story above our present rooms so we could do some bugging of our present rooms to see if anyone tries to go in. I already talked to Norman about this and she has some other plan to make sure we can identify who might search the room. Now as to our reasoning on using the upstairs room here in the hotel. We could stay in that warehouse in the north part of the Fergana Valley that the CIA has rented under a shell company, but there are no showers and security would be poor. So the only option is that extra room and, by the way, we can leave the hotel by going down to the basement and out the back door. If we leave the car parked in the parking lot owned by that company next to the hotel, we should be able to pull this off."

"Look at who we've got," Lawson objected. "We've got you, me, Gunny and Norman. Add to that Benson, Murodov and Izzy."

"Not Izzy, he's Blanding," Myers corrected.

"True, but let's keep calling him Izzy," Lawson advised. "If we accidently call him Blanding while other people are around, that will blow whatever cover he has left. Now as to our personnel situation, we have seven people and a car that will only carry five. We either get another car or we find some way to send two people home."

"You're right about Izzy's cover," Myers replied. "As for the situation concerning the personnel, we put four people up in the CIA warehouse and the rest here in your 'John Rochester' room.

We can cycle people around so that the people in the warehouse can get rest in the hotel every other night. We really should have people in the CIA warehouse anyway since it is only about a quarter mile from Zhu's building at the other end of that row of buildings from Zhu's facility. That way, if something of importance happens at Zhu's location at night, we have people that are more apt to witness what is going on. Besides, Gunny says that we should be on offense and this arrangement makes it easier to set things up by putting a lot of our equipment and ops clothing in the warehouse, close to the action." Lawson thought about Myers suggestions and agreed. It was time to tell the others.

The team headed out the back door of the hotel, each of those with keys checking to make sure their key worked on the back door lock. Satisfied that they could all get in with their keys, Benson, Murodov and Norman went back into the hotel through the back door after leaving their gear in the other parking lot with Lawson, Gunny, Izzy and Myers. The building next to the hotel's parking lot had a view that was blocked from the view of the hotel parking lot by a long line of Cyprus trees. Gunny noted where to park in the other parking lot that would hide them from view including even the highest story of the hotel. Gunny took Lawson, Myers and Izzy in the car and all of the gear then left to the northern part of the Fergana Valley. It would take him an hour and a half to get to the CIA warehouse.

Once they arrived at the warehouse Izzy unlocked the small personnel entrance door that was to the left of a very large loading dock door with a large padlock securing it. As they stepped inside, Lawson could see a large number of crates of all sizes stacked the full length of the left side of the building. As Lawson looked over the layout, a text came in from Chief

Rasulov. Lawson answered it and went back to assessing the building they had entered after showing the text to Gunny and Myers.

"This building is 68 meters by 68 meters," Izzy announced. Lawson did the quick calculation in his head and figured it was 75 yards by 75 yards inside. The outside walls were corrugated steel which was different from most of the other buildings along the frontage road. Those buildings were made of preformed concrete walls which meant that this building had been here much longer than the other buildings. The roof was a typical peak roof of corrugated steel with the top of the roof slanted in opposite directions from the peak at the center of the building. It was obvious electrical power had never been installed in the building as there were no lights hanging from the top rails inside the building. Most of the space was open except for the crates on the left side and stacks of barrels, pallets and machine parts on the right side.

The room was dark so Izzy lit a kerosene lantern then closed the door they entered through. Lawson found a couple more lanterns and checked them for fuel. Satisfied they had sufficient fuel, he lit each lantern and handed one of them to Gunny. Lawson then motioned for Myers to come with him. As they walked down the line of crates, they both realized many of the crates were labeled with NATO identifiers. One crate was combat boots, another camouflage uniforms, and still another was web gear for weapons, ammo pouches, grenades and canteens. Izzy just stood watching them as they walked down the line. Suddenly the labels changed to scripts that Lawson and Myers were not familiar with.

"Those crates are full of Uzbeki uniforms, communication gear and equipment," Izzy explained. "We tried to get uniforms for each of the armies that are located in the area so you will see Kyrgyz, Uzbek, Russian, NATO and Kazakh uniforms, weapons and equipment. We can outfit at least ten people in whatever uniform is needed. One other thing, Colonel Zhu's or shall I say Cho Ming's defense people have their own distinctive uniforms. No explosives are stored here but ammo is. Most of it is 9 millimeter and 7.62 millimeter."

"You said 7.62," Gunny interrupted. "Does that mean there are weapons that support 7.62 ammo?"

"Yes, we have some M-14 combat rifles and R11 RSASS Remington sniper rifles," Izzy reported. With that acknowledgement Lawson noticed Gunny's face light up.

"Here we go again," Myers jested as everyone started laughing as Gunny wrapped his arm around Myers head.

"Wasn't it such a weapon that kept you guys alive in both Iran and Washington, DC?" Gunny said as he started walking down the crates looking for the labeling for the sniper rifles.

"It's in this crate," Izzy said while pointing to the crate in question. "I don't have match rounds so previous experience is not indicative of future results." Everyone laughed as Lawson helped Gunny get the crate down. As they got the crate to the floor Lawson saw another crate that was USMC labeled with 'M17-0560 Experimental' on the crate. Lawson pulled the crate out as he watched Gunny go to the other side of the building to get a hammer or crowbar to open the crates. As he did so, Lawson began to wonder if all of this stuff was brought in to support the team's effort.

"So, when did you rent the building?" Lawson asked as he decided to test his hunch.

"We rented it last week," was Izzy's response. "I know what you're thinking. You think that all of this was put together for your mission. Well, you're partially right. The NATO weapons, camouflage uniforms, web gear and associated communications gear was brought in for your mission. The rest of the stuff is for ongoing missions we are doing in the region. We had to move our storage operations out of Tashkent due to some stresses with the government. They didn't like the fact that we temporarily stored five nuclear artillery shells overnight while they were in transit." Lawson looked at Gunny while Gunny just rubbed his chin and thought about the comment about the artillery shells.

Lawson pulled the crate with the rifles to where Gunny could open the crate using the metal bar he found. Once he got the crate open he pulled out the sniper rifle, scope and magazines. As he was attaching the scope to the rifle, Lawson took the metal bar and opened the crate with the USMC markings. Inside were ten M17 pistols with silencers and extra empty magazines for the pistols.

"Look at this," Lawson shouted. "M17 pistols with their silencers and plenty of clips." Gunny stopped his assembling of the sniper rifle as he looked into the crate Lawson just opened.

"We'll use these pistols instead of the Maxim 9 pistols on out mission," Gunny instructed as he picked up one of the pistols and turned it over in his hand. "I'll check each weapon we're going to use to make sure they are operational and have firing pins."

"You must understand that these pistols are experimental and not yet approved for use," Izzy advised. "They are untested which is something to be considered if you're going to use them in actual service. I brought them here so we could test them without interference."

"Well I'm sure these pistols don't know that they are not approved yet," Gunny quipped as he sat down the sniper rifle and checked the chamber on the pistol he had picked up. Everyone went back to what they were doing while Izzy smiled at Gunny's comment.

"What about that satellite dish for me to hook up to my computer?" Myers posed as he looked around for any electrical connection.

"We just moved into the facility and we can't install electrical as it would have to be done by a local and we can't afford some local to see what's in here," Izzy remarked. "However, the sat link kit operates by battery. It's the same kit they use on US Navy lifeboats. I'll pull one from the crate and help you set it up. The kit also has a signal meter with it that allows for you to set the azimuth to a specific satellite and there's also a calculator that shows you the compass direction for the satellite you want to connect to. By the way, did you charge up your computer before bringing it out here?"

"Yes," Myers acknowledged as he looked at the computer. "It has an 11 hour battery and is fully charged."

While Izzy was getting the satellite link kit, Gunny was checking out the sniper rifle. As he did so, something was rolling around in his head. As they were waiting, a knock was heard at the door.

"Shut down the other two lanterns," Izzy whispered as he headed for the small door. Gunny and Lawson brought the flames on the lanterns down then blew them out. Once they did that Izzy opened the door to see Norman standing there.

"I thought you were staying at the hotel tonight," Gunny called out while Lawson looked out the door to see what car she came in. Lawson started laughing as he saw the police car leave.

"Well, everyone is fed and put to bed at the hotel, so I called Rasulov at the precinct and asked him for an officer to drive me over," Norman stated. "I noticed activity at the hotel on the third floor where our previous rooms were at. I left an exploding packet of bank dye in the room safe with a trigger string. Blanding gave me the packet and the recommendation on what to do with it. Anyway, I went to the front window of the hotel on the fourth floor and looked out front into the parking lot after I heard a lot of yelling and people running below us. I saw two men running out to their cars. One man had a purple face and the other man was covered in purple all across the front of his suit. That stuff will not wash out. With the damage the ink probably did to the carpet, I also think we may have exhausted our welcome, at least for those registered in the room. Since Lawson registered under a different name, I don't think they will put it together that 'John Rochester' is part of our group." Gunny and Myers started laughing while Lawson just stared at Norman.

"How do you know that police officer won't go tell one of Zhu's people where we are?" Gunny grilled as he stared at Norman. Myers quit laughing as the question was realized.

"It wasn't a smart move on her part," Izzy declared. "However, the guy dropping her off happens to be one of our people, so she got lucky." Norman looked at Lawson then Gunny then Myers as she realized how stupid that decision was.

"I'm so sorry, Guys," Norman whimpered. "I wasn't in the mood to babysit and I took a shortcut I shouldn't have."

"Apology accepted," Lawson said as they all broke out in laughter. "We covered for you, Norman. Rasulov sent me a text asking me if he should send one of his officers to pick you up. He knew where you were going from your request and told me that he will send someone that will not expose any of us to Zhu's people. I texted him back and said that would work. I didn't know the guy he sent would be one of Blanding's CIA buddies but that works."

Norman gave a sigh of relief then realized Gunny was polishing up a sniper rifle. She looked but said nothing as Gunny sat down, put the weapon across his lap and formed a perplexed look on his face. While all this was going on, Myers had connected the sat link kit, locked onto a satellite and brought up maps of the area. Gunny moved uncomfortably as a question formed in his mind.

"So why is Qiang Zhu operating here rather than somewhere else?" Gunny inquired as he was operating the action on the rifle. Everyone looked at each other as to why no one had raised the question before. "I mean, he had a number of other areas to go to in Africa, Southeast Asia, South America and many other remote spots. What makes this one so special?"

They all sat thinking about the Gunny's question and what was Zhu's true intent. Both Norman and Lawson were about to speak at the same time so Lawson motioned for Norman to go ahead. She looked down at the ground while frowning then looked back up at Gunny.

"What I see, Gunny, are the needs and capabilities that Zhu sees are necessary which provides us an avenue to understand his reasons," Norman began. "Being in Africa or South America would make him stand out in a crowd. If you've noticed, half the people we see in this city look oriental because of the Kyrgyz's background. So Zhu would blend into this culture better than in others. The second point is that there are a lot of former Russian special forces people that retire to this area due to the climate, so it would be easy to hire a wide range of security expertise to cover his tracks. The third point, he needs some place where he can get quick delivery of parts and materials while also being close enough to uninhabited land to do his testing. Does that help?" Gunny nodded 'yes' as Lawson looked at Norman, at which point she nodded for him to go ahead. Confirmed to provide his opinion, he sat down near the table in the room and leaned back in the chair. Lawson glanced at Myers then at the map on the computer that Myers was pointing at which immediately caught Lawson's attention. It was precisely what Lawson needed to make his case.

"The city has highly trained technical resources," Lawson said as he continued to look at the map. "It is also a very large city with many places to hide and, because of its location, it's like a magnet to intelligence groups from around the world. The presence of so many intel people recently coming to Osh raised Rasulov's attention but the fact of the matter is that Osh is a great place to share intel information between countries. It truly is the city that acts as a bridge between the East and the West without having too many rules. It's the same that Geneva, Switzerland was for Russia and the US during the 1960's."

"But why test here?" Gunny probed.

"Look at this map," Lawson instructed. "As I zoom out you can see Kazakhstan near the Kyrgyz border and here in Kazakhstan you can see the Russian Space Launch Complex. They have sent many missiles into space with some of those launches supporting the International Space Station. People living in this area are not going to think it unusual to see test aircraft and rockets flying across the sky. It's a perfect location for Zhu to develop and test drones."

After Lawson finished everyone agreed that Norman's and Lawson's explanations were a good summary of Zhu's reason for being here. Yet Gunny felt something in his gut that told him something was missing. What bothered him more is that whatever they were missing, it was something lethal. Lawson motioned to Gunny as the others prepared their equipment. Gunny came over to Lawson then looked back at the others as Lawson spoke.

"I know what you're thinking, Gunny," Lawson whispered. "We all are feeling the same thing but no one wants to raise the question until we have more information."

"And what would that be that everyone be feel'n?" Gunny asked in a rather Irish-accented irritating voice.

"That there is something we are missing that could cause us great harm," Lawson replied. In an instant, Gunny's expression changed from a frown to a relaxed expression. So, once more, they were ahead of him in seeing the threats.

"How do you do that?" Gunny questioned as he smiled. "How do you know what I'm thinking?"

"Remember when we were getting ready to kick off the mission in Iran and you asked me to think of something then you said I thought of an elephant. I wondered how you would have guessed that then I realized that that's what a lot of people would answer with the way you posed the question. You went on to say you did that to show that if you knew how I thought, you were more likely to trust me. Did you ever consider that I might have felt the same way until I could read you?" Gunny stopped, thought for a moment then patted Lawson on the back as he laughed and picked up his duffle bag and rifle.

"You ready, my friend, to do some serious mismanagement?" Gunny quipped as he headed for the door. They both laughed at the results of their conversation as they went out the door. "We're going to do some reconnaissance to see what the terrain looks like. We'll be back in about an hour." Norman felt nervous with them going out as it was near sunset and they would be back well after dark.

"Don't worry about them," Izzy counseled Norman. "They're dressed normal for this area so they won't stand out."

"Yea, right," Norman shouted. "We're just two normal guys walking down the street or whatever carrying a sniper rifle. Real normal!"

"Most of the people in the outskirts of the city carry weapons to protect themselves at night," Izzy instructed. "Going out without some visible weapon in this area would be more suspicious. Besides, Lawson took one of the new M17 pistols along with a silencer and three clips of ammo. He also took one of the extended holsters for his belt that supports an external silencer. They are both armed for bear." Norman sat back down as she watched Myers pulling up screens of active satellite scans of the local area. While everyone was talking, Myers had somehow retasked a satellite to give him a present view of the area. Izzy noticed it too and wondered what level of authority Myers was given to retask a satellite without going through proper channels. Both Norman and Izzy looked at each other with the same question. As Izzy was contemplating Myers' actions, he looked to see that Gunny had opened a small crate earlier that held night-vision goggles. It was obvious to Izzy that Gunny intended to get close to Zhu's facility and that made Izzy uncomfortable.

Lawson and Gunny returned at 10:33 PM. Once they confirmed who they were at the door, they entered into the warehouse and set down their equipment. Gunny pulled out his phone and pulled up some pictures.

"I was able to get pictures of the east side of the facility," Gunny said as he looked at the pictures. "They have a roving patrol operation around the building with at least eight guards on just the east and north sides. The north side is the back of the building that sports a very large entrance with a single roll-down door. There were three large open trailers that are normally used by 18-wheelers to move product. I saw drones that looked almost like miniature P-38 aircraft from World War II being loaded in the last of the three trailers, as seen in the picture here. They appeared to be stacked five high and there were five pallets of drones on each trailer." Myers looked at the pictures as Gunny talked.

"Five high by five pallets," Myers said as he heard Gunny's description. "If there are three trailers all loaded the same that would put the total number of drones at 75." Myers began to walk back and forth across the warehouse as he continued to think about the information Gunny and Lawson brought back.

"You've got something?" Gunny asked Lawson as he watched Myers.

"What was the number on the miniature engine we photographed at the hotel?" Lawson posed.

"I think it was '1020'," Myers replied.

"So we know that 1020 sounds like it's the number of the engines made," Lawson continued. "So why would they need 1020 engines if the demonstration appears to be about 75 drones and an assassination would probably require the same number? Gunny, you remember you said something was missing and it might create great harm?" Gunny nodded as Lawson turned to Norman, "What was that last message you got from Admiral Roedl?" Norman brought up the texts on her phone and read back Roedl's message.

"It says, message intercepted and decrypted from Fort Gordon. The message reads 'From Peacock: Discovered. Target - President of the United States, President of Russia, Prime Minister of Great Britain, President of China, President of France or Chancellor of Germany'."

"That's what we've been missing," Lawson remarked to Norman's comment. "Now look at this, I think we've been reading the message all wrong. The part of the message saying 'President of France or Chancellor of Germany' is just for a selection of those two. They are trying to decide whether to target France's President or Germany's Chancellor. The rest of the names in that list are already designated targets. That's the reason why the first message we saw in Roedl's office stated five possibilities and we see six. Everyone in that list is an active target!" Everyone else looked at one another as they began to realize that Lawson was onto something. The shock of that fact also brought them to the realization that Qiang Zhu was planning to do five simultaneous assassinations of five of the world's top leaders.

"As your sure this is a real possibility?" Norman asked as the reality of the suggestion began to sink in. "That would cause world-wide chaos for at least a day to maybe a week or more."

"It could also be the trigger for a world-wide collapse of the monetary system as well as cause the chaos to go into uncontrollable expansion," Izzy observed. "This is the very scenario we were taught was the tipping point of civilization when I was in intelligence training."

"Look, it's after 11:00 PM and we all need to get some sleep," Lawson advised. "We should also get the others out of the hotel and into this building."

"I'll go get them," Gunny volunteered. "I'll get some food on the way back." They all nodded agreement as Izzy was working on finishing setting up a portable latrine at the back end of the building.

"I'll have the portable potty and field shower set up in half an hour," Izzy reported as he sprayed the inside of the portable latrine with disinfectant and pointed to the far right side of the building.. "I need someone to get me about 50 gallons of water for the shower. There is a faucet on the outside of the building next to us and we've got 10 gallon containers against the wall over there."

Myers moved to get a couple of water containers while Gunny walked out the door to the car to pick up the people from the hotel. Gunny knew it would be a short night as he and Lawson had to take a walk about 4:00 AM the next morning to look at the field that Myers discovered while scanning the area with the retasked satellite. It was about a mile northeast of their location and they had to get to the location and scout it at first light. Gunny calculated it would take him 3 hours round trip to pick up the others at the hotel and get them to the warehouse. As it was already past 11:00 PM, that would give him about 2 hours sleep before getting ready for the patrol.

Chapter 11

The Admiral's Decision

"This whole mission has been a mess from the start. People traveling all over Europe and Asia, communications seriously in question, CIA personnel being exposed and messages from a team member that seems to indicate the whole team is wandering around with no objective. Lawson really appears to have screwed up this whole operation and Norman is not doing much better. All we know is the threat is real but we don't know what it is. It's now July 16th and they've been on this operation for 5 days without any real progress. Admiral Roedl needs to make some moves." – Commander Blaine Samoylev, Group Commander, Special Operations Group, ONI

US Navy Commander Blaine Samoylev sat down in Admiral Roedl's office as the Admiral read the report and messages on his desk. The Admiral would read some pages, flip some other pages on his desk to the left of the main document to verify what he was reading, then go back to the main document to continue. Once he finished reading, he took the eyeglasses from his face and set them on the desk. He looked up at Commander Samoylev, "Your thoughts, Blaine."

"Well, Admiral, I think this effort has stalled and the team is floundering," Samoylev tersely stated.

"What brings you to this conclusion?" Roedl inquired.

"I've been getting texts from Joanne Benson, you know, the Pentagon analyst you assigned to the team. She has given a serious thumb's down on the team's activities and what they've accomplished so far."

"I understand your concerns, Blaine, but are you considering that Benson has no field experience and may not be in tune to what is going on?" Roedl asked as he put his glasses back on and looked down at the report.

Samoylev shifted in his chair and responded, "Benson's a top notch analyst and she would know if something is not right as she analyzes team actions after the fact at the Pentagon. They've not set up any plan, they don't communicate well with one another, they leave themselves open to attack and they keep jumping from one fire into another without any resolution. The team has even exposed a CIA asset in Osh which has raised some hackles at the CIA."

Roedl looked at Samoylev and leaned back in his chair. Thoughts raced through his mind as he remembered that Samoylev had not seen the messages from Inspector Bernardakis from Crete, Captain Pavel Volkov from Russia or Chief Rasulov from Osh. He was also wondering why Joanne Benson was sending reports to Samoylev and Roedl was not seeing them.

"First thing, Blaine," Roedl started, "you refer to messages and conditions I have not been told about. I don't see any of Benson's messages here in your report yet you are referring to her as the main source of your impressions of how the mission is going. Second thing, Benson may be able to assess things from the viewpoint of a person seeing the after action reports when everything can be better explained. However, she is in the middle of the fog of war where most things are still to be explained and half of the stuff is yet to be acted on. I've been getting updates from Commander Norman via Professor Murodov's phone as Commander Norman's phone has been hacked. They traded phones so that Norman could continue giving me reports. One more thing, I gave Myers permission to retask a satellite to get a better idea on what the present layout is in the area they are working in."

"You did what?" Samoylev exclaimed.

"You have a problem with that, Commander?" Roedl challenged back.

Samoylev paused for a moment as he realized the Admiral could assign anyone to retask one of their satellites. He also realized the Admiral had a lot more on-the-ground information of what was going on in Kyrgyzstan than Samoylev got from Benson.

"No Sir, no problem," Samoylev sheepishly admitted.

"Now that that's resolved, let's go up to SAL and see what Myers is looking at," Roedl ordered as he got up, checked the pistol in his holster and headed for the door.

After leaving his office and going through the security vault to get into the outer hallway, they went to another part of the building and up some stairs to get to the SAL. After doing a finger print and eye scan, the door to the SAL opened and they walked in.

The Strategic Analysis Lab, also known as SAL, was a central monitoring and command station for ground activity being captured by satellite, radio, phone and text transmissions sent by other countries and for encrypting and sending rapid response messages. The center was manned at all times by no less than twelve analysts and command personnel.

The SAL center consisted of electronic stations on three walls toward one end of the room with the second half of the room laid out with seats in a theater-like arrangement. The seats were facing toward the electronics portion of the room and the associated screens. On the wall on the left was the equipment with stations for satellite tracking, assignment and recording of events. It had eight large monitors with keyboards and controls at four different stations. One station was for satellite retasking and satellite tracking. The second station was for real-time monitoring of information and video captured by satellite. The third station was assigned recording and playback tasks on demand. The fourth station was used by drone controllers for strike missions and dropping messages or small supply packages. The information and control of the satellites was provided by Schriever Air Force Base in Colorado, having over one-hundred and seventy satellites under their control with the data and control being linked to the SAL facility as well as numerous other military installations around the world.

The back wall, which the theater seats would be facing, held the large main screens used to display both recorded and real-time information. These screens could be controlled by commanders wanting to see events as they occurred or playback events that had been previously recorded. They were able to partially control what was to be displayed on the main screens once the proper station was linked to one of the main screens. They could also call up documents and information on persons, organizations, statistics and governments using controls on one of two seats in the front row of the theater seats.

The right wall held the communications tracking, analysis, recording and encryption capabilities. It supported a dozen smaller displays with eight keyboards and controls. One station was used for decrypting messages acquired from both U.S. and international sources. Another station was used for creating and encrypting messages going out to units. A third station was used for assimilating messages so that communication threads between parties could be tracked and printed. A fourth station was used for verbal capture of phone, radio and intercepted conversations. The fifth station was used for Presidential, State Department, National Security Agency, FBI and CIA communications. Three other stations were used for various tasks and to manage the overload of information during crisis times.

Admiral Roedl and Commander Samoylev sat down in two of the seats in the front row of the theater seats as Roedl pushed a button on a hand control on one of the two seats. The main screen began displaying a satellite video from a satellite that had been retasked by Schriever AFB as a request from Petty Officer Myers to observe the area north of the Fergana Valley. The video was captured video that Myers had gotten about an hour earlier and recorded it for Roedl to play back.

"Now look there," Roedl pointed out. "This is the area we are interested in. Does that match with your map?"

"It appears to be that," Samoylev agreed. "I see two people here on the lower part of the screen to the east of that building." Roedl looked at what Samoylev was looking at and started laughing. Samoylev's questioning look required a response.

"Blaine," Roedl quipped, "that is nothing other than Gunny Glendenning and Lieutenant Lawson. I can tell because, if you look closely you can see Gunny flashing a message using the laser sight on his rifle and pointing it up into the sky. Can you read what it is saying?"

"It just stopped," Samoylev complained. "Can you play that back again?" As Roedl rewound the video and replayed the portion in question, Samoylev continued, "My Morse code is rusty but it looks like 'G' 'U' 'N' 'N' 'Y'. OK, now I know how you know it's Gunny and Lawson. It looks like they're scouting that facility. What's the interest of that particular building?"

"That's Cho Ming's building," Roedl explained. "Norman texted that it is known as the Propheta Nostri Corporation."

"Propheta Nostri," Samoylev said slowly. "What a peculiar name for a corporation. Naming it for something that typically represents ..." Samoylev stopped talking as a realization of truth hit him.

"Represents what?" Roedl posed while smiling at Samoylev.

"The name represents the progress of control toward total domination," Samoylev answered. "Admiral, I owe you an apology. It looks like the team has made considerable progress and is on the verge of owning the field."

"Apology accepted," Roedl acknowledged. "Now, if you look northeast of the facility that Gunny and Lawson are scoping out you'll see a field that has some structures on it," Roedl said while zooming in on the area. "It appears to be a large field, about 400 yards by 300 yards in size with what appears to be a set of bleachers on one side and some type of bunkers on the other side. What's these things to the sides of the bleachers?" Roedl asked as he zoomed in further on the items in question.

"They appear to be cameras," Samoylev observed. "It makes sense if this is the testing range where some test is to occur. They would be filming it to look at the details of the tests later."

"We need to get back to my office," Roedl instructed as a comment from Samoylev triggered something in the Admiral's memory. "I need to check on a message we intercepted this morning and no one can make sense of it." With that comment, they left the SAL and headed back to Roedl's office. Once inside the office, Roedl went to his desk and shifted through the stack of messages for Operation Shiny Object.

Samoylev sat down as he pondered, "That field is too large for some ground demonstration. It has to be something airborne that they are testing." Roedl nodded agreement as he pulled out a piece of paper with a short message on it.

"This was sent from 'Peacock' to 'Trechko'," Roedl commented as he read the message. "Now, we've figured so far that 'Peacock' is Cho Ming but we don't know who 'Trechko' is. The message says 'Usb Field 19'. Samoylev looked the message over and provided his input.

"This is not something we can determine here," Samoylev began. "We need to give it to the team in Osh so they can look into it. It has something to do with things going on in Uzbekistan and they would have a better chance to figure it out. Let me send the message to Norman and see what the team can make of it."

"Sounds good," Roedl agreed as he looked over the other documents in the file then wrote down a phone number on a piece of paper and handed it to Commander Samoylev.

"Remember to send it to this number as that is the phone number Norman has now. As I said before, her phone was hacked."

"Aye, Sir," Samoylev acknowledged as he turned to go to the SAL.

Admiral Roedl leaned back in his chair as he looked at the documents then got up. Going over to the cabinets on the right wall of his office, he opened a cabinet door which exposed a safe. He turned the dial on the safe and, once done, put his head up to the top center of the safe for an eye scan. Once the scan was completed the safe opened to expose four drawers. Roedl put a key into the second drawer down, opened the drawer and pulled out a sealed folder. The folder had a diagonal red line across the front of the folder with a 'TOP SECRET – SCIF' in large letters on the front of it. At the bottom of the folder was the title in large letters 'OPERATION CHAOS'. Roedl closed the safe door and waited for it to latch. Once he heard the click of the latches and saw the flashing green light on the front of the safe indicating the safe was locked he closed the cabinet door.

Stepping to where the picture was situated behind his chair on the back wall, he pressed the center screw of an electrical outlet on the wall. Once he did so, a small keypad and camera swung out from the space where the outlet was situated. Roedl punched in a series of numbers into the keypad which caused the camera to swing upward. Roedl put his eye up to the lens of the camera and a moment later, a section of wall that the picture was on rose up exposing a vault door. Once more, Roedl put his eye to a scanner to the left of the vault door that verified him which unlatched the vault door. At the same time this happened, all the doors to Roedl's office closed and latched then the lighting in his office changed from regular lighting to red light. Roedl put the folder under his arm and entered the vault. As he did so, a message came from a speaker in the wall inside the vault, 'THIS IS A SENSITIVE COMPARTMENTED INFORMATION FACILITY ALSO KNOWN AS A SCIF FACILITY. REMOVE ALL CELLPHONES, ANY OTHER COMMUNICATION EQUIPMENT AND ANY COMPUTER EQUIPMENT BEFORE ENTERING. USE ONLY THE COMPUTER PROVIDED IN THIS VAULT FOR DOING YOUR WORK. HAVE A NICE DAY'.

Roedl laid his cellphone on his desk and entered the SCIF. Once inside, he pressed a button on the wall next to the vault door which caused the vault door to close and latch.

Roedl sat down in the chair in front of a desk holding a laptop computer, secure phone, clock, lamp and a shredder in the corner opposite the desk. The computer had a LAN connection that would encrypt any information he needed to send and direct the information to the proper recipient. He laid the folder down on the desk and proceeded to break the seal on the folder. Once the seal was broken, he pulled out the paperwork and a jump drive. He booted up the computer and looked through the paperwork as he waited for the computer to come up to full operation. Once the computer came up, he typed in a password to bring up the home screen then plugged in the jump drive. Plugging in the jump drive resulted in a password screen being displayed on the computer screen with a message below it that said, 'THREE ATTEMPTS ONLY FOR ENTERING PASSWORD. IF NOT SUCCESSFUL AFTER THREE ATTEMPTS, ALL DATA ON THE DEVICE WILL BE ERASED'.

Roedl reached into the pocket of his uniform jacket and pulled out a postcard-size, leather-bound book that had the title 'Metrics and Measurements' on the front cover. Laying the book on the desk he reached into the folder and pulled out a thick plastic ruler. Holding the ruler on each end he bent the ruler up and down until the ruler broke in the middle. He pulled the two sections of the ruler away from each other exposing a thin sheet of Mylar plastic with the characters 'AB21C04W3CHECK' printed on the surface of the plastic. Picking up the small book he had laid on the desk, Roedl turned to page 21 then looked at a table to find line 4 and went to row 3. That cell in the table showed the sine value for 60 degrees as being '.8660'. Seeing the result, he typed '60-8660' into the password field on the screen. Once he did so, the password screen disappeared and a screen of documents came up.

Roedl clicked on a document that was titled 'Activation'. The document came up displaying the requirements needed in order to activate 'Operation Chaos'. The personnel needed would be provided by the United States Marine Corps Forces Special Operations Command (MARSOC). The persons doing the operation would come from the Marine Raider Regiment, 1st Raider Battalion. Roedl determined he would need one man with a 'United States Marine Corps Critical Skills Operator' designation to carry out Operation Chaos. He selected the appropriate personnel and clicked on the 'Submit' button on the screen.

Next, he identified the code required for Operation Chaos to go active and perform the type of function he required. In the field labeled 'Activation' he entered 'RED LILAC', double checked that he had selected the right activation code from the numerous codes available on the screen then clicked once more on the 'Submit' button. He waited several minutes, looking through the paperwork as he waited, then heard a 'beep' and saw that his order had been received and verified.

Satisfied that all was in order, he turned off the computer, picked up all of the material, including the jump drive, and ran them all through the shredder. Once the shredding was completed he checked for any leftover items. He left the SCIF once he was satisfied everything had been accounted for, putting his office back in order after he exited the vaulted room. As he brought the wall back down to its original position, the doors to his office unlatched and the lighting went from red back to regular lighting.

Samoylev entered Roedl's office a couple of minutes later with a sheaf of papers in his hands. Roedl looked up at him then back down at his desk as he pondered whether Operation Chaos would be successful or run into snags. He knew a snag would be fatal to a lot of people.

"You send off the request?" Samoylev asked as he thumbed through the stack of paper in his hands.

"It's not a request, it's an order, and yes I did," Roedl tersely remarked as he looked up at Samoylev. "Sorry Blaine, I'm just a little stretched right now with the needs of Operation Shiny Object. Our people are hanging out there and we have unknowns as to what's facing the team and can they be successful. As you know, they are playing in a field where things are much different than they appear."

"I think you said 'radically different than they appear' at the Joint Staff meeting at the Pentagon yesterday," Samoylev observed. "Operation Chaos will only muddy the waters as time goes by."

"I know your concern on the Chaos Operation but if we don't act, someone will and we will lose the whole team," Roedl commented as he wondered if he had made the right move. "At least in Iran, the team had you covering for them. We're trusting the CIA and Blanding to help us in this one and that doesn't give me much comfort with the magnitude of threats the CAT team is facing."

"We'd have much less of a chance of success without the CIA's help," Samoylev responded. "Lawson is good but even he has his limits. The team all working together is exceptional but even with Lawson's reading of situations with his devious methods, Myers' ability to work through the technology, Gunny's combat experience and Norman's ability to coordinate such disjointed efforts, all they need is one team member to be lost and they all fail." Roedl nodded his understanding as he went back to his paperwork and Samoylev turned to leave the room.

"You do realize, Admiral, that this could be just a big game being played by the Pentagon," Samoylev suggested as he got to the door of the office.

"That thought had crossed my mind more than once," Roedl acknowledged. "If that's true, it's a pretty expensive game because, according to Norman, three people have lost their lives already. I don't think it's a game but we're always surprised at what lengths some people in our government will go to."

"Scary thought," Samoylev said as he walked out the door.

Chapter 12

Ground Zero

"There's no question something is about to happen. As to when it happens, time will tell. The field test of these drones has to fail to give us more time to ascertain the intentions and targets of this unknown cabal. From what Admiral Roedl has reported, it seems that the CAT205 team may be insufficient to carry out this mission to completion. They've surprised me before so I guess a little faith would be in order." – Admiral Ted Johnson, US Navy, senior officer at the US Pentagon for the United States Special Operations Command (USSOCOM)

It was 3:50 AM on July 17th as Gunny and Lawson put on their packs and checked their weapons. As they left out the door of the warehouse they both looked back to see Myers on his computer ready to call for the retasking of a surveillance satellite once he got the call from Lawson that they were in position at the field in question.

The air was warm and humid with a slight breeze from the south. There was no moon in the sky as they walked across the road going behind the warehouse and started up the small, rolling hill to the northeast. The ground was compacted soil with tufts of green grass growing in spots that, although Lawson couldn't see them, he could tell by the smell of the grass and the impact of his boots against the little mounds set up by the grass clumps.

"According to Myers, the field is to the northeast bearing 43 degrees from the warehouse," Gunny stated as he looked at the compass app on his cellphone. "It's supposedly 40°52'38.13"N by 72°35'1.05"E so I'll set my GPS destination to that location."

"It's as dark as Batman's cave," Lawson observed though he could see light starting to form on the eastern horizon.

"Let ye eyes adjust to the dark and we'll move slowly til we get better adjusted," Gunny advised in a slight Irish accent while knowing Lawson already knew what to do.

"I can tell you're a little apprehensive about this patrol, Gunny," Lawson stated as they stepped forward. "You always start going back to your Irish lilt when you're not sure where things are going."

"Aye, that I do," Gunny responded as they both laughed and proceeded forward.

Back in the warehouse Myers was already up and at his computer. "78 percent battery power left on the computer," Myers pronounced to himself as he brought up the screens that would provide him the links necessary to gain access to the surveillance satellite that was due to be accessible in approximately one hour.

"That should be plenty of power for the computer but what about the battery on the satellite antenna?" Izzy asked as Myers turned to see Izzy standing behind him.

"The antenna unit has 85 percent power which should give us six hours of power," Myers responded. "I didn't realize anyone else was up."

"They're all soundly asleep," Izzy commented as he looked around the warehouse. The darkness extended through most of the space with the light from a lantern next to Myers providing the only illumination outside of the computer screen. Myers reached over and picked up a book then proceeded to go to the page that had a marker inserted. As he began to read, Izzy sat down beside him.

"Is it an interesting book?" Izzy questioned.

"I've read through it twice and I'm still finding things I never caught the first two times I've read it," Myers said.

"What are you reading that would have you go through a book this thick three times?" Izzy inquired.

"It's the Christian Bible," Myers uttered.

"Oh, that's right, you're the agent that was going to be a pastor," Izzy whispered. "I was raised Catholic, as was most of my family. I still consider myself a Catholic but I don't practice it that much. What religion are you?"

"I don't have a religion," Myers disclosed. Izzy was taken back by the statement.

"You were going to be a pastor, you read the Bible and I hear you praying once in a while yet you say you don't have a religion?" Izzy exclaimed. Myers smiled and set down the Bible.

"How about speaking a little quieter, people are sleeping," Myers advised as Izzy nodded agreement while he waited for Myers to collect his thoughts. "I don't have a religion, I have a relationship with God. You see, in my perspective, religions are formed by people with rules made by people. I'm not rules oriented. My relationship with God is based on his rules only and the rules are very simple and straight forward. I've seen too many miracles in my life to believe any other way but that's just me."

"Don't you have a conflict between killing people and your beliefs? Doesn't the Ten Commandments say 'thou shalt not kill'?" Izzy challenged.

"That's not how the original Hebrew seems to state it," Myers started. "The term used in the Hebrew is 'lo tirtsah' which means to murder. Also, if God had meant that the commandment instructed that person killing anyone was prohibited then why, on two separate occasions, was Jesus amazed by the faith of Centurions when Centurions were the Roman soldiers that were chosen for their ability to end uprisings very quickly and almost always with death. Another example is in the 22nd chapter of Matthew. Jesus told his disciples to bring two swords to the Garden of Gethsemane the night he was arrested. I had questions about that part of the story for some time until I realized that Jesus was telling his disciples that it was ok for them to defend themselves if attacked. I kill in self-defense and I won't kill an unarmed person unless I am threatened by them to the point that I am in jeopardy. My Commander understands this and always asks us at the beginning of each mission, that if based upon what we are told about the mission, do we have any reservations about the mission that conflicts with our beliefs. He's smart enough to know that a person with reservations in what we do will be a threat to the team if the actions required goes against a person's core beliefs."

"So, why do you stay with this team?" Izzy inquired. "It seems that there is a lot of killing associated with the missions our teams have to handle and you would seem to be fatigued by the constant exposure to death based upon your perspective."

"It is exhausting," Myers explained. "However, I don't have to justify to myself why people die in these operations. There are actions that have consequences and death may be one of them. I have, on a couple of occasions, rendered medical attention to a person I've wounded. I don't view those against me as my enemy. I figure they are fighting for what they believe in and I'm fighting for what I believe in."

"And what is it you believe in?" was Izzy's response.

Myers looked at the computer screen then back to Izzy. "I believe that every person has the right to live free, to choose the God they need to worship or no God at all, to live in society where people can disagree without being disagreeable and where they live and work without fear."

"So you believe that a person can believe in no God at all?" a perplexed Izzy contended.

"A person must be the one to choose who they will serve even if it's no God," Myers started. "Beliefs forced on you are not beliefs but mandates. God wants us to worship him freely and without a bunch of binding rules that take our focus off of him. He wants us to relate to him and rely on him while treating those around us with value. Yes, I hate the killing but I also hate to see evil win out and subjugate people to one leader's whims. One other note, every society needs some level of common values to exist and grow. God's commandments of loving him and loving one another was a good place for the laws in the US to start to bring some semblance of order."

"Interesting perspective," Izzy stated. "I can see why your team works so well together. Gunny the tactician, Norman the strategist, Lawson the analyst and you the scientist. Though I have to admit that Lawson has a unique skill of being devious yet truthful and I can't seem to find a label for his character. He's a chess game with few rules. That is also what I find disturbing in your team, no rules."

Myers sat staring at Izzy as he thought through Izzy's assessment. "I'm confused with your observation. Disturbing? What you find disturbing, Izzy, is that Lawson's character has become the character of our team. Without him, we would be predictable, mediocre, and not very beneficial to the ONI. We've all picked up Lawson's characteristics and adapted to it. That devious nature you're not so sure about is the very jewel in the midst of our team. Norman has got so good at thinking like Lawson that she will finish a thought or plan he has placed forth. Gunny has picked it up as well. We've all learned to not believe what we see until we've vetted the situation. That's Lawson's doing as he's a pro at creating situations that look different than what they really are."

"You have some unique insights, my friend," Izzy stated as he patted Myers on the back. "You're an interesting group. Now we'll just sit back and wait for the lads, as Gunny would say, to call."

Myers went back to reading while Izzy checked on the equipment in the NATO section of crates.

Lawson and Gunny had gone over two hills and were able to move more quickly as the sky lightened up. It was 5:35 AM when they got to the top of the second hill and looked down on a field about 500 yards to the north. The sun was about to rise as they positioned themselves next to a small out jut. A small indentation in the top of the hill allowed for them to get a full view of the field while still not being exposed to those that would occupy the field. The ground was dusty with clumps of grass surrounded by large areas of dirt and small rocks. Gunny positioned himself with his rifle and checked his surroundings to ensure that they couldn't be seen.

"This is as good as any position up here to set up a sniper's post," Gunny observed as he looked the full 360 degrees to see if they could be surprised from any direction. While he was talking, Lawson got on the cellphone and called Myers. After Myers got the call, he activated the signal for the satellite that was retasked.

"You've got ten minutes before the satellite will be in position to give me a view of the area," Myers texted Lawson. "I've got an infrared detection satellite and, it being about 20 degrees cooler at your site than human body temperature, I should be able to detect if anyone is anywhere in your area. You'll need to get out of the area by 9:30 AM as the air temperature will rise high enough to make the infrared detection difficult. Do you understand?"

"Yes," Lawson acknowledged, "9:30."

Lawson pulled out a pair of binoculars and began to scan the area while Gunny did the same thing with the sniper scope. "Why do they call this a pair of binoculars when the 'bin' at the start of the word comes from the Latin word 'bini' meaning 'two'," Lawson questioned as he looked through the eyepiece. "Shouldn't it be called a pair of oculars? Otherwise we're saying we're looking through a pair of a pair oculars." Gunny just grunted at Lawson's comments as he thought how Lawson needed to get a life. Finally the comment became too much for Gunny.

"Ye seem to rip apart the English language at every opportunity ye get," Gunny protested. "Remember when ye said 'why do they call pants a pair of pants'? You went on to say 'does that mean one pant covers one leg?'. Maybe when pants were made, there were a lot of amputees with only one leg." Lawson looked at Gunny for a moment then started laughing as Gunny broke out in laughter as well. "Ye know, me lad, ye got too much rumbling inside. I'd be knackered listen'n to ye all day."

"Knackered, what's that?" Lawson probed.

"It means exhausted. It's what we Irish say," Gunny responded

"Gunny, you realized you've gone totally Irish in your comments over the past hour. You stressed out brother?" Lawson questioned.

Gunny sat the rifle down and thought for a moment, "Ye got me there. You're right, I don't feel right about this whole mission and it's getting more confusing the deeper we get into it. None of this makes sense and I got a feeling that nothing is at it appears. That's what's got me bugged."

"I know, Gunny," Lawson whispered. "I've felt that way ever since Crete. I know nothing makes sense but, like when you're playing poker, if you have no feel for where everything is going you just play that hand."

"I get you, buddy," Gunny agreed, "you're saying to play the play we have right now and don't concern ourselves about all the other stuff until we're in a safe place to do so."

"Right on," was Lawson's retort. They continued to scan the area for another 15 minutes when Gunny's phone vibrated. Gunny answered to hear Myers voice.

"Gunny, you've got four people north-northwest of you about 700 yards," Myers advised. "They appear to be guarding three large truck trailers that have their contents covered. That may be the aircraft on trailers you saw last night."

Gunny scanned the area the responded, "I can't see what you're looking at. They must be down in a ravine or low spot where we can't see them."

"Do you see the bleachers on the far end of the field and the bunker close to you?" Myers continued.

"I see the bleachers but not the bunker," Gunny answered. "Lawson says he sees the top of something flat about 150 yards north of us and down about 40 feet lower than we are."

"You've got movement behind you about 500 yards coming up the hill just before you," Myers exclaimed. "Get to some cover!" Gunny motioned for Lawson to lay low in the indentation they were in. Gunny swung the rifle around and checked to be sure a round was in the chamber. Lawson pulled his pistol, tightened the silencer on the end of the barrel and quietly chambered a round. They waited and, after several minutes, heard footsteps drawing closer and closer. The footsteps stopped somewhere down the hill as it was obvious from a conversation that an argument was in full bloom. Neither Gunny or Lawson could understand the language but the emotions were on full display. A moment later, another voice was heard but it was coming from the opposite side of the hill from where the argument was taking place. It had become a screaming match where all three voices were involved. Both Gunny and Lawson stayed frozen in their positions as the first two that were arguing walked past the indentation where Gunny could see them and make out their faces. They were both so involved in their argument that they passed by the indentation without ever looking down. After they passed and were out of earshot, Gunny looked over to Lawson and was about to say something when Lawson held up three fingers and pointed to the rock out jut. Gunny slowly turned his head to see the third person sitting on the out jut just some 20 feet away smoking a cigarette. Lawson thought for a moment then, as the man turned to leave, jumped up and stuck the end of the silencer against the man's neck. Gunny was startled by Lawson's move as Lawson grabbed the man's collar and pushed him forward.

"What are you doing?" Gunny frantically whispered as Lawson moved quickly down the hill toward the south as he pushed his prisoner along. Gunny looked back to see where the other two men had gone. They were out of sight.

"You said that things don't appear to be as represented," Lawson whispered back. "Well, we've got to get some answers and this is the guy to do it. You see, he's a supervisor and he can tell us a lot with Murodov's help."

"And how do you know he's a supervisor and can help us understand what's going on," Gunny asked.

"It's simple," Lawson explained. "You see you've been a leader for so long you've forgotten how you come across to other people. Well, this guy may speak languages we don't understand but his voice and inflections say he's a supervisor and, based upon those inflections, pretty high up the management ladder." Gunny just said 'humm' as they quickly moved from one hill to the next.

Once they came near the peak of the last hill, they checked behind them to make sure no one could see them before going over the ridge then looked up the back road toward Zhu's facility. Once they saw it was safe to move they went down to the warehouse. Gunny looked down at his phone to see that Myers had called him five times and Gunny didn't feel the phone vibrate. Gunny texted Myers with 'be there in 2 minutes'. Myers responded back 'if you've gone to the burger place, I want fries with my order." Gunny just laughed as they pulled their prisoner in tow into the warehouse. Everyone's weapons were pointed at the two prodigals as they came through the door with their prisoner.

"Aziz, what have you done to get yourself caught?" Izzy inquired in English as they pushed the man forward. The man said something in another language that sounded to Lawson like a threat based upon the way it was presented.

"Don't worry, he just called me a traitor and some other less acceptable names," Izzy said as he took the man and sat him down. "May I present Aziz Azamatov, senior engineer and confidant to Cho Ming, or shall I say Qiang Zhu." At the mention of Qiang Zhu's name, Azamatov jumped up and was immediately and forcibly pushed back down by Gunny. "By the way, he speaks perfect English and he is the perfect capture to be made in Zhu's little army. He probably knows every detail of the drones and the plans to use them. I worked with the guy at the Propheta Nostri facility until he may have discovered I had taken a full listing of the software program they were working on. I'm not sure if he knew or not but I couldn't take any chances. I didn't go back as I discovered that they had started to monitor my computer just after the printout of the program was completed."

"You know about the drones?" Azamatov asked as he looked with amazement at his captors.

Commander Norman stepped into the conversation, "We not only know about the drones, we also know about the new fuel mixture for the new fuel-injected engines, the shaped charges, the software for three different drone configurations and have a good idea of the potential targets."

"I commend you on your excellent intelligence efforts," Azamatov declared. "You wouldn't be the CAT205 Team, would you?"

Lawson, Gunny, Norman and Myers all looked at each other as they contemplated how to answer the question. Before they could respond, Benson spoke up, "These are one and the same, the CAT205 Team you've heard so much about."

"Impressive," Azamatov proclaimed as he smiled while looking at each one of them. "Such rumors creating such legends that you all have become. You don't look like giants with superpower skills. Is it true that you four took out a whole Iranian regiment?" At that Gunny started laughing. As he did so, he looked at Lawson and saw Lawson nod his head 'yes'.

"Actually, mate, there were only three of us on that mission and it wasn't a regiment, it was a battalion," Gunny explained. "We probably wouldn't have had to wipe out that battalion had our fourth team member been present."

"Well, how is it you were able to take out 3000 soldiers in that mission?" Azamatov returned.

"Someone moved a decimal point in some report," Gunny shot back. "It wasn't even 300 soldiers unless you count all of those at the Iranian military base." Lawson motioned for Izzy to cover the prisoner as Lawson motioned for Norman, Gunny, Myers and Murodov to follow him outside. Once outside, they went to the side of the building and moved behind a tree to talk.

"Well, did you get enough info to determine his value," Gunny asked Lawson as the rest listened.

"Not a lot but enough to know where he fits," Lawson stated. "He is in the top command of Zhu's organization. I know that because the rumors he mentioned would have come from the Russian government to the Chinese government as a probe for the Russians to see what the Chinese knew about CAT205. That information would have had to come directly from Zhu. All of his numbers and sizes were approximately ten times larger than what was actual, meaning that he knew the real number to start with. He was giving high numbers to stroke our egos and get us to talk. In other words, he was doing a reverse interrogation. Gunny, you did a great job playing along so now maybe we can get some of your questions answered and get an idea of what is real in this whole mess."

"What's our approach," questioned Myers as he looked at his cellphone.

"From what I've seen he's going to be a tough nut to crack," Norman warned. "He has a big ego and a lot of confidence in himself. So, Lawson, what's your approach?"

Lawson lit up a cigarette as he contemplated their next move. "You're right. He is going to be hard to break. Remember when you were kids and were to be punished for something you did. What was the one thing that created the greatest fear in you regarding that punishment?"

"The long wait before my dad carried out the punishment," Myers reminisced. "The worse the violation the longer I had to wait and my dad was a pro at making me sweat."

"That's precisely the plan," Lawson directed as he took a puff on his cigarette. "We'll just have him sit. Myers, check with Izzy and see if there are any restraints we can put on Azamatov." Myers nodded he understood as they turned to go back into the warehouse.

After they entered into the warehouse, Izzy located a crate that had handcuffs and leg restraints. He put the restraints on Azamatov then secured him to the lower frame of the building. After that was completed Myers went back to the computer and checked on the condition of the satellite.

"The satellite is out of visual and I'll need a new order to retask it again," Myers complained as he looked around at the others. "Look, it's after 9:00 AM and I've had this computer on for almost five hours. I've got another five and a half hours of power left before it's in need of recharge so I'm shutting the system down."

"You've also got about three hours left on the satellite kit so I'm shutting that down as well," Izzy stated as he proceeded to shut the satellite link down. "One more thing, if I remember correctly, I've got a vertical drone somewhere in these crates. Let me check the manifest as see which box it's located in. We might use the drone to replace the observation capabilities of the satellite."

There was an eruption of laughter as Izzy turned around to see what was causing the commotion. There was Lawson standing near the crates wearing a pair of coveralls over a brown shirt. On his head was a dark gray Greek fisherman's hat, also called a Lenin hat, with the low crown and a small visor covering dark brown shoulder length hair.

"Where'd you get the outfit and what's with the hair?" Norman asked as she tried to keep from laughing.

"The outfit was in one of the crates along with several wigs and other clothing," Lawson explained. "My guess is that Izzy has a lot more going on than we previously suspected." Izzy just smiled as Lawson walked over to one of the other crates marked with script that Lawson suspected was Uzbeki and selected a Mauser 7.92 mm bolt action rifle and a box of ammo.

"Good choice of weapons," Izzy approved. "Many of the farmers around here have the German Mauser as it has a large round that works against bears, wolves and jackals in the area. A lot of the Mausers around here are weapons captured from the Germans in World War II. The locals care for them like a family heirloom. The residents in this area also carry the weapons to protect themselves against marauders that show up once in a while. The mountain areas are good hiding places for outlaws and bandits so it's typical to see farmers checking their fields with a rifle or pistol on them."

"You going out by yourself?" Gunny asked as Lawson headed for the door.

"They're less likely to pay attention to one person walking down the road than two people," Lawson advised as he checked to make sure a round was in the chamber of the rifle. "Besides, I am checking on something that doesn't concern the rest of you." Gunny just nodded and sat back down as Lawson exited the warehouse.

Lawson walked west down the road past the Propheta Nostri facility, all the while watching for the number of people around the building. He continued walking about a mile beyond the building as the road took a gradual turn to the north and proceeded to where the road made a sudden turn to the east into a loop before going north again. He stopped at the farthest eastern point of the loop and leaned back against a large rock as he lit up a cigarette. From his vantage point, he could see rich farmlands down in the valley. The lush green and fragrances of plant life reminded him of the spring time in Iowa. As he was searching memories, a car came up the road in Lawson's direction. Lawson moved his rifle so that the rifle barrel was pointed down but in the direction of the car. The car slowed up as it approached Lawson and finally stopped with a man exiting from the driver's side.

"Mister Lawson, it's been a long time," came the voice from the visitor as he laughed at the outfit Lawson was wearing.

"It has, Captain Volkov," Lawson responded. "You were an excellent teacher. I'm trying to look like a farmer from the area. You're ruining that image I have of me."

"You'll pass for a farmer, just not a very good one. As per your request, I got this picture sent to me by Inspector Bernardakis in Crete. This is the man that was trying to get you in Crete and presented himself as an Interpol agent. His name is Mark Dietrich, a German assassin. He does not appear to have anything to do with Qiang Zhu so I suspect he is operating for another group. He is tied in with the guy that tried to kill Commander Norman in Volgograd. That man's name is Pax Dominici, which I suspect is not his real name as the meaning is similar to the Vulgate Latin for 'working for peace'. He's Italian and a contract killer. By the way, we've tracked Mark Dietrich to Washington, DC. General Machinko thinks that Dietrich believes you went to Washington after leaving Dubai. One other note, we broke part of the code for the message 'Usb field 19'. From other messages we've intercepted, we've determined it means that Zhu is doing a field test of the drones on July 19th. That's the day after tomorrow."

The determination of the test date caught Lawson's attention as he looked long and hard at the photo of Dietrich then handed it back to Volkov. "Thanks, Captain. This helps a lot. Tell Machinko that he left quite an impression on Commander Norman. The date of the testing really helps us to set up a plan."

"You're welcome, Lieutenant," Volkov said as he headed for the car. "By the way, I'd take a different route going back to your location. You guys stirred up a hornet's nest when you took Azamatov. Zhu's soldiers are checking everyone on the road and anyone walking in the area. I've already informed Rasulov of the situation and he is sending several police cars to stop the illegal searches and roadblocks."

"Thanks, Captain," Lawson pronounced as he wondered how Volkov knew about the capture of Azamatov and how he was able to circumvent the road blocks.

"If you want to get something out of Azamatov, tell him you know about his message from the past," Volkov stated as he turned back toward Lawson and wrote down some words on a piece of paper. Lawson took the paper and looked at the words 'Mene, Mene, Tekel, Upharsin'.

"What does this mean?" Lawson queried as he looked at the paper. "It's definitely something foreign and looks like some phonetics in English that comes from some other country."

"Right you are," Volkov responded. "We had some trouble determining the meaning of the words but after we found out that Azamatov's mother was from Iraq and he was primarily raised by her, we sought out a linguist from Iraq to give us a definition. After being sent to three different people, we found a linguist in ancient Persian-Babylonian languages that was able to translate some basics of it. He said it meant 'numbered, numbered, weighted, divided'. We don't know why it has such significance to Azamatov but it seems to be a gateway to his soul, if you catch my drift."

Lawson was more perplexed than ever. "How did you find that piece of information?"

"We knew Azamatov was key to getting to Colonel Zhu so we did a lot of background analysis on him," Volkov instructed. "A guy he went to technical school with in Osh said that

Azamatov was very superstitious and had some emotional issues with certain ancient Persian phrases, probably a result of being brought up by his mother. This was one of the phrases that seemed to impact him the most. Why that is, we don't know but it could be an opening to getting him talking."

"Thanks, Captain," Lawson called out as he put the piece of paper in his pocket while wondering what Volkov had on him.

"You didn't get the football scholarship you wanted for college so you paid your way through college but couldn't graduate because you ran out of money," Volkov shouted as he opened the door to his car. "I figured that's the general topic you were thinking about after our discussion. By the way, cut the hair shorter and lose the coveralls. It's too hot during the day to wear them this time of the year."

As Volkov drove off Lawson just smiled and started on his journey back to the warehouse by a different route. "How is it that people can do that to me, always knowing what I'm thinking? Am I that easy to read?" Lawson questioned himself as he started his walk.

It took Lawson until almost 2:00 PM to get back to the warehouse as he had to take a long way around going through farmlands to the south to avoid any of Zhu's security people. Rasulov's officers had been successful in breaking up the roving bands of Zhu's men but his men were still out individually watching the roads for cars and travelers. Lawson got to the east side of the main highway going north to the complex of buildings the warehouse was in. He quickly crossed the east-west road that ran in front of the warehouse once he saw one of Zhu's men that was about 100 yards to the west turn to look the other way. Carefully entering the warehouse after giving a Morse code tap of 'LA', the door was unlatched from the inside and opened slowly so he was not to be spotted. After entering and walking to the nearest stack of crates, he sat the Mauser rifle down on a crate and caught his breath. The others sat waiting for him to fill them in on what he found.

"You get what you went out for whatever that was?" Gunny tersely posed as he looked at Lawson.

"Yes, and a lot more, Master Gunny," Lawson snapped back. Gunny stepped away as he could tell his challenge set Lawson off and Lawson was in no mood for it as Lawson continued, "Zhu's got this area covered like a blanket so any of us going out right now would be foolish."

Gunny took a deep breath and moved to sit down next to Lawson. "I didn't mean to snap at you, good buddy, but we have been in a tense situation here since just after you left this morning," Gunny whispered. "Commander Norman made it very clear that if Azamatov makes any noise that brings any of Zhu's people into the warehouse, he'll be the first person shot. That kept Azamatov quiet when a couple of Zhu's goons tried the door to see if it would open. We've been operating on silence protocol so no one has been talking. Myers has a good position next to a small hole where he can see someone coming toward the building in the front and Murodov is keeping watch, looking through a nail hole in the back of the building. There has been no one anywhere near the building for the past two hours so I figure they have written the warehouse off as a building of interest. So, what about you?"

"I've been able to verify that the 'Usb Field 19' message indicates that the drone field tests are to be July 19th, day after tomorrow," Lawson reported.

"I won't ask you how you got that," Norman said as Lawson turned to realize Norman had been sitting on a crate just above him. He knew he was fatigued.

"I met with Captain Pavel Volkov about three hours ago and got a number of key pieces of information from him," Lawson conveyed.

"Volkov is here!" Norman exclaimed then put her hand over her mouth as she looked at Myers at the front of the building. Myers just provided Norman a very disgusted look then went back to looking out through the little hole that was his observation post.

"He is here but he's going to remain hidden until things are settled," stated Lawson as he looked toward Myers for any indication that Norman's outburst might have created an interest outside of the building.

"We interrogated Azamatov for nearly an hour until Zhu's patrols started putting a crimp in our conversations," Norman recounted. "He's clammed up and hasn't said anything since you left. He feels he has all the cards."

"I thought we were just going to let him stew and not talk to him at all until he had ample time to think through all the possibilities," Lawson said.

"We were but Azamatov kept making noise and egging us on," Gunny related. "He was driving us all nuts and when Zhu's patrols started doing their thing, Norman knew she had enough of his rantings and smacked him across the face with her pistol then gave him the threat that he would be the first to die if anything went wrong." Lawson smiled at Gunny's description as Lawson looked up at Norman realizing that this is the woman he plans to marry. A gun across the face…it could just as easily be a frying pan. He started laughing as everyone wondered what brought that reaction on.

"It looks like Zhu's people have gone back to their facility," Murodov observed. "However, I wouldn't put it past him to leave some observers out there to watch where we might be hiding." Everyone agreed as Lawson motioned for Norman, Myers, Gunny and Izzy to the far back end of the warehouse. Myers protested for a moment as he wanted to stay watching the front but realized Lawson was right. Zhu's people weren't going to do any more probing for the moment.

They all took seats near each other on crates at the back of the building. Lawson started off the discussion with a whispered question as he pulled a piece of paper out of his pocket. "Anyone knows what significance these words have?" Gunny took the paper first and nodded 'no'. Norman looked at the paper and handed it to Izzy.

"So, what is 'Mene, Mene, Tekel, Upharsin," Izzy whispered as he handed the paper to Myers.

"I've seen these words before," Myers remarked as he thought for a moment. "I remember that they're from the Book of Daniel in the Bible. The words 'Numbered, Numbered, Weighed and Divided' written below these words match with the words meanings." Everyone looked at Myers wondering what the words had to do with the Bible.

"It appears to have great significance to Azamatov, but what, I'm not sure," Lawson reported.

"Well, here's the background of the words," Myers began. "Daniel was a prophet in Babylon back during the time of Nebuchadnezzar until the first year of King Cyrus of Persia. Belshazzar became king of Babylon after Nebuchadnezzar died and one night during a banquet, Belshazzar used the gold items that were originally taken from the Jewish temple in Jerusalem to drink to the Babylonian gods. While they were drinking, words were written on the wall by an unknown hand that gave these words, 'Mene, Mene, Tekel, Upharsin'. Belshazzar was disturbed by the message as was all the people at the banquet. He called for Daniel to come in to interpret the meaning of the words and Daniel proceeded to tell Belshazzar the meaning. For the two first words 'Mene, Mene' meant that 'Your days are numbered and your kingdom will be taken from you'. The word 'Tekel' means 'God has weighed you in the balance or on the scales and found you wanting'. The word 'Upharsin' which can also be 'Parsin' or 'Peres' in the Persian language means 'Your kingdom will be divided and given to the Medes and Persians'. That night, Belshazzar died and Cyrus, King of Persia, took over the kingdom."

"So, what does this have to do with Azamatov," Norman asked as she was confused why a Uzbekistani citizen would be involved with Persia or Babylon.

Lawson was immediate to respond. "Captain Volkov stated that Azamatov's mother was Iraqi and he was raised by her through most of his childhood. Now, if I remember correctly, Babylon, the city and its present ruins, are in Iraq. Furthermore, Iraq is part of what used to be Persia and many Iraqis and

Iranians today still consider themselves Persians. That being said, if Azamatov was raised in Iraq, he probably knows the intimate details about the Daniel story."

"My question is why does he put so much credence on the words written on the wall?" Gunny posed. "It has to be something that had a great impact on him for some reason. Maybe the story scared him so much when he was little that it stayed with him and just grew over the years."

"Or maybe it was an immediate event concerning the writing on the wall that impacted him," Norman offered. "The only way we'll find out is to bring the words up to him in some way as to get a response and go from there. Lawson, this is your bailiwick. You're going to have to fly blind and hope as your conversation goes along where you can determine the way these words impact him."

"OK," Lawson answered, "it's probably going to be Gunny's thought that the words gained meaning over a long period of time or Norman's thought that it could be an immediate event such as a confrontation or a dream that stayed with him."

"The only way you're going to find out is by trying and see what happens," Gunny interjected. "I suggest that we all go over one at a time with Lawson showing up last. We can sit and start up conversations with each other until Lawson gets there. Once Lawson starts to talk, everyone else keep quiet so Lawson can thread the needle in the conversation. I know we will all want to jump in to give some direction to the conversation but I think Lawson needs free reign on this effort. Agreed?"

Everyone nodded 'yes' as they looked to see who would go first.

"Norman, you need to stay away from the conversation," Lawson advised. "You smacked him in the head with a gun and he's not going to be receptive to conversations if you're there with us."

"You're right," Norman winced as she responded. "Go get him."

Later, as Lawson was preparing to discuss the topic of the Daniel interpretations with Azamatov, Myers came over to Lawson.

"You might want to wait until tomorrow morning to talk to Azamatov. I just took food over to him and he's upset about Norman putting tape over his mouth," Myers recommended as Lawson listened.

"I was thinking the same thing. I'm not ready yet to hold that discussion with him," Lawson declared. "I've got to get my hands around how to approach the conversation before we continue." Norman came over with Gunny and Izzy as Lawson and Myers were talking.

"By the way, Gunny said that from your conversation with Volkov that the meaning for 'Usb field 19' was determined," Myers stated as Lawson realized the topic had totally slipped his mind to let the others know about the conversation.

"It's true," Lawson responded. "Volkov said that, from other messages they had deciphered, the testing of the drones is to take place on July 19th, day after tomorrow."

"Ok," Norman reflected as she sat down, "I know there are a lot of things going on but you can't keep information like this from the others. I know you told me and Gunny earlier but you have to be the one to tell those others that need to know."

Lawson sat next to her as he leaned his head back to stretch his neck. "You're right. Listen, we are all tired, not getting much sleep and feel closed in by having to stay in this warehouse and keep quiet. I suggest that we set up our nightly security watches for the rest of the day and get as much rest as we can for the rest of the day then proceed to plan and prep tomorrow for Wednesday's actions."

They all went to their air mattresses while Myers unshackled Azamatov and brought him over to one of the air mattresses.

"I know you're an honorable man," Myers told Azamatov as they both laid down. "If you give me your word you won't do anything that can threaten us or try to escape, I'll leave the handcuffs off of you so you can get some sleep."

"You have my word," Azamatov said thankfully.

Myers laid back on the mattress as he opened a book. Reaching under his mattress, he felt for the M17 pistol and, once assured that it was placed where he could reach it, he began to read. As he did so, he could hear Azamatov say something but didn't recognize the language. Myers realized at that moment that Azamatov was praying. Murodov came over and laid down on the mattress next to Myers.

"Gunny's got the first watch, 4:00 PM to 6:00 PM," Murodov explained. "You've got the 6 to 8 watch then Norman has the 8 to 10 watch. By the way, Azamatov was praying in the native Persian language. I learned the language at the Institute and he was praying that God protects you all and it sounded like the way a Christian or Jew addresses their God. He is a strange one."

"Maybe not so strange," Myers perceived as he smiled and went back to his book.

Chapter 13

Prophesies and Panic

"It seems everyone is at war in some sense with everyone else. My mother used to say 'trust no one, not even yourself because there is some evil in each of us'. I would like to add 'there is also good in each of us'. The question is whether we allow good or evil to win out in our daily lives. I hold no grievances against these CAT205 people. They are trying to keep the world in some form of stability and I support that. I hope they know that, in his own way, Colonel Zhu is trying to do the same thing though they would probably disagree." – Aziz Azamatov, Colonel Zhu's Chief Engineer

It was 6:35 AM on July 18th as Gunny handed a plate of food to Azamatov. Myers was up and using the portable latrine as Norman was taking a shower in the field shower unit. Lawson was cooking food while concerned that the smell of the food would be detected by one of Zhu's people outside somewhere in the area. He became less concerned as he could detect the smell of a dozen different farms in the area cooking breakfast. The strong smell of mutton and of onions could be picked up as the light wind from the south carried the fragrances across the valley.

"You're smelling the scent of pilaf," Azamatov instructed as he picked up food from his plate with his fingers. "Pilaf is a rice dish with onions and carrots with or without meat. They're using meat this morning and it smells like mutton." As he was speaking, Lawson picked up a bowl of water and a cloth for Azamatov to clean his hands after eating. "You know something about our ways," Azamatov continued. "Only a person that knows that we eat with our hands would also know to provide us water and a cloth to clean our hands."

"Actually, I didn't know that," came Lawson's response. "I gave you the water to drink as we didn't want to break out the canteens from the crates yet and I knew you would need the cloth to wipe your hands." Azamatov laughed as he heard Lawson's explanation and realized he was dealing with people that were exceptionally honest. His view of Americans was different than what he had been told about them.

Myers came over and sat on one of the crates near Azamatov as Gunny handed his plate to Lawson for some food. Norman went to the far end of the warehouse to check on her messages while Izzy handed his cleaned plate back to Lawson for storage then sat down next to Myers. Lawson put the last of the food in his plate and turned off the gas jet that fed the flame for the hot plate. As he did so, he shifted his body as he turned to face Azamatov.

"I believe you had a dream and your dream has come to fruition, Aziz. In it was Mene, Mene, Tekel, Upharsin," Lawson whispered loud enough for everyone to hear him. As he finished speaking, Azamatov's face turned pale as he sat his plate down on the ground.

"It is as I dreamed," Azamatov said in terror. "In my dream I saw I would be captured then I would hear those words. It has come to be. I have feared this moment all my life. How do you know these words and how do you know of my dream? I've told no one of the dream."

"You had the dream while you were young," Lawson stated as he started gambling on the time, depth and meaning of the dream and the words that caused Azamatov's distress. "Your mother told you stories about the glory of Persia and particularly of Babylon, Daniel and Kings Nebuchadnezzar and Cyrus." Myers felt for Azamatov as he heard Lawson speaking and wished Lawson had not taken this approach as Myers realized Azamatov was a Christian. Myers was upset until he heard Lawson continue. "Today, you are going to be freed from that fear and it will be gone from you for the rest of your life." Myers looked at Gunny as he couldn't believe the change in direction Lawson had taken. Gunny just smiled at the brilliant move Lawson had just made.

"I will tell you whatever you want to know," Azamatov lamented as he realized his hidden burden had been exposed. "Just free me of this demon I have had to deal with throughout my life."

"I don't have the power to free you from this," Lawson declared, "but by exposing it, you can remove its power." Myers was taken aback by Lawson's statement as he continued. "It's like confession. Once you confess you remove the burden of having to keep it secret. That's freedom in itself."

"You're getting to sound like Myers," Gunny opined. "What you just said is as good a sermon as Myers has ever given me. It's amazing what holds us down and it's usually our own fears."

"What do you want to know?" Azamatov asked.

Lawson could see the relief in Azamatov's face as Lawson asked, "I know there are 75 drones being moved out to the field for tomorrow's exhibition. Where are the other 925 drones?"

"The other 924 drones are being moved to the Chinese city of Chengdu in western China," Azamatov answered. "We made exactly one thousand drones. The other 76 drones are being used for the demo tomorrow."

"So Zhu is going to demonstrate 76 of his upgraded fuel-injected, engine-driven drones tomorrow," Lawson supposed. "But we only counted 75 drones on the flatbed trailers."

"Zhu is demonstrating his 75 carburetor-based drones tomorrow," Azamatov stated as he picked up the plate and attempted to spin it on the tip of his finger. "The 76th drone is a fuel-injected model. He wanted to use one fuel-injected drone to see how it would behave with the increased power." Myers and Lawson looked at each other as they both came to the same question.

"Why is Zhu demonstrating the carburetor-based drones and not the fuel-injected ones," Myers queried. "According to messages that have been decrypted, the demo appears to be planned for an hour flight demonstration and the carburetor-based drones will be able to fly only about 20 minutes before the engines overheat and they fall from the sky."

Azamatov looked perplexed as he thought over Myers comments. It was a good question, one that he hadn't considered. "Your question makes sense but also raises some interesting questions," Azamatov commented as he put the plate down. "They really went all out on this demo. Zhu had them order cold meat slices, different types of cheeses, grapes, melon, various vegetables, shellfishes, salmon and sheep liver. He also ordered a large supply of drinks including alcoholic beverages for the non-Muslim attendees. This is a first-rate layout for entertaining big time players in this area of the world. So why would Zhu show them inferior products?"

Lawson sat thinking as Norman heard the topic being discussed and came over. She proceeded to sit down, which made Azamatov nervous, and asked, "Who are these people Zhu is demonstrating to?"

Azamatov uneasily watched Norman's hands for any moves that would indicate she would attack him. Finally, realizing that she was not acting in a threatening manner, he replied, "They are leaders of the Propheta Nostri cells from all over the world. There are some seventy to ninety of them that were invited and they all accepted as they see the drones as a great instrument to create chaos in their protests and marches. These people attending are the top leaders of the organization."

Lawson got up and paced the floor as Azamatov watched. He was mystified by Lawson's sudden change of disposition.

"Don't worry about him," Myers advised. "He does this when he goes into thinking mode. When he sees too many variables, he has to go into this mode to sort things out."

"Is he a mystic or Magi like Daniel was?" questioned Azamatov as he watched Lawson pacing back and forth. "Otherwise, how could you explain his knowledge of my dream or how it affected me?"

Myers smiled as he answered Azamatov's question, "He's not a mystic or someone with supernatural powers. He got just enough information to know there was something about the four words Daniel interpreted that made you uncomfortable. He also put together that it had to be a dream and something you've lived with since childhood. He's good at putting pieces like that together."

"But he does have powers," Azamatov gave as a retort. "He sees things different than you or I do and he sees them in ways that makes sense out of a puzzle. That is a gift and one that's not from learning. It's a God-given, natural skill that doesn't come from DNA. It's part of the human spirit." Myers was taken back by the level of intelligence and wisdom Azamatov demonstrated. He exhibited a sense of depth and understanding of the human soul. He was really getting to like this guy.

Lawson came back and sat down. "We need to get things together and lay out a plan for our activities tomorrow," he said as he was still contemplating all Azamatov had exposed. There were details that didn't make sense, and yet, somehow he knew that Azamatov was telling the truth.

At Lawson's comment Gunny exclaimed, "It's about time," as he grabbed a large pad of planning sheets and some pens and put them in front of Lawson.

For the next six hours they mapped out the layout of the terrain, where everyone should be, what types of weapons and gear they would need and what outside support may be required. Izzy indicated that they could not call upon any US or Russian military help as that would be seen as an illegal incursion. He also warned that any major confrontation could result in a new outbreak of hostilities between the Uzbeks and the Kyrgyz in Osh. Everyone knew that a major confrontation was a high probability if the team was to fight their way in to get to Zhu.

Lawson picked up Norman's cellphone to check on any emails or texts coming from Admiral Roedl. The first text from

Roedl stated that the woman that was in the lobby with the small aircraft engine was Margret Halpern, a design analyst for the Dolotecque Corporation. She was on the 'Shiny Object' watch list. As Lawson looked over the other texts that Norman had received, one stood out. It was from a Russell Mejia, Senior Technical Hobgoblin at the Pentagon.

"What's a Pentagon Hobgoblin?" Lawson asked as he looked at the texts.

Norman was first to answer, "It's a Strategist, sometimes formally called a Storyteller. The term 'Hobgoblin' was first used by one of the members of the Joint Chiefs of Staff. However, the Storyteller and the Hobgoblin are slightly different. Storytellers lay out commentary and make comparisons of the viability of different strategies where the Hobgoblins try to match defense budgets with organizations and personnel needed in the planning of future conflicts. Why is that a concern to you?"

"Well," Lawson began, "this text to you comes from a Pentagon Senior Technical Hobgoblin named Russell Mejia and states 'Orders are to eliminate Cho Ming at earliest possible opportunity'. Now why would someone doing planning in the Pentagon give us orders to assassinate a foreign national? Isn't that something we would get from Admiral Roedl?"

"Let me see that!" Norman exclaimed as she grabbed the cellphone from Lawson. "I didn't even notice the role, just the order. I was going to inform you all about the order later this evening as it would have to be a planned insertion. You will all ignore this order! Something is really going fishy here."

"I think she means that something is fishy here," Myers corrected. "It's not going fishy, it's already fished." Everyone laughed at Myers' observation while Norman frowned at him and shoved her cellphone into her pocket.

Lawson pulled out his own phone as he explained his next step, "I'm going to text some questions to Admiral Roedl on who this Russell Mejia is and what's going on. Maybe he can clear some things up."

"Sounds good," Norman acquiesced. "Let's get back to planning and prep for our mission tomorrow."

They continued through the planning until they were satisfied they had covered all the bases. At least that is what they all thought until Norman raised another issue. "We go up to see what the demo is supposed to do, we identify anyone we can in the group of spectators but what are we to do to stop them from using the drones?" They all looked at each other as they realized that in all their planning they forgot to deal with the most important question.

"I've got a couple of the ID designations from Izzy," Myers informed. "They both appear to be leader drones as we found from the software in that they have multiple cameras installed. I can hack into one of them, put in new coordinates and send them off where they will lead the other drones in an unexpected attack against a friendly target."

"What type of target?" Lawson asked

"How about their own facility," Gunny offered. "I suspect that all of the security people and personnel will be out on the field to observe the demo so why not hit the building with their own drones? It will destroy their ability to manufacture any more drones and probably destroy their records and notes." Everyone started laughing as they heard Gunny's solution. It was obvious that they all agreed with the recommendation.

"Myers, do you have the ability to enter the coordinates for one of the lead drones?" Lawson asked as he saw the software code being displayed on Myers' computer screen. At that moment the loud sound of a large metal door being opened caught their attention. Myers sat the computer down and ran to the small hole to look out to the front of the building. He couldn't see anything moving.

Gunny ran toward the back of the building as he shouted, "I'll go around to the front and see what's going on."

"Hold on, Gunny," Izzy loudly whispered. Opening up a lid to one of the crates, Izzy took out a small mirror attached to an extendable rod. "You'll need this to look around the corner and see what they're doing without being seen." Gunny grabbed the mirror and went out the back door.

A couple minutes later he came back in and handed the mirror back to Izzy. "They appear to be going from one building to another," Gunny reported. "They're cutting the locks off of the loading dock doors and going inside. There are also two men with AK-47 rifles about four buildings down from where the men are at. I suspect they are lookouts. The three men entering the buildings appear to be very professional and very cautious as they enter. It appears that they are going into each building on this road and they're being very methodical. I figure they will be at our build in 10 to 15 minutes. So what do we do?"

"I know who they are," Azamatov admitted. "They are probably one of the three man teams sent out by that killer Ergashev and his brutal associates. Just after I left his office, I overheard Zhu giving Ergashev instructions to send out three teams of three men each to wipe out your group. I think this is one of those teams."

"Alright, we don't have much time to react," Lawson announced. "Where is the car?"

"It's three buildings down east of us and behind the building," Gunny explained. "We had to do that so they wouldn't see a car parked outside our building."

"Great," Lawson responded. "Izzy, I saw you have several MP5 9 millimeter automatic rifles. Where are they?" Izzy ran to a stack of crates and moved the top crate over then pulled the next lower crate out. After setting the crate down he gave a hard hit with his boot to the top of the crate which caused the lid to pop up. Lawson grabbed one of the rifles causing Gunny to give a sigh of relief as he saw that they were already cleaned and ready for action.

Izzy pulled the magazine out of the weapon and proceeded to load it with 9 mm rounds using an autoloader strip as Lawson grabbed Gunny and asked for the car keys. Gunny immediately recognized the plan.

"I'll drive and you shoot," Gunny suggested as Izzy put the loaded clip into the weapon and handed it to Lawson.

"I've set the weapon to full automatic," Izzy reported as Gunny and Lawson ran out the back door.

"They better hurry," Myers exclaimed. "I can see by some motion that they are moving to open the door to the building next to us. They're going to each building in sequence."

Gunny unlocked the car using the key fob as they ran toward the vehicle. Lawson got in the front passenger side as Gunny got into the driver side. Gunny started the engine and put the vehicle into gear. He headed east on the back road that went behind the buildings and parallel to the main road. Lawson was baffled by Gunny's driving as he was going the opposite direction of where they needed to go.

"It's simple," Gunny stated. "If I came out from the side of the last building, they would know we're somewhere in one of those buildings. However, if I come down the road from nowhere, they will think that we are just making a hit on them and not that we may be in one of the buildings."

Lawson was starting to panic at the length of time it would take to make it back. Finally, Gunny drove the car to where there was a lower spot that was present in both roads. Going across the grassy area between the two roads, he turned onto the main road and headed west. Knowing that the lookouts down the road could not see where the car was at or its entrance onto the main road, Lawson understood Gunny's plan. As Gunny accelerated the vehicle, Lawson checked to make sure a round was chambered in his weapon.

"This is a drive-by shooting," Gunny explained as they raced toward their target. "You need to be effective and accurate with your shots. Full automatic. Once we pass our building and the building after that I will be turning south on the main north-south road which means the two lookouts won't be able to intercept us.

If you don't get all three at the building, they will be firing on us so be sure that you get everyone."

As Gunny was talking Lawson was texting Myers 'everyone down on the deck' to let those in the building know that bullets were coming their way. Lawson wasn't sure if the corrugated steel was enough to keep the bullets from going through walls. After he sent the text, Lawson looked up to see that they were approaching the buildings. He could see three men outside of the building next to theirs with one man moving forward to that building's door with some bolt cutters.

"I'm going to quickly slow for you to take the shot. They will think we're slowing down for the turn," Gunny shouted as Lawson rolled down the window. Lawson kept the barrel of the rifle below the window until they were almost up to their target. As they approached the buildings the men just looked at the car but didn't react to its approach. As Gunny slowed down, the men proceeded to turn toward the building they were about to enter. One man looked back and shouted something as Lawson put the barrel out of the window. The men tried to swing their rifles up as Lawson opened fire. The speed for the rate of fire surprised Lawson as he fought to keep the barrel down and on his targets. Lawson kept firing in the general direction until Gunny tapped him on the shoulder.

"I think they're dead," Gunny gently said while he turned the car down the road to the south. They heard a crack and then small particles of glass fly as Gunny stepped on the gas. "Those are 7.62 rounds they're shooting at us! They'll go through the metal of the car. Any rounds left in your rifle?" Gunny shouted. Lawson could see the two lookouts shooting at them. He could also hear the impact of bullets against the side of the car. Lawson flipped the selection lever on the rifle to single fire. He carefully sighted in on one of the lookouts, lifted his sight about 6 inches above the man's head and pulled the trigger. A moment later the man fell and the other lookout ran. Lawson pulled out the clip from the weapon, no rounds left. Opening the chamber of the rifle re realized that the round he fired at the lookout was his last one. He sat back in the car seat and took a deep breath.

"You ok, Gunny?" Lawson questioned as he looked at Gunny and saw the crease on the side of Gunny's head. The passing bullet had shaved his head so close where it passed that it took the hair down to the skin but didn't draw blood. The very top part of the windshield exhibited the point where the bullet exited the car.

"You still alive?" Gunny responded as he felt the place where the bullet passed. "There goes my hairdo." They both laughed as Gunny proceeded to plot how to get back to the building without being seen. He knew he had to do it soon as Zhu's people would be out shortly to collect the bodies. Gunny took the next side road, went down about a mile to the east and caught another dirt farming road to the north. Once he got to the main east-west road, he crossed it and went to the secondary dirt road that would take him behind their building. They arrived and parked the car back to where it was originally parked. Once they got out of the car they could see the damage.

"I don't think this rental is going to be used much more," Lawson observed as he counted 11 bullet holes in the passenger side of the vehicle and a broken side window. They went back into their building and reported on their success.

Lawson leaned back next to Gunny and closed his eyes about the time Myers came over. Lawson didn't want to do more talking but he knew Myers had something that needed to be completed. Lawson heard the footsteps and opened his eyes to Myers smiling at him.

"Zhu's people just picked up the three you killed," Myers said. "There was a lot of swearing and anger among them as they picked up the bodies. Murodov says that they were arguing that the attack came from east of the area and why were they so busy breaking into these buildings. They are worried the police will trace the break-ins back to the Propheta Nostri people."

"Great, mission accomplished," Lawson responded. "Anything else?"

"Now, Lawson, as to your question concerning if I can program the coordinates into one of their lead drones. It's a piece of cake," came Myers' response. "All I have to do is enter the coordinates when the drones get airborne. They have to be on-line for me to make the change. I can do it by connecting my cellphone up to my computer and send the string of commands to change the contents of the data tables in the lead drone. They are using cellphone frequencies to command their drones so I suspect they are also using cellphone towers to extend the range of their control of the drones. I'll pull up the mapping program and get the coordinates for the rear of the Propheta Nostri building."

"Why the rear of the building?" Norman queried as she approached.

Lawson answered Norman after he realized only he and Gunny had seen the layout of the outside of the building. "We hit the back of the building because, unlike the front of the building with its heavy loading dock doors for individual trucks and cement pillars between each door, the back of the building has that big loading dock with one large, flimsy aluminum door that extends about 80 feet across the back. The drones should have no problem taking that door down and entering the building."

"That's great but then the drones won't know what to hit," Gunny observed.

"All I have to do is tell the leader drone what type of target to hit and it will send that order to the other drones," Myers instructed. "Remember that these are smart drones that supposedly can pick their own targets using artificial intelligence once they are informed by the lead drone." Everyone agreed the plan was a good one.

Izzy and Myers ran a power cable from the outlet of the building next to theirs and pushed the other end of the cable through a small hole into their building. After some manipulation of cables and connectors, they were able to get everyone's electronics connected up and charging.

While Izzy and Myers were doing their tasks, Gunny, Lawson and Norman were laying out the gear, weapons, ammo, food and water for each individual. While they were doing this, Lawson looked over to see Benson reading messages on her phone. It was at that point he realized he had a dilemma. Benson had no experience in direct contact operations and Lawson was not sure if he could trust Benson to be left alone. Looking around, he realized that Murodov would also be a limiting party to this effort.

"I think I'll have Benson and Murodov stay in this building with Azamatov while we go on our mission," Lawson stated.

"No," Norman shot back. "I need Benson with me. It's essential. Murodov can keep an eye on Azamatov." Lawson just shrugged his shoulders in response as he went back to putting items in each person's stack of gear for the next morning's mission.

Chapter 14

Into the Mouth of the Dragon

"From everything I'm getting from Admiral Roedl, it appears that Operation Shiny Object is about to go into overdrive. The CAT205 Team believes the testing of the drones will happen at any time. They also believe several world leaders are targets once the test is completed. There are forces at work here in the US that appear to be working against our operational success." – Captain Harry Wallace, US Navy, Pentagon Intelligence Operations Coordinator

It was 3:30 AM on July 19th as Gunny moved from mattress to mattress in the warehouse waking each person and pointing to the dim light given off by the gas burner with a pot of boiling water on top. "For coffee and oatmeal," he said as he sat down to eat his bowl of oatmeal. "We leave at 0430 hours, so eat then do whatever you do. We'll need 15 minutes to get the gear on and weapons checked before we go." Everyone started moving around as a line formed outside of the portable latrine while others were making coffee and oatmeal. By the time 4:15 AM came around everyone was putting on their gear from their specific stack of materials that were laid out the night before. Once they got the gear on and checked the contents of their backpacks, Gunny stepped forward and proceeded to direct them through the checklist. They opened the backpacks and checked as Gunny called out the contents.

"One medical kit, three meals, three clips ammo for the M14 rifle, six clips ammo for the M17 pistol, two morphine syringes, three packets blood clot powder, one pair miniature military binoculars, one compass and one regional map."

"Why do we need a compass if we have one on our phone?" asked Benson as she put the items back into her backpack.

"What are you going to do if you get lost and your phone loses power?" Gunny responded. Benson made a face at him as she picked up the clothing.

"We are going to dress with the clothing Izzy brought and Lawson used to dress up like a farmer," Gunny continued. "You're going to wear brown pants with gray shirts. Some of you have brown vests, some have green vests and some have gray vests. We're not wearing military camouflage today as that would stand out like a sore thumb. Everyone will wear an M17 pistol that Norman will hand to you. Lawson and Norman will be carrying M14 rifles. The M-14 clips you have in your packs are to provide all of us extra ammo if we get into a firefight. I will be carrying a 7.62 millimeter sniper rifle. Everyone carries two canteens of water and make sure you put a purification packet into each canteen to kill off any bacteria. Communications will be by cellphone and each of you has an earpiece so that your phone won't ring and give our position away. Anyone needs to take a restroom break or have a cigarette, now's the time to do it."

Once Gunny finished, Norman handed out the M17 pistols to each person. They each chambered a round in the pistols then put the pistols in new holsters that Izzy pulled from one of the crates after Lawson found the pistols. The new holsters were made to provide extra space to put a pistol into holster that had an optional silencer on the barrel. They put their backpacks on and followed Gunny to the back door of the building. One by one, they exited and proceeded to the northeast across the hills Gunny and Lawson had reconnoitered two days before. They moved slowly until it became light enough to see some of their surroundings and it was much slower than before as they were moving as a larger group. They arrived at the place where Lawson and Gunny were before. It was 5:10 AM and things were easier to see. Lawson estimated it was about a half an hour until sunrise.

Gunny took the position in the indentation along with Myers. Lawson, Norman and Izzy went west about 50 yards west from the indentation and set up their observation positions in small drops in the ridge. Izzy watched the small tufts of grass spread throughout the hillsides. Watching the wind blow the grass, Izzy told Norman to set her rifle scope one click left to adjust for the wind. When she questioned his reasoning he pointed to the breeze blowing through the grass. Norman understood immediately and adjusted the sight.

While Lawson, Norman and Izzy were preparing their position, Myers had taken the satellite link unit and computer out of his backpack and set them up behind the rock out jut. "Don't turn that on until we see some real activity down there," Gunny advised. "We don't know when they'll start and we need to conserve power." Myers agreed as he took out his pistol, checked it and sat it on top of the computer. Everyone waited as the day became hotter and the humidity was rising as the wind shifted from the south. The wind brought the humid air up to them from the Fergana Valley. The result was stifling. Lawson was elated that he made everyone take two canteens of water and everyone else was happy with the decision as well.

It was approximately 8:05 AM when Izzy approached Lawson. "I've got to go back to the warehouse as I've been texted that we've got some items being delivered," Izzy said as he showed Lawson the text. Lawson agreed and sent Izzy on his way.

Izzy came back around 9:10 AM and pulled Lawson aside. "These came for you," Izzy stated as he handed Lawson some miniature electronic receivers and instructions.

After reading the instructions Lawson instructed Izzy, "Make sure Myers, Gunny and Norman each get a set with the instructions and make sure Benson doesn't see you doing it." Izzy nodded he understood as he walked up the hill toward where the others were positioned.

It was approximately 11:15 AM when things started happening. A refrigeration truck pulled up at one end of the field next to the bleachers. Men started pulling out tables and binding covers on the tables to keep the wind from blowing the table cloths around. Next, they brought out tray after tray of food which resulted in everyone on the CAT205 team taking out their binoculars and calling each other on what they thought the food items were.

"Everyone get off the air unless you see something important," Lawson texted everyone. "They may be able to pick up our communications and determine where we are." At that moment, everything they had that was electronic went silent.

They continued to watch as the people on the field brought out the last of the food then set up the table for the drinks.

"Oh no," Gunny said loud enough for Lawson and his group to hear him. Lawson got up to see Gunny looking down the hill to the field through the scope on his rifle. "They've got Irish Whiskey and it's my favorite brand," Gunny exclaimed as he wished he was down on the field.

Lawson went over to Gunny's position to check on everyone. "How far are we from the bleachers?" Lawson probed as he looked at the activity taking place on the field.

"The bleachers are about 600 yards from us," Gunny estimated.

"And how far does sound carry with the wind at your back?" Lawson posed.

Gunny caught onto the question instantly, "I guess I was a little loud there, wasn't I. They could have heard it if they were all still at the time I made the comment. Sorry for the risk."

"Thanks, Gunny," Lawson replied as he moved back to his position. As he was moving, he heard a quick set of whistles. At first Lawson thought it was a bird then realized that it was coming from Gunny's direction. Looking back toward Gunny, Lawson saw Gunny pointing to a string of cars entering the valley to the east that goes to the field. Nodding to Gunny that he understood, Lawson motioned with his hands for Myers to open the computer. Gunny tapped Myers on the shoulder, said something to him and a moment later Myers was bringing up the computer.

Gunny used the rifle scope to see each of the cars and their occupants. "Looks like they pulled all of the cars available in some salvage lot to bring those people here," Gunny whispered to Myers as Myers brought the satellite link online. "There's lot of the little Lada cars, a number of the 2107 models. There are also a couple of large, old Russian military four-wheel drive trucks and a couple of worn buses. They're all loaded with people."

They all watched as the vehicles came down the narrow valley and parked in a row at the east side of the field. Using the sniper rifle scope, Gunny could see them all get out and follow Zhu to the area where the food and drinks were set up. Lawson also watched as the large group of people followed Zhu to the tables and realized something didn't seem right. The next moment it was apparent to Lawson that none of Zhu's security people or workers were on the field. He crawled over to where Myers and Gunny were positioned and was about to speak when Gunny motioned for Lawson to come into the indentation.

"You notice that there are no security people on the field," Gunny reported.

"That's what I came over to tell you," Lawson replied. "Something is way out of order here. Zhu's got a bunch of unknowns on the field and where are his security teams? Doesn't make sense. See if you can use the satellite to determine where the security people are."

Myers began to scan the area for any presence of the security people. After approximately 15 minutes he saw the door to the back of the facility open and a number of people come out and set up chairs in the shade in the back of the building. As they did so it appeared that others were coming out with plates of food and drinks and sitting down.

"I can tell you where they are," Myers interrupted. "I've got the satellite picture on the screen and it looks like they're at the back of the facility. A lot of them are going in and out of the facility while some are sitting and, it looks like, they're eating and drinking." Lawson was about ready to go over the two hills to get a look at what Myers reported when the sound of a lot of engines started up. Lawson thought it sounded like a whole neighborhood of lawnmowers all starting up at once. As he turned his attention back toward the field, he could see wave after wave of drones taking off. As they did so, the people around the food and drink tables all went up to the bleachers and sat down.

The drones assembled in flight about 200 feet above the field and started doing acrobatics as a group. At each turn the crowd could be seen giving an 'ahh' and applauding but their reactions could not be heard due to the noise of the drones. As they did so, Myers brought up the lead drone on his computer and looked at the data tables. As he was about to enter in the coordinates he realized the coordinates they originally agreed to was the back entrance of the building that was now occupied with all the people from Zhu's operation. Myers was at a loss what to do.

"Lawson," Myers called out, "we can't send the drones to destroy the building with all those people there. What do we do?" Lawson was busy putting the pieces together.

"Try to send the drones into the ground where the bunker is at." Lawson ordered. Myers acknowledged and proceeded to look down the data table for the coordinate's entry. He brought up the map to determine the coordinates for the bunker. As he was doing so, Gunny tapped Lawson on the shoulder.

"Where's Zhu going?" Gunny asked while watching Zhu walk across the field and go south while everyone was watching the air show. "I can take him out now on your orders. He'll be off the field and beyond my view behind the hill in another 15 seconds!"

Lawson pushed up in Gunny's rifle. "Don't shoot," Lawson ordered. "Nothing is right about all of this and we don't want to make a mistake."

"The original coordinates in the data table are almost identical to the coordinates I was going to put in," Myers called out as Gunny and Lawson watched the drones break up into two groups. One group of ten drones was dropping lower as the other group went higher group. The higher group circled once and started heading south.

"What are you saying?" Lawson yelled over the noise of the drones.

"Zhu's target is his own building and I'm trying to change the coordinates!" shouted Myers as he hammered on the keyboard of the computer. "Zhu's going to kill…" Myers stopped as they saw two drones heading for where Gunny, Lawson, Myers and Benson were. Gunny swung his rifle but couldn't sight in on the drone as it was moving too fast and dropping toward the group. It was about 50 yards from them as Lawson pulled out his pistol and saw the red flashes of light indicating that the drone was scanning Gunny's face. No time to react. Just as Lawson raised his pistol, the drone suddenly changed course at about 25 yards away and headed in the direction of the other drones. Both Gunny and Lawson looked at each other while wondering what just happened. Gunny sat down the rifle and took a deep breath. Lawson was trying to make sense out of it all.

Their thoughts were broken by Norman shouting out from her position to Lawson. Lawson and Gunny looked to where Norman was pointing and saw a line of 10 drones traveling in single file about 40 feet above the field and 100 yards in front of bleachers. Myers looked up from his computer to see what all the yelling was about. As the drones came into a line in front to the bleachers, they suddenly made a 90 degree turn flying straight toward the bleachers. As the people saw what was happening, large numbers of individuals were screaming and started to get up to run as others were frozen in their place or oblivious to the threat. It was too late. At the speed the drones were traveling, those in the bleachers had no time to react as the drones were on them in approximately 3 seconds. At that point there was a loud roar as each of the explosive charges in the nose of the drones detonated all at the same time and a huge cloud of smoke and dust obliterated the view the CAT205 team had of the people or the bleachers.

The team stood up in shock at what they had just witnessed. A black object flying in the sky caught Lawson's attention as it was being carried south by the winds higher up and would show a bright silver flash on occasion. "Was this another of Zhu's weapons?" Lawson thought to himself. The object dropped from the sky to the south as Lawson became aware of a distance sound of a continuous roar, sounding like thunder in the distance that lasted for almost 40 seconds. Lawson realized it was something else as there were no clouds in the sky. As Lawson was contemplating the events Myers grabbed his sleeve and pointed to the computer screen.

Lawson looked at the screen then realized he had been oblivious to the other events taking place. Norman, Gunny, Benson and Izzy were looking at the screen as Myers just sat in shock. Norman looked up at Lawson as she had tears running down her face. Lawson took a closer look at the screen. There was smoke coming out of the back entrance of the Propheta Nostri facility. There were also several bodies outside of the big door. He could also see a person moving toward the building but still about a half mile away. Lawson assumed that it would be Zhu.

"Let's pick up our gear, check our weapons and prepare to move out," Lawson ordered. "Leave the rifles here as they are too bulky to use in close quarters." The others looked at him for a moment but, even though they were in shock, they did as they were told. Except for Gunny, they were much too disoriented to do otherwise. "Izzy, go over to the warehouse and bring Murodov and Azamatov and meet us at the front of the Prophets Nostri building. Don't go into the building. Stay by the cars in the parking lot. We'll come out the front." Izzy left the group as the rest of them slowly moved forward in single file patrol formation with Gunny on point and Lawson about 25 feet behind him.

It took them a while to make it to the back of the Propheta Nostri building, an hour and 6 minutes to be exact. As they entered the building, Lawson motioned for Myers and Norman to check out the main building corridor while Gunny and Benson checked the back storage area. There was broken cement, tangled wires and metal framing lying all over the place. Bodies, blood and lost life was vividly apparent as they entered and began their check of the building. As the others made their checks, Lawson checked what was obviously the executive office area. Most of the office walls were either down or heavily damaged. No one was in the offices and some of the offices had never been occupied.

As Lawson turned the corner, he came into a large area that appeared to be a reception area for the executive suite. There appeared to be one office that was untouched except for some embedded shrapnel in the door and a sign on the door said 'Cho Ming, CEO'. It was obvious that the office had been intentionally protected from the devastation that had taken place throughout the rest of the facility. Lawson pulled his weapon as he prepared to push open the door.

Chapter 15

Lawson's Dilemma

"Too many variables, too many things that can go wrong and it always seems to be that there is one more thing to consider that we missed. A giant game with only one rule – find the truth and determine how to deal with it. However, all the variables don't seem to connect well and I'm leery about taking out Zhu without having those anomalies answered. Well, sometimes the events overtake the ability to decide and I fear that this is one of those times." – Lieutenant James Lawson, US Navy CAT205 Special Operations Group Commander, ONI

As Lawson entered Cho Ming's office he stood facing Colonel Qiang Zhu as the Colonel leaned back in his chair. The Colonel knew it was not in his best interest to move his hands anywhere toward his desk. As Lawson stood facing him, Myers and Gunny stepped through the door with their weapons drawn. Benson followed behind them and moved toward the desk as she kept her pistol pointed toward Zhu. As she stood at the side of the desk, Norman entered the room as Gunny was first to speak.

"I'm having trouble understanding why you sent those drones into your own building. I mean, you wiped out your whole security contingency and engineers in the process. What's up with that?"

"You may think that I was after the leaders of the major countries, but the fact of the matter is, I was targeting the anarchists that set up the whole plan to do the assassinations," Zhu answered as he adjusted his position in his chair. Everyone tensed up on their weapons as Zhu moved.

"What do you mean anarchists?" Lawson questioned as he started putting pieces together. "Everything pointed to this test being a setup for multiple assassinations and the numbers relating to the number of drones bears that out."

"I know you came here to kill me and, if I were in your shoes, I would have pulled the trigger and already left," Zhu observed. "The fact that you didn't do that tells me you are starting to put the puzzle together. Don't you realize I knew you were coming based upon the number of eyes I have on you throughout the facility. That being said, I had to risk you would hesitate even though I know you have so little trust for me that any explanation I give you would be seen by you as another effort for me to manipulate you. It would be safer for you to just pull the trigger and leave." As Zhu was talking, Norman moved herself closer to Lawson which put her closer to Zhu.

Lawson adjusted his position to the front-right side of the desk where he could see everyone then said, "I hesitated because the pieces don't fit. You see, Colonel, your lead drone didn't go after Gunny. Your drones scanned Gunny and, once they identified him, they continued on to your building. The fact that the lead drone scanned Gunny's face and didn't see Gunny as a target meant that they were scanning faces, not buildings. So that tells me the security people you employed were the targets, not us. Furthermore, if that's the case, we were not targets at all which means the attempt on Norman in Volgograd was not you and the attack in the hotel against Gunny, Myers and Benson was not you. I believe you gave the guy with the fedora hat orders to take us out probably so that you would not raise suspicions with your own people and you also figured we could take care of ourselves in that situation. Am I right?" Zhu nodded his head 'yes' at the question.

"So your target was the security people in the building, why?" Gunny probed as he was seeing Lawson's logic.

"It's simple," Zhu replied. "They were already in the planning stages to take out the major world leaders working with a guy by the name of Rod Lavlery. I know you remember Rod Lavlery. He was the aide to Congressman Latershan and was the leader of this plot to take out the major leaders of the most powerful nations. I killed Lavlery on board the Pacific Jade. I happened to come into the picture when they were considering several plans to carry out the assassinations. You succeeded in your last mission to stop Lavlery's plan to start World War III in which they would use the programmed launch of nuclear missiles into North Korea. However, I had already put conditions in place to prevent the launches from happening. Lavlery figured the plan was in motion to launch the nukes and figured the plan could not be stopped, so he escaped on the ship which I arranged. I shot him on the ship because I knew he would take the 5 million dollars and use that to accelerate the second part of their plan to take out the world leaders. The rest of his group knew me well by then so they trusted me. Killing him didn't stop the rest of the anarchists from continuing with the plans so I offered them a better solution by convincing them that the drone attack on the world leaders was the best approach. You see, they could see the logic that, at the present, there is no good defense against a drone swarm when they attack a person in the open. That was my method for shutting the anarchists down."

"What's with this anarchist bull?" Benson called out as she chambered a round into her pistol. "They were just a bunch of militia wannabes."

"That's not true," Zhu responded. "Remember that it was an anarchist that killed the Archduke Ferdinand that started World War I. These guys Lavlery hired were all highly trained mercenaries from Russia, Germany, France, Indonesia, China, Great Britain and, yes, even the United States. They were all former Special Forces personnel that felt they could gain power by bringing chaos to the world. You know the name of my company, Propheta Nostri? They chose that name as their organization before I was ever involved with them. It's a name that has become known through history for complete victory and control."

"Now it's starting to make sense," Lawson said as he moved his weapon to his left hand. "Propheta Nostril is also the story of the Masters of the Order of the Dutch knights. They were the Dutch Templars. There are a lot of mysteries concerning the Templars activities and the associated legend of the Illuminati. They supposedly formed a cabal that was meant to rule the world in the background as the Illuminati. I don't know whether the Illuminati was real or not or if it exists now under a different name. However, there are a lot of people that believe the legend and many of those people are trying to form organizations to overthrow governments of which the anarchists are one of them so Zhu's story holds some water."

"That's not true!" Benson exclaimed as she pushed her weapon closer to Zhu's head. Lawson started to move forward but stopped when Norman grabbed his sleeve. "Don't you see that the Colonel is just playing with your minds? He's got you roped, Lawson," Benson continued as everyone looked at Lawson. Lawson just smiled as he motioned for Zhu to continue.

"You can shoot me but before you do, please let me finish the job I need to do," Zhu pleaded.

"What job is that?" Lawson queried.

"The question of Lenny Kover," Zhu answered.

"Who's Lenny Kover?" Myers asked.

"I remember the name," Lawson recollected. "That's the name Benson gave us of the person that gave her the ammo clips with the sabotaged rounds."

"Lenny Kover was the guy that made me aware of Rod Lavlery and his plot to do something with North Korea when Lavlery sent pictures to North Korea during your last mission," Zhu explained. "To explain, Commander Norman's texts were intercepted by my people. The rest of your phones were not accessible but Commander Norman's was. You see, when she called Chief Rasulov at the police headquarters the same day you were met by him at the restaurant, we were tracking Rasulov's number and, in the process, picked up her number. She said something about getting police uniforms for the team and when you all arrived the next day in police uniforms, I went back to that number and all of the captured phone calls and text messages we had. You see, we were recording all of Rasulov's calls and texts over the past 3 months. We also recorded all calls and texts from anyone that had made contact with the Chief. Her number wasn't hard to find since we only had to go through 2 days of calls and texts and pulled up the text she sent. Her name popped up in a text from Rasulov at which point we had the number she used. She sent a text to someone in the US asking about Lenny Kover. That raised my suspicions as I already had known Kover. When I saw the question being that Commander

Norman thought that Lenny Kover had given Joanne Benson sabotaged ammo, I knew it couldn't be true. I was sure…"

At that moment Benson turned her weapon toward Lawson, shouted, "you're a fool!" and pulled the trigger. There was just a click. Quickly ratcheting another round into the chamber, she pulled the trigger again as Norman pulled Lawson's weapon away from pointing at her. Another click but the gun didn't fire. In a panic, she ran for the door and was tackled by Gunny as she tried to get by him.

"Zhu's playing all of you!" she screamed as Gunny pushed her to the ground, put the barrel of his pistol against her head and calmly stated, "You move, you die." At that moment, Lawson looked to Norman for an explanation.

"Jim, I know I left you in the dark but I couldn't tell you what was happening as Benson was always with us," Norman started. "I got a message yesterday from Admiral Roedl that just said 'Ben defending yourself, MamaSon?'. At first I thought 'Ben' was a misspelling of 'Been'. I couldn't figure out what the message related to but it was obvious that it was relating to my question about Lenny Kover. I was laying on the air mattress in the warehouse when something came back to me that happened in Volgograd. Remember I told you about the guy who tried to kill me with the shotgun by shooting at the door peephole when he thought I was looking through it."

"Yes, I remember it," Lawson acknowledged.

"Well," Norman went on, "the man at the door said it was a message from Ben. I was thinking about that incident when I remembered the hash message method of communication we used during my training. The first word would be part of a name or location and the last part of the message would complete the word or location based upon where the last word showed capitalization. So the first part of the message was 'Ben' and the last part of the message from the point of capitalization was 'Son'. The merging of the parts resulted in 'Benson'. Based upon the rest of the message, Roedl was telling me to defend myself from Benson."

"So what did you do?" Myers asked.

"I waited until about 2:00 AM to make sure Benson was in deep sleep and removed the firing pin from her M17 weapon while she was asleep," Norman expounded. "When Gunny collected all the weapons in the morning to replace them with the new M17 pistols you found in the crate, I made sure Benson got her weapon back. That's the reason I pulled your weapon away from you. I knew her gun wouldn't fire and I didn't want you guys shooting her as we need to find out who else is involved with her."

"I had come to the same conclusion concerning Benson and was putting the pieces together which is the reason I wanted to confront Zhu rather than just shoot him and why I didn't just open fire on Benson when she pulled the trigger," Lawson informed them as he looked back toward the desk and Zhu. "I found a link between 'Trechko' and Benson. Myers mentioned a message on Benson's phone that came in the first day he met Benson that said, 'Usb field 19', the 'Usb' being the identifier for 'US Benson'. That's the same message Admiral Roedl sent to you, Norman, several days ago after it was decrypted noting that it was originally sent by 'Peacock' to 'Trechko' which means Joanne Benson is 'Trechko' and has been working for the anarchists or some Deep State group in Washington. My meeting with Captain Volkov confirmed my suspicions. I had further evidence when I sent Roedl a message asking him to see who Russell Mejia, the Senior Technical Hobgoblin that ordered us to execute Cho Ming, had as coworkers in his office. One of the names one the list of 11 people was an Eastern Asia Analyst by the name of Joanne Benson. So it all links together. Also, Roedl sent me back an order yesterday not to kill Colonel Zhu as there were other extenuating circumstances he couldn't tell us at the present time. Now comes the question of what to do with Colonel Qiang Zhu. Colonel, I don't know whether you are friend or foe. To be honest, I've come to like you and your character. That being said, I don't know what your intentions are or what you are really doing. Where does reality end and the games begin?"

"I was actually working for the Chinese government, and I'm not 'Peacock," Zhu began. "We knew that there were intercepts of messages that indicated that senior Chinese leaders were targets of some plots. I was sent to draw the players in this plot together and eliminate them. As I said, Lavlery was their leader. I had to take over the leadership, so removing Lavlery was necessary."

"Then who is 'Peacock'?" Lawson questioned.

"As close as I can figure, he is a German ex-patriot by the name of 'Mark Dietrich'," Zhu explained. "He is a known assassin working for the highest bidder. Lately, he has gone into the business of kidnapping agents and operatives and delivering them to those that paid for the kidnapping. I heard that he may be responsible for the death of a German Interpol agent in Berlin several days back and somehow that may tie into your activities. Lawson, did you happen to be in Crete just a few …"

"I see you have all been busy," came the voice of Chief Rasulov, having positioned himself in the doorway to Zhu's office with Russian Captain Volkov standing behind him. "I saw all the damage and dead bodies around. It looks like some questions have been answered and others have been raised. Colonel Zhu, I received orders two hours ago to place you under arrest and escort you to the airport. You are ordered to leave the country. Your presence in our region is no longer acceptable." Zhu got up and walked toward Rasulov while Gunny pulled Benson up off the floor.

"Please take her as well and put her in one of your cells until we can get someone from the US embassy to escort her back to the US," Gunny requested as he pushed Benson toward Rasulov.

"With pleasure," Rasulov stated as he put handcuffs on Benson. "I will send out a team to recover these bodies and do the forensics. Meanwhile, I will take Zhu and Benson to headquarters." Looking at the CAT205 team he continued, "Do you all need a lift into town?"

"No," Lawson answered. "We have our vehicle and we have some cleanup to do. We'll walk you out." Rasulov nodded and handed Zhu and Benson off to the police officers that were with him.

As they walked down the corridor through all the debris left from the attack, Lawson asked Rasulov, "How did you get here so fast?"

"We had been informed much earlier by Captain Volkov that things were about to get interesting in the Fergana Valley," Rasulov responded. "We left right after he informed us about his suspicions at which point Volkov asked to come with us so we agreed. That was about three hours ago."

Zhu whispered to Lawson, "Mark Dietrich was not at the demonstration. I thought he would come but he didn't. He's still out there somewhere very much alive." They all walked out the front door of the facility together with Lawson, Norman, Myers and Gunny standing at the front entrance as the officers walked their prisoners to the vehicles and got into the police cars with Murodov and Azamatov joining the police officers.

"Azamatov should be under arrest," Lawson yelled across the distance as he saw Azamatov along with Colonel Zhu get into the back seat of Rasulov's police car. Volkov stood by the passenger side of Rasulov's car, watching the CAT205 Team as they stood in front of the building.

"Azamatov's ok," Myers answered quietly. "He helped us get the whole group and he was instrumental in keeping us from being discovered in the CIA warehouse. Let him go." Lawson looked at Myers and the others then agreed that Myers was right.

"Azamatov will be checked out," Rasulov shouted back. "By the way, Azamatov said that Izzy got on a motorcycle he had hidden in the warehouse and has left the area." Lawson thought it interesting that Izzy would just pick up and leave without even a 'by your leave' to the team.

As Lawson watched, Rasulov open the car door and turned to wave to the team when a man dressed in all black with a black face mask stepped out from the side of the building and opened fire on the team with an Uzi weapon firing full automatic. As the team members swung their weapons to respond to the threat each of them fell before they could get off a shot. Rasulov could see blood splatters from the bullet hits on the team members as he started the engine to his car. At that moment Captain Volkov jumped into the passenger side and they raced off with the other police car following immediately behind them. Rasulov looked in his rearview mirror as the man turned to fire at the police cars but it was obvious that the cars were too far away for the man to succeed in doing much damage. Rasulov's last view in the rearview mirror was of the four team members on the ground with the man checking them to see if any of them were still alive.

"I'll send out a team later to pick them up," Rasulov commented to his police sergeant as he continued to drive. "What a waste of good people. I'm sure there will be an international spat over this. Maybe not in the press but surely within government back channels and I was just getting to like those guys. Well, let's get Zhu to the airport and Benson to a cell. Now, Colonel Zhu, you know that your government is requesting we send you to Beijing."

"Yes, I know," Zhu responded. "It was my plan all along as my mission is completed. Too bad about the Americans. I was growing fond of their antics and I just lost a good adversary. I will honor him when I get home."

"Why didn't we see this coming?" Captain Volkov called out. He had grown fond of Commander Norman and was at a loss concerning the reason for the death of the four team members. Then he remembered General Vikovny's threat about needing to wipe out the CAT205 Team after Zhu's demo. Apparently it wasn't just talk as Volkov looked through the car's back window at the distant building while barely seeing the mounds that were once living people and the form of the darkly-dressed man standing over them.

Zhu caught a flight to Hanoi, Vietnam then to Beijing. Benson was put in a cell in Osh and later transferred to US Marine custody and sent back to the United States. The madness came to an end.

Chapter 16

LAB214

"The US has so many intelligence agencies that it appears they tend to operate against one another. Is it just the bureaucratic mess we've created or are they intentionally operating at times against each other to position themselves for more power?" – Captain William Michaels, Executive Officer, Office of Naval Intelligence, Special Operations Group

Admiral Roedl sat behind his desk while five people sat facing him in the chairs in his office. He looked down at the numerous reports, photos and diagrams spread across his desk as his administrative aide took his cellphone from the desk and put it into the phone charger on the cabinet counter on the right side of Roedl's office. He watched her leave then picked up one piece of paper and looked at Commander Blaine Samoylev.

"What's this bill from the Osh hotel for $2,480 dollars?"

"It's for damage caused by one of our team members due to a packet of blue dye damaging carpeting and paint in a hotel room. I think it was a bank dye packet," Samoylev answered while looking at the others. "We're also to receive a bill for $2,305 dollars for damage done to a rental car that got shot up during the mission," Everyone else sat and said nothing as Roedl just nodded and went on to other papers.

"So we have decommissioned the CAT205 Team," Roedl questioned as he looked at Samoylev.

Yes, Sir," came the response as Roedl looked at the four people sitting in the other chairs. "They have all been verified 'Deceased' on the final team report and the team designator has been decommissioned. Another message I got from our staff in the SAL was received from Assistant Chief Rasulov in Osh. It states 'We went back to the Propheta Nostri facility with our forensic people and found the bodies of your people were already removed. There was lots of blood around but no bodies. I figured that the guy we called Izzy was responsible for their removal as he was the only one that could have known about the activities at the site and the only one that could have communicated to the outside on the deaths. I thought he had already left on a motorcycle but my guess is that he is a U.S. asset that you or someone in your government put into this episode and he stayed around until the CAT205 Team had safely left, which they didn't. So my best analysis is that he arranged for their removal to keep this from creating an international incident. Nice move, Admiral Roedl, but it still doesn't match with my initial report so I have some explaining to do with the Chief. Thanks a lot!' "

"Send a message to him that we have already straightened it out with his boss," Roedl ordered as Samoylev took notes.

"Are you four ready to form a new access team?" Roedl questioned as the four people all nodded 'yes'. "Do we have a new team designator for these people?"

"Yes, Admiral," Samoylev replied. "Captain Michaels has come up with the new designation identifier for this new team. You see, we came to the conclusion that having the name 'team' in the team title raises the interest of foreign powers of what the team is. Since we have official organizations called 'boards' for different internal functions that nobody cares about, we came up with a very creative approach to your new team name. It will be called 'Labyrinth Analysis Board' or 'LAB'. So looking at that designator and the next sequential team number being 214, your designator is now 'LAB214'. It's a good solution."

"Sir," the Marine team member questioned, "why 'Labyrinth' for the name?"

Roedl opened the screen on his computer to the word 'Labyrinth', "It fits as a Labyrinth is a complex series of paths. Isn't that the description of what the team will do?"

"Sir, it works but I still think we will need some assistance in learning the ropes on how to do this job," one of the four answered to his question. At that comment, everyone laughed as Roedl leaned back in his chair.

"Commander Norman, the last thing in the world you need to learn is ropes," Roedl quipped. "Now with the definition I gave you does it answer your question, Gunny?"

"I guess so," Gunny agreed as he thought about the ramifications of the choice. He could see how the designator would hide the team's exposure as far as a name was concerned.

"So, how about giving us some idea of what we just went through on in our last mission," Myers requested. "Some details on Benson's involvement, Zhu's real function, Blanding's orders, what anarchist group we were dealing with, where does Rasulov fit is all this, you know, things like these."

"There are a number of things you ought to know," Roedl explained. "First, the false hit on you at the Propheta Nostri Facility. That was an operation called 'Operation Chaos'. We knew you all were getting too exposed to the rank and file intelligence communities around the world. We couldn't let that stand as a lot of your capability is based upon your obscurity and the lack of information about your team and its function. We'll use Operation Chaos when an agent has been exposed and must be removed from a threat. Most times, they are removed from the ONI and given a new identity and a new life. In your case, it was to remove you from the view of other countries. One note of warning, you are to avoid going to the Pentagon or the Defense Intelligence Agency. According to what Joanne Benson saw, you are all supposed to be dead. Let's leave them believing that for a while. By the way, we defined your supposed real names in the verification of death. Those names are different than your real names so that, when you retire, you will still get your pensions and VA benefits."

"What about Joanne Benson? What happened to her and what was her role in all this?" Norman asked as she thought about Benson pulling the trigger while pointing the gun at Lawson.

Roedl thought for a moment then spoke, "Benson's role was to stop your team from succeeding. A number of deep state people in the Pentagon were working with the anarchists, Benson being one of them as was Russell Mejia. We knew this when Norman sent me back a text stating that Myers had seen the 'Usb Field 19' text on Benson's original phone that Gunny confiscated when she first met Gunny and Myers in Osh. Lawson figured out the message meant 'Usb' for 'United States Benson' then Captain Volkov's team figured out that 'field 19' meant they were going to do the field testing of the drones on July 19th. It was discovered from several other messages that Lawson's, Volkov's and Norman's assessments were correct. Another message we intercepted that was sent to Colonel Zhu from one of the Propheta Nostri organizations verified this assumption. Now remembering that his name in Uzbekistan was 'Cho Ming', the intercepted message copied to him was 'Chm Field 19'. So 'Chm' meant 'China' and 'Ming'."

"How did you know when to set up the Operation Chaos effort?" Gunny asked.

"I knew when we discovered that Benson might be a mole," Roedl stated. "Norman's message to us on her suspicions about Benson started the ball rolling. We suspected it on the 16th and activated Operation Chaos on that day but didn't get confirmation of Benson's involvement until the 18th, the day before the drone demo."

Gunny appeared to be perturbed as he continued his questioning, "Why did we get notification of the plan and the timing to take us out only two hours before it happened? Luckily, Blanding was able to get us those exploding blood packets and instructions on how to use them and where to position ourselves in time to carry out the operation. Otherwise, we would have been exposed and it would have gone for naught. One other thing, how did the assailant that shot us know which people to shoot?"

"First," Roedl responded, "your assailant was a highly trained Marine Critical Skills Operator from the 1st Marines Raider Battalion. He had your pictures and knew where you would be standing. He knew that you four would have been instructed to stand apart from everyone else and also knew to wait until everyone was in the cars that were going to leave before he opened fire. His timing had to be perfect so they could see you getting shot and they would run rather than fight or he would be in a shootout with the police and he only had blanks in his weapon. It came off as planned."

"OK, we got all that but what about Colonel Zhu and his function?" Lawson queried.

"Colonel Zhu," Roedl pondered as he looked down at notes on his desk. "Now there is a real enigma. Colonel Zhu set himself up to be this super villain and he really put his life on the line to play the role. He was responsible for taking down Caper's organization and getting rid of Rod Lavlery without exposing that he was targeting them. He got all of Caper's group together and used us to eliminate them as a threat. We didn't know this until we talked to him after Red Draper's funeral and, yes Norman, we did meet with him after our discussion with you recommending on not meeting with him. The drone approach he used was quite creative. As to your involvement with Zhu and what was to be done about it, we had a problem that Zhu could help to solve without knowing it. Once the 'Shiny Object' operation was completed, we would have the problem of using the CAT205 team on another operation because the international intelligence community would know your team by name and would react at the slightest indication that the CAT205 team was operating on a mission. So, the best way to convince our adversaries that the CAT team was wiped out was to have one of our more trusted voices in the intelligence community be a witness to your execution. Zhu fit the bill as he didn't know anything about 'Operation Chaos' or that your deaths were faked. As the Chinese leadership becomes persuaded that you've been eliminated, the rest of the world will be convinced, as well."

"So what about Chief Rasulov in Osh," Gunny asked.

Roedl looked at his notes then answered, "Inspector Bernardakis from Crete, Captain Pavel Volkov from Russia and Chief Rasulov from Osh were all in contact with me once one of you made your presence known at their location. For Lawson, it was after he got on the plane to Dubai from Crete. I got indirect communications from Bernardakis that a fake Interpol cop was trying to get Lawson. The real Interpol cop he replaced was killed in Berlin the night before. We're in the process of tracking down the fake Interpol guy, named Mark Dietrich, and who he belongs to."

"As for Captain Volkov," Roedl continued, "he was greatly impressed by Norman's ability to act on her feet. We've got the identity of the guy she killed with the shotgun in the Volgograd Hotel but we haven't been able to link him up to any group yet. He definitely wasn't working for Zhu. Volkov and I have been communicating frequently. By the way Lawson, he says to tell you 'hi'. I found out you guys had him for a Russian language instructor during your active family living training at the language school in Monterey, California."

"Only Lawson had him for his training," Myers reported. "Each of us had individual trainers during the family living exercises. The trainers we got were American citizens. Volkov was a visiting instructor, a part of the language exchange program at the college."

"Now for Chief Rasulov in Osh," Roedl continued. "We had contact with him several weeks before I sent you all out on this mission. He knew who the CIA agents were in the city and has communicated with me on several occasions over the past month. He is one of the reasons the trigger for 'Shiny Object' was tripped. He reported the suspicious activity to the

Kyrgyzstani leadership and they, in turn, gave Rasulov the ONI phone number. His call was transferred to me and, during my first discussion with him, he informed me he had already talked to people at the Defense Intelligence Agency (DIA) in the form of a contact with an Admiral Johnson at the Pentagon. A Captain Wallace at the Pentagon was the person that opened the activation folder for 'Shiny Object'. This was done after General Machinko of the Russian Army informed the DIA that he had information from soldiers in Syria that a major strike against world leaders was in the planning stages."

"General Machinko?" Norman questioned. "Is he related to Colonel Machinko of the Russian Air Command in Syria?"

Roedl pulled the pen out of his desk pen-holder as he answered, "He is. His rank is General. He was dressed as a Colonel while in Volgograd because the main issue he was to discuss was not about defeating ISIS, though your conversations on ISIS helped us negotiate further on the combat situation in Syria. He didn't want anyone to know that he was dealing with the 'Shiny Object' protocol. The Russians don't know the anarchists in their government any more than we do about anarchists internal to our government and he didn't know who he could trust in the Kremlin. They have the same problem and Machinko didn't want to let anything out on our progress in dealing with the assassination plot. Let's take a rest break and be back in here in fifteen minutes."

Everyone got up and left the office through the main door while Roedl left through the conference room door. As he was in the conference room an analyst gave him a note. It said that they had identified where Mark Dietrich was staying in Washington,

DC. Once they came back into the room, Roedl continued the explanations.

"Now, as for Blanding. He was sent out with a load of equipment and weapons on a C-17 aircraft several weeks before we sent you. He rented the warehouse and moved the materials to the warehouse a week before the first of you arrived in Osh. He introduced himself to Professor Murodov at the Osh Technical University as Nurlan Isakova early in his tenure in Osh. You see, Blanding has his degree in micro-energy generation. The same discipline we know as the core science of solar panels, so it would be easy for Murodov to take to him in. Blanding is also a capable software programmer and spoke excellent Kyrgyz. So, with Zhu's need for skilled programmers, it would be easy for him to get a job working at Propheta Nostri Corporation, particularly since Zhu was pulling a lot of programmers from the Technical University. First, Blanding had to find out which company in the area was part of the assassination plot. He interviewed with several companies over a two week period to try to locate someone doing technology that would seem similar to designs that could be used for assassinations. He communicated 3 days before we sent you out that he thought Propheta Nostri was a viable suspect and they were getting close to completion of a working system. Don't know when he actually got the job at the corporation. He didn't know what they were making the software for but he knew it was some type of targeting system. That was key to activating your part of Shiny Object. He had trouble getting the materials to Osh as he had to drop them off at a port area, have them shipped up river to Termez, Uzbekistan then 1,400 miles by road to the warehouse you stayed in. We were concerned the materials wouldn't get there before you needed them."

"What about the anarchist group, who are they?" Norman questioned.

"They are the group with the same name as the corporation, Propheta Nostri," Roedl explained. "They are an international organization responsible for a number of May Day riots around the world last year. We think they have as many as 5,000 members, many with key positions in different governments, and the group you ran into is a radical arm of the organization. The main organization, in general, is more involved in using the general populace to create chaos. The group you got involved with was more set on making the chaos by removing major nations' leadership. Same group, different targets. Zhu's attack on the spectators during the demonstration of the drones wiped out about 90 percent of their leadership. That's what he sold us when he wanted to negotiate not being tracked down by the US after Red Draper's funeral. A number of Deep Staters in the Pentagon didn't want to let up on getting Zhu even after we had an agreement with him. You see, Zhu's efforts were putting a crimp in the Deep State efforts as he was impacting them by drawing off some key Deep State people to do his work. When Zhu gave us his explanation of what he was doing, his arguments were very convincing. We decided to go with his plan but to treat him with caution. There were those in the Pentagon that wanted to close down 'Shiny Object' so you can see there were multiple competing forces at work within our bureaucracies. Putting Benson into our effort was a gamble as we had some doubts as to where her loyalties lay. Any further questions?"

"What about Azamatov?" asked a concerned Myers.

"We found him to be no threat," Roedl replied. "His knowledge of flight dynamics and the fact that he was the senior engineer for the drone program made him a particular benefit for the Osh Technological Institute. While we're talking about that, Professor Murodov was reinstated as a Senior Professor at the Institute once the Institute Committee found the reason for the fire in his lab. Azamatov now works with Murodov as a replacement for Izzy Isakova."

"There is one question that nobody is asking but seems just as important," Lawson stated as Roedl winced at Lawson's comment being that Roedl knew what was coming next. "What was China and Russia to gain from working with us?"

"I suspect you have some ideas, Jim," Roedl assumed.

"I do," was Lawson's response. "It's true what they would gain by stopping the attempt on world leaders but I don't think that was what Zhu was focused on. You see, he had the anarchists dead to rights. He knew he could take the whole group out with 75 drones. So, what is he going to do with the other 900 plus smart drones? My guess is that China agreed to his effort in Uzbekistan because, in exchange, they would get a full complement of anti-personnel smart drones as part of their military upgrade. That would put China on par for progress with the US. Zhu would also be able to hide several million dollars in cash and a large number of anti-tank launchers and missiles he got during our 'Operation Scarborough' mission to use to barter in exchange for his own regiment. One more thing the Chinese would gain is the ability to see how our CAT205 methods work in the field. Something I'm sure Zhu would like to understand."

Roedl realized at that moment that Lawson was onto something that had completely passed the by the American intelligence community so he asked, "So, what about Russia? What do they have to gain?"

Lawson took a drink from a soda can and continued, "Remember that Russia lost a number of soldiers in Iran due to a small team they came to know as CAT205. They had a tremendous incentive to find out who we were, what we did and how we operated. They pinned the assassination of Russian agent 'Tripoli' on our team even though we know it was Commander Samoylev that took the shot. The gain for the Russians was obviously to protect their President but they also wanted to know who we were. They got some idea of our techniques with Norman's activities and her meeting with Captain Volkov in Volgograd. They also wanted to know how we operate and what our methods were. Norman gave them a good taste of the methods. They are still mystified as to how we operate. The Russians don't go to the restroom without an instruction book so they are going to have a lot of trouble trying to copy what we do. I was told by Bahram Khaliqi one time that watching us gave him a good idea how American cowboys thought. He said we think like the Kurdish people, we move to the need."

"So you think the Russians can't figure out how we work?" Roedl probed.

"They can figure out how we work, they just can't replicate it because it's not in their upbringing," Lawson expounded. "They are used to playing a game of chess with set rules and limited moves. We operate with few rules and unlimited moves and they have trouble with that. The Chinese are very different. They are constantly adapting to the situations laid out before them. Colonel Zhu was a tough adversary because he was not restricted with having tunnel vision. He recognized that we operate with no rules and he played us with that piece of information."

"How so did he play us?" Gunny challenged as the others wondered where Lawson got that opinion.

"It may not be obvious but it is recognizable," Lawson instructed as Roedl smiled at Lawson's ability to see the simple things everyone else misses. "Zhu was intentionally sending us a message when he had the one drone scan Gunny's face before it went back to the other drones to the facility. Why did that drone go completely off the path to the facility to pass by Gunny? The simple answer is that Zhu knew where Gunny had positioned himself as it was the most obvious position for a sniper. Zhu was doing two things. He was distracting Gunny long enough for Gunny not to take a long shot at Zhu at the time when everyone would be watching the drones. By the drone scanning Gunny's face and then not taking action against Gunny, he was telling us that we were not his target. Second, he was inviting us to go to the facility to see the result of his actions. Zhu knew we would be somewhere in the area where we positioned ourselves during the test and demonstration but that we would take the time and be cautious on our way to the facility. He knew we would come and do so slowly. That would give Zhu time to get back to his office and wait for us."

"So you didn't just catch Zhu at his desk when you entered his office," Gunny interjected.

"No, no surprise there," Lawson answered back. "Anybody wonder why the rest of the facility was in shambles but Zhu's officer was untouched?" The team all looked at each other then at Roedl as they let the question sink in. Roedl motioned with his hand for Lawson to continue.

"Are you saying he was expecting us," Myers asked.

"Exactly," Lawson continued. "He had to have a place that had some order to it. He understood that people are more likely to stop, think and listen if the environment is orderly and not a mess of mangled metal and concrete. I knew what he was doing the moment I stepped into the room. He had no weapon near him, he had backed away from the desk so I could see he was unarmed and he had the look on his face that he was at peace and not concerned. I also figured that he had watched me come into the building using any of the cameras that were still operational and I could see from the monitors behind him that some were. I realized the moment I stepped into the room that things were different than what they appeared to be. First, why did he take out all of his key security and planning people? Second, why did he stay behind when he had plenty of routes to escape with all the chaos that occurred with the attack? And third, I knew he had something significant to tell me because he waited for me to tell of my intentions before he was willing to talk. That is the actions of a person that has the upper hand."

"Why don't you tell them the main point in Zhu's actions?" Roedl directed.

"You know my thoughts on that?" Lawson questioned.

"I do," Roedl acknowledged. "Tell them what you know."

Lawson was perplexed as to how Roedl would know what conclusions Lawson had come to. Looking, almost staring, at the Admiral, Lawson continued, "Zhu was playing us from the very beginning, probably in the early stages of Lavlery's involvement. I suspect that Zhu was the one that convinced Sam Ginty to become Rod Lavlery because Ginty would not have had the ability to reenter government employment without outside help and contacts. Yet Ginty was one of the main leaders of the anarchists so Zhu had to put Ginty in a position where Zhu could get control of him. Zhu had the contacts in our government and Zhu directed those contacts. Ginty's value was that, being one of the main leaders in the anarchist movement, many of those people in the anarchist movement were also active in the US government and could be drawn out by Zhu using Ginty. The Capers organization was drawn together by forces I couldn't understand until I put Zhu in the mix. He was the driving force. The assembling of the anarchists bent on destroying national governments was Zhu's intentions and he used a number of people to accomplish that. As we could see, he wasn't doing it to form the group but to destroy it."

"So why did the Chinese get involved?" Norman inquired.

"They were probably one of the first governments to realize what was going on," Lawson explained. "Zhu probably discovered the presence of the anarchist group and heard rumblings of a plan developing for multiple simultaneous assassinations when he was trying to recruit spies from different nations for China. As he interviewed more and more people, the presence of the threat probably took form. You have to remember that he was dealing with the undercurrents of society, so he was talking to the criminals, sociopaths and rejects of society, those that had a bone to pick with their governments. I suspect, Zhu put the pieces of the developing plot together and the information hit a tipping point where he had to do something. I should also note that Zhu is not this super patriot trying to save

China. More likely, he saw an opportunity to gain some position in the Chinese social structure while getting financially secure at the same time."

"Thanks, Lawson. Well, we've got a lot of answers and we'll find out a lot more as we dig deeper into our investigation of what had occurred," Roedl said as he got up from his chair and shook hands with each of them. "You all did a magnificent job. Lawson, stay behind." They all got up and left the room as Lawson sat back down.

"You comfortable with the results, Sir?" Lawson asked as he watched Roedl take the folder to the cabinet on the right side of the room, open the safe and put the folder into it.

"That part, yes," Roedl responded. "You know that Mark Dietrich is in Washington, DC and I want you and Norman to smoke him out and apprehend him."

"I figured that's what you were going to do, Sir," Lawson acknowledged. "We knew about his location but couldn't tell anyone. We already have a plan in place and are already putting it in motion. Dietrich is at the Watergate Hotel and we are in the process of getting a Captain that Gunny knows from the Washington Police to aid us in arresting Dietrich once we have him where he can't do any harm to people around him. We have an operation already in play to neutralize Dietrich's firepower."

"I trust in your timing," Roedl affirmed. "Why didn't you tell me about him being in town?"

"It's simple, Sir," Lawson stated. "Can you call your administrative aide in here?"

"I can but I don't like to leave the front desk unattended," Roedl protested. "However, I can bring her in for just a moment." Roedl pressed a button and sat down. Moments later, a US Navy Lieutenant came in.

"Yes, Sir," came the woman's voice as she stepped through the door and approached Roedl's desk.

"Lieutenant Lawson, I would like to present to you Lieutenant Sheila Medford," said a smiling Roedl. He was caught by surprise by Lawson's next move as Lawson put the barrel of his pistol against Medford's neck. "What are you doing? Roedl exclaimed.

Lawson pulled Lieutenant Medford's pistol from its holster as he spoke, "Knowing how you work, Sir, there are only two other people in Washington outside of yourself that would have possibly known Commander Norman's burner phone number. Remember that we got the burner phones so that no one had information on our whereabouts except you. Zhu told me how he got Norman's number by tracking Rasulov but Zhu would not have provided that number to anyone at the Pentagon or the DIA. Why would he? I also know that you would not have given anyone Norman's number while the operation was active. Yet, a person in Joanne Benson's group had the number to send a fake text to Norman to take out Zhu. I checked Benson's phone while she was sleeping. She didn't send texts to her own group, only ones to Commander Samoylev. So how did the person in Benson's group get Norman's phone number? Commander Samoylev had Benson's number by way of the texts she sent to him but he didn't have Norman's number. Samoylev would have used the SAL Center to communicate with her. Follow me so far?"

"I think so," Roedl replied.

Lawson continued, "The only other person that could have seen her number is Lieutenant Medford when she took your phone to put on the charger, just as she did when we came into your office. So unless Samoylev somehow got Norman's number and suddenly changed his character, Medford had to be the leaker."

At the moment Lawson finished his comment, Medford grabbed his hand, slammed it against the table to knock the pistol loose. He didn't release the pistol so she slammed his hand with the pistol in it into his face. She made two more swift moves that knocked Lawson to the floor. Roedl realized at that moment that Medford was highly trained in martial arts and started to pull his weapon from his holster. As he did so, she already had pulled a small caliber pistol from a hidden holster under her skirt and swung it toward Roedl as a shot rang out. She grabbed her leg and dropped the gun as Lawson pulled himself up from the ground with his pistol pointed toward her.

"Next shot will be fatal," Lawson charged as he saw her try to reach for her weapon on the floor. Slowly, he pulled himself to a chair with blood dripping from his mouth all the while watching her every move. She sat on the floor as she held her bleeding knee, crying in pain as the Marine security officer raced into the room from the vault entry area and ordered Lawson to drop his weapon. Roedl waved the officer off as Lawson wiped the blood off his mouth with his sleeve. The security officer just stood with his weapon pointed in Lawson's general direction as Roedl sat down then turned his weapon on the woman.

"Now, how did you know that shot would stop her from shooting me?" asked a troubled Roedl.

"One place where a person has an immediate reaction to pain in the leg area is when they hit their kneecap," Lawson explained. "I had plenty of time to sight in on her kneecap because she was so focused on you." Roedl gave a sarcastic grin and nodded as he threw a box of tissues to Lawson.

"Cuff her, get her medical attention and clap her in irons," Roedl ordered to the Marine officer. "And be careful, she is a highly trained expert in hand-to-hand combat. Charges are espionage, attempted murder and exceeding her authority."

Lawson's bleeding stopped and he was ok except for the welt on his lip.

"Thanks for your assistance," Roedl expressed as he looked at Lawson. "That was some good detective work. I wish, however, you wouldn't fly by the seat of you pants when there are better ways to engage a questionable person. You've done enough today. Put some ice on that lip, now get going." Lawson got up and put a hat on his head.

"What's that?" Roedl questioned as Lawson put the dark gray fedora hat on with a silver band on it.

"I got this on my last mission, Admiral," Lawson replied. "Its previous owner thought highly of it but didn't want to keep it. It came floating through the air and landed near the back entrance of the Propheta Nostri facility. It has the name 'Guljigit Sukhrab' printed in it."

Roedl smiled at Lawson then said, "It probably has lice in it" which caused Lawson to immediately take the hat off and look around the inside rim. Roedl laughed. "Get out of here; I've got work to do. Lawson just smiled and started to leave.

"Yes, Sir," Lawson acknowledged.

"Did you say 'Guljigit Sukhrab'?" Roedl questioned which caused Lawson to turn to face the Admiral.

"That's what's in the hat and it's formally stitched," Lawson identified.

"Bring it here," Roedl commanded as Lawson handed him the hat. "Guljigit Sukhrab is, or was, a deep mole in Zhu's organization. We don't know what group he worked for but we do know that he was the person sending out assassination teams to take out key people in the intelligence community. By being a part of Zhu's organization, his hits were made to look like they were orders from Zhu's group and not the group he was a member of. Chief Rasulov verified that Sukhrab was one of the people killed by the drone attack sent against those in the bleachers during the drone demonstration. Apparently Zhu knew of Sukhrab's real role."

Roedl took a small toolkit from his desk drawer and pulled out a pair of needle-nosed pliers as Lawson looked in panic at what the Admiral was about to do with his hat. Roedl checked the silver band on the hat until he found a connecting pin that held the silver band together. Looking up at Lawson, the Admiral smiled as Lawson cringed. Roedl pulled the pin out of the silver band which released the tension on the band. As Roedl laid back the band, a small electronic chip fell out. Roedl was about to smash it when Lawson stopped him.

"I don't think that's a bug, Sir, I think it's a data storage device," Lawson stated. Roedl put his hand down then picked up the phone.

"Get Petty Office Myers back in here right now and tell him to bring his tech tools," Roedl called out as he looked up at Lawson. As Roedl put the phone down, Lawson picked up the silver band and looked at the back of it. As he did so he could see a series of small numbers and letters engraved on the inside of the band.

"Do you have a magnifying glass, Sir?"

"I have an eye loupe used for looking at aerial photos. Will that work?" Roedl answered as he handed the eye loupe to Lawson. Lawson looked at the side and saw that the eye loupe had a 10 times magnification lens. Lawson picked up a note pad from Roedl's desk then pulled the gold pen from Roedl's desk nameplate. As Lawson looked at the characters engraved on the back of the silver band, he proceeded to write down what he was reading 'Fg3UwT56GGh3'.

"I think this may be the code for getting into the chip," Lawson explained as he handed the sheet of paper with the characters to Roedl. Myers arrived moments later and sat down his tech bag. After getting a description of what was found in the hat band, Myers took out a jump drive from his bag, disassembled it and installed the chip found by Roedl into the jump drive frame. Once completing that task, he disconnected Roedl's computer from the LAN network and plugged in the jump drive into the USB port. He clicked on the drive icon for the jump drive causing a password screen to come up, at which time, he entered the code Lawson had written down. Moments later, a set of directories came up.

"You both know that whatever you see here is to be considered top secret, highest level," Roedl commanded as they both looked at the screen.

"We understand, Sir," Lawson acknowledged followed by pointing to the screen, "open that folder." Myers opened the folder Lawson pointed to. It was labeled 'Surgeries' which brought up 5 documents. The first document Myers clicked on, labeled 'Dorothy' brought up SF-86 interview background check forms for Elizabeth Norman. It wasn't just one form. It was many forms and supporting data on her personal life. As they clicked on the other folders and documents they found the same forms and information for James Lawson, Arnoud Glendenning, Nicholas Myers and Blaine Samoylev.

"This is more than just intelligence gathering," Roedl commented as he saw the different pages. "These are raw files of security clearance interviews and investigations. They had to come from someone within the Office of Personnel and Management for the US government." Lawson clicked on another folder labeled 'Targets'. He clicked on the document labeled 'Dorothy' and saw the contents of a word document that had Commander Norman's picture, an itinerary of her stay in Volgograd, Russia and an 'Assigned' block with the name 'Pax Dominici'.

"Wait," Lawson shouted as he took a small notebook out of his pocket and flipped through the pages, 'that's the name of the man Commander Norman killed that tried to assassinate her in Volgograd!"

"How do you know his name?" Roedl shot back.

"Captain Volkov told me the name when I met Volkov in Osh," Lawson replied as he went to click on the other documents in the folder. Roedl realized at that moment that they were enmeshed in two operations without knowing it.

"Try the folder labeled 'Scarecrow," Roedl ordered. Lawson clicked on the folder and brought up one of the four documents that were in the folder. One was a document with a picture of Lawson and his itinerary in Osh. Lawson scanned down to the 'Assigned' block on the page. It held the name 'Mark Dietrich'. As Lawson went from one folder to another, he found each folder had a name for a character from the 'Wizard of Oz'. The folder labeled 'Tinman' had Gunny's information and 'Lion' had Myers information. Roedl wanted to go into each to see who was assigned to each of them but Lawson ignored his order as something caught Lawson's eye, a folder labeled 'WickedWitch'.

He opened the folder to see several flowchart documents that were made using an organizational mapping tool. Roedl didn't have the mapping tool on his computer but that didn't stop Myers from being able to open it up. He looked for a document conversion tool in the editing tool and opened one of the flowcharts. As it came up they all were looking at the screen in disbelief. The flowcharts were actually organizational charts for several media outlets and large lobbying organizations with the top of the main group for all the organizations being a group called 'Rogue World'. Lawson pointed out that the name of a member of 'Customer Service' for one of the media outlets was 'Mark Dietrich'. Myers pointed to one of the person's names in one of the lobbying organization's 'Delivery Service Group' as

'Pax Dominici'. Roedl knew they had hit the motherlode. He sent out an alert for Gunny and Norman to come to his office while he told Lawson and Myers to remain.

While he was doing so Lawson continued to open folders. One document caught his attention. It was a memo from someone code named 'Valence' to 'Peacock'. In the message in Russian was a sentence that read, 'and you must remember Guljigit that we have a very short window to finish our commitments to Vilsig. He's to meet at the fish place in Washington DC'. And here's another to 'Peacock'. It says, 'Guljigit the three advocates from South America will meet with Ryles at the fish place. Make sure Demetri leaves the fish place before they get there'. "Sir, this proves that Guljigit Sukhrab, the guy who owned this hat, was 'Peacock'," Lawson exclaimed. "That means that Zhu was telling the truth. Zhu wasn't 'Peacock'. That also means that Zhu's belief that Mark Dietrich was 'Peacock' was not accurate."

Roedl nodded his head then clicked on the documents closing them one by one. "Let's wait for the others to arrive before we continue.

Chapter 17

Dietrich

"The Deep State is well entrenched and versatile. We have people in the most important key positions in world governments and it's just a matter of time before we can take control and create a global government. We will have the power and the people of the world will provide us with all we need to complete our goal. Free people are the enemy of a peaceful world." – *Mark Dietrich, Anarchist and assassin for the organization 'Rogue World'*

It was an hour later when Gunny and Norman arrived at the Admiral's office. Lawson, Myers and Roedl had been talking during the time they waited. When Norman and Gunny came in, Roedl ordered for them to sit down and explained the reason for their return and the discovery of the information inside the hat band Lawson had brought into the office.

"So Lawson, Myers and I have been discussing approaches for dealing with the people assigned to deal with each of you from these discovered files," Admiral Roedl stated as they waited for his plan. "Lawson and Gunny will go to the Watergate Hotel and wait in the lobby for Mark Dietrich to appear. They will not be apprehending Dietrich. Gunny's captain friend from the Capitol Police Force, Captain Ben Garrison and his officers, will be doing the actual arrest. Gunny will be there since Garrison knows Gunny from many different activities, so that should make everyone comfortable working together. Lawson will be there to point out Dietrich to the Captain. Lawson and Gunny, I want both of you to stay out of sight as far as anyone at the Watergate knowing who you are. Is that understood?"

"What about my part in this?" Norman queried.

"At the present, you do not appear to be targeted so I have another task for you," Roedl responded. "Pax Dominici was killed by you in Volgograd and it appears that no one else has been assigned to you. Did you do the switch?"

"Yes I did, thanks to help from the Marine Corps Recruit Depot at Parris Island. Now, assigned by who?" Norman shot back.

"The 'who' part we are still working on but we found that each one of you had different shadow figures assigned to come after you," Roedl explained as he leaned back in his chair while looking at the screen. "I think it's something that is outside the realm of the Propheta Nostri group. From the organizations we see, those that were assigned to assassinate each of you appear to be from the European Union. There were three people from Germany and one from France. The guy you killed was from Italy. I just got word that the guy assigned to Gunny was picked up in Bermuda and he's one of the ones from Germany. Well, Gunny and Lawson, change to suits and go to the Watergate Hotel. Captain Garrison just texted me that he and his officers just arrived there and are taking up positions. You'll find Captain Garrison and his men in business suits in the area where the gold couches are off from the main check-in counter. According to one of the bellhops, Dietrich requested a luggage cart to his room about ten minutes ago so you need to change and leave now."

Lawson and Gunny went to the change room located on the other side of the conference room from the Admiral's office. Opening up a closet, they slid one suit garment bag after another until they found their suits hanging in the closet. They quickly got dressed, left the change room and headed out the door of the Admiral's office through the security vault and to the hallway that took them out of the facility. At that moment, Lawson got a text that said 'Helo waiting at edge of facility parking lot. It will take you to Georgetown Medical Center Helo pad. Capitol Police car will be waiting for you next to the exit from helo pad. It takes 6 minutes from there to the Watergate Hotel. Hurry. Roedl'.

Lawson ran out the door to the edge of the parking lot with Gunny following him. As they entered the helicopter, it took off without Lawson or Gunny buckled in. Lawson grabbed on the overhead rail of the helo as Gunny hooked up his safety harness then held on to Lawson so he could put his harness on. Lawson figured that the pilot had been ordered to rush and to forget the passenger safety checklist. The trip took less than 5 minutes to get to the Georgetown Medical Center. Once there, Lawson and Gunny ran down the stairway to the parking lot where a man in a dark blue sedan shouted 'Gunny'. Both Lawson and Gunny ran to the car as the man flashed his badge and ID to them.

"It'll take us five minutes to get to the Watergate Hotel," the man said as he raced through the town toward the area known as 'Foggy Bottom'. It took him 4 minutes and 15 seconds when he pulled into the Watergate Hotel front entrance. Jumping out of the car, he threw the car keys to the valet on duty and raced into the main entrance with Gunny and Lawson following him. Once they went through the main entrance they slowed to a normal walk as they walked across the main lobby to a group of gold couches.

Lawson was struck by the layout and colors in the lobby. The lobby was expansive with horizontal gold piping making up the many enormous pillars spread throughout the lobby. There was horizontal gold piping along the whole counter area with the gold piping going from the floor to the countertop of the desk. There were exquisite silver cords spiraling up from several places on the check-in countertops with the counter estimated to be approximately 60 yards in length. The whole scene broadcast a sense of luxury and opulence.

As Lawson was taking in the beauty of his surroundings, Gunny shook hands with Captain Ben Garrison. Lawson watched their interaction out of the corner of his eye while he scoped the area and the people in it. Finally, he turned to hear their discussion.

"So he hasn't come down yet," Gunny said while Garrison looked at Lawson.

"No he hasn't, Gunny. Who's this," Garrison questioned as he faced directly at Lawson.

"Oh, Ben, this is my associate, Jim Lawson," Gunny answered as he realized he had jumped ahead without the general courtesies. Garrison shook Lawson's hand and turned back to Gunny.

Glancing over to the entrance area to the elevators, Garrison continued, "According to the bellhop, he hasn't come down yet. I don't know what the guy looks like so that's why you're here."

"Lawson knows what he looks like so he should be able to point him out," Gunny responded.

Lawson was slightly perturbed with the conversation as he could see they had no plan and didn't fully understand the risks. "Before you guys go off and put a bunch of people at risk, I think I better give you the full layout on what's going on and we need to do it quickly," Lawson abruptly advised as Gunny and Garrison looked at him with a startled expression. "Mark

Dietrich is an assassin. He will most likely be armed and have armed security people around him. He also knows what I look like and he may know what Gunny looks like, that part I'm not sure. Don't trust the bellhop. In every hotel I've been to in the world, they like to sell information and your wanting to know when he comes down is the type of information that's easy to sell." Gunny and Garrison looked at each other as they realized Lawson had full understanding of the threats and the need to change the approach.

"What do you advise us to do?" Garrison asked as he realized that this was an agency operation and not just a typical apprehension. "I have 5 armed men, and with you two, that makes 7. How do you recommend we place ourselves?"

"Before we do that, let me talk to the lady at the counter," Lawson stated. "It's typical for a person to check out of hotels like this by doing the checkout in their room. I can check to see if he has checked out from his room and if there are any instructions like 'bring my car to the garage or have a taxi pick me up in the back'. Something like that." With that comment, Lawson walked over to the counter while Gunny and Garrison continued talking. Moments later Lawson was back.

"The bellhop just texted me that he's on his way down," Garrison updated Lawson. "I guess this bellhop is one of those people that has some ethics."

Lawson smiled as he pointed to one of the police officers to move away from the hallway entrance that went to the elevator. "Dietrich has to come down as the lady at the counter told me he has to pick up something he left in the hotel safe," Lawson declared while starting to move to where he could step behind a pillar but still see the people coming from the elevator hallway. "I'd be getting into positon now. Gunny, you need to be at the counter looking at some brochures. Captain, your men need to spread out a little more in case there's gun play. Gunny and I will support you if things get dicey. Otherwise just watch me from the side of the pillar I'll be on. I'll motion to you who Dietrich is." Garrison nodded 'yes' as he turned and positioned his men. Lawson got Garrison's attention, pointed to one of Garrison's officers then pointed at Gunny. Garrison understood immediately and motioned for one of his men to go over to where Gunny was standing at the counter looking at brochures. Once the officer got over to where Gunny was at, they both acted like they were looking at the brochures together while Gunny watched the elevator hallway out of the corner of his eye.

About three minutes later three men walked out of the hallway to the check-in counter. Lawson could clearly hear one of the men ask for Dietrich's property from the hotel safe. None of the three men were Dietrich but Lawson distinctly heard one of the men say 'it's Mister Dietrich's items, here's the claim check'. Garrison was about to move when Lawson motioned for him to stay in place. Lawson knew the lady was not about to give the man Dietrich's property without proof of identification.

"I'm sorry but you may have a claim check but you are not the person that put the items in the safe," she said as she handed back his claim check.

"You don't understand," the man protested. "Mister Dietrich is very sick and has been taken to the Georgetown Medical Center. We need to get his property and get it to the hospital." Lawson pulled a piece of paper from his notepad he kept in his pocket, wrote something on it and walked over to the counter.

"Excuse me ma'am," Lawson interrupted.

"Don't you see we are talking? How rude can you be?" said the man with the claim check while facing Lawson.

"I'm sorry, sir, but you see I've got a flight to catch and I'm late," Lawson exclaimed as he moved his hand across the counter while holding the attention of the man he was addressing. The lady saw Lawson's move and the piece of paper he shoved under the reservation slip she had been working on.

"Well, you can just wait your turn," the man shouted as he turned back toward the lady. While the man was shouting at Lawson, the lady read the note. It said, 'stall him for 3 minutes'. She smiled and put the paper in her pocket as Lawson motioned to Garrison with 5 fingers. Garrison understood completely. He motioned one of his officers to follow Lawson as Lawson headed down the hallway to the elevator. Five seconds later Garrison motioned for Gunny and the officer with Gunny to go down the hallway. This went on until they all had gone down to the elevators where they waited until the three men came into the hallway. Lawson pushed the down button on one elevator and the up arrow on the elevator next to the one he had pushed the down button. As the elevator going down arrived, Lawson pushed one of the officers into the elevator and told him to hold the door. He did the same thing to the elevator arriving to go up.

"Was that the funniest thing you ever saw," Lawson exclaimed as he stood with his back to the three, laughed and motioned the others to laugh too as they looked at him, wondering what he was talking about. Realizing that Lawson was playing a con job, they immediately started laughing.

"I can't believe the buyers were coming to the meeting without any authorization to sign the agreement," Gunny chuckled as the others laughed at his comment. The three men pushed the down button and, seeing that the light went out immediately, realized another elevator going down had arrived at the lobby level.

"Oh, the elevator is here," Lawson shouted as they proceeded to enter the elevator. The three men followed them into the elevator before the doors closed.

Gunny hit the button for the lowest garage level then asked, "What level you guys need?"

"Level 2" came the answer. Gunny pushed the 'L2' button. At that moment, both Gunny and Lawson leaned against either side of the elevator where the button panels were located allowing for them not to be seen by anyone outside of the elevator when the doors opened.

The elevator stopped and, as the doors opened, Lawson took a quick peek and saw a man standing next to a car. "It's Dietrich," Lawson informed Garrison. At the same time, Lawson grabbed the box from under the arm of the man he had the confrontation with at the lobby counter as the man exited the elevator. As Lawson took the box, the man turned to see Lawson then felt the barrel of a pistol touching the back of his head as he heard Gunny say, "Do as I tell you."

Garrison followed the man and Gunny. He stepped out of the elevator then two of his officers stepped out right after he did. Dietrich immediately reached for his weapon in his belt holster when Garrison said, "I don't think you will want to complete that action," to Dietrich. Realizing he was outnumbered, Dietrich slowly pulled out the weapon and handed it to Garrison.

"You realize I have diplomatic immunity," Dietrich stated as he slowly pulled out his wallet and showed his diplomatic identification to Garrison. Garrison looked at one of his officers then back at Dietrich. As he handed Dietrich back his identification, Garrison realized his hands were tied, he had to let him go.

"No so fast," Lawson called out as he pushed the three men out of the elevator while pointing his weapon at them. "His immunity has been revoked by the German government after he is suspected of murdering an Interpol agent and taking his ID."

"James Lawson," Dietrich announced. "I should have known it was you behind this catch and grab. That was a good trick you pulled in Crete." Turning to Garrison he continued, "Do you realize I had Lawson dead to rights and he pulled a great shell game by getting himself ticketed on 4 different airlines. I figured you'd come back here, you know that."

"I know," Lawson acknowledged.

"You probably didn't count on me having a backup plan in case you followed me down here," Dietrich declared. As he did so, four men stepped out from two vans armed with Uzi machineguns. "I figured that you would walk into my trap."

"What have you gotten me into, Gunny?" Garrison asked as he realized Dietrich could not leave them alive. Gunny just shrugged.

"So, just as a professional courtesy, what's in the box?" Lawson solicited as he looked around at the people with guns on them and handed the box to Dietrich.

"Mister Lawson, don't you know that you could never overcome this much firepower. You've lost," Dietrich stated. "As for what's in the box, it's papers that gives me control over the European Union's funding program. In other words, when I get back to Germany I'll execute these documents and I will control seventy-two percent of the EU's monetary wealth. The Interpol agent I killed in Berlin was just about to deliver the papers to the assigned courier when I stopped him. You see, these papers are guarantees for payments from the EU headquarters in Brussels to nine member countries for loan guarantees. Without these documents, those countries will have their loans default in three days."

"But the EU headquarters can just reproduce the documents and sign them again, can they not?" Gunny probed.

"Actually they can't," Dietrich responded. "The papers include bank account numbers and access codes that are only located in one place, right here in this box."

"Well, I guess you can't fault us for trying," Lawson quipped.

"I'm glad I could answer your questions," Dietrich pronounced as he moved out of the way of his four armed killers.

"Did you get enough?" Lawson called out.

"We got everything, great job," came back Norman's voice. Dietrich turned and waved for his men to fire. They all hesitated when they saw SWAT team members and US Marines swarm the area. Two of the men pulled the triggers which resulted in a 'click' for each of their weapons just before the Marines took away the weapons from Dietrich's people and handcuffed them.

"How did you know our weapons wouldn't work?" an amazed Dietrich whispered.

"One of our agents accidently heard you talking to your people as they went out of the garage entrance here in the hotel," Lawson articulated. "You were heard to say that you had a scheduled appointment at the firing range and they were to fire all the old rounds they had as you had received a new shipment of match rounds for their weapons. We got into your room and switched out your rounds with dummy rounds the Marines use for training their people on how to load and chamber weapons. We figured you wouldn't look too closely at the rounds if we put them in the match round boxes. We figured we only had two hours to make the change so it was close but we were able to get the rounds flown in from the Parris Island Marine Recruit Training Center and exchanged them with your rounds in less than an hour and a half."

"You do realize that we are trying to stop the insanity that started in your government," Dietrich stated. "We are progressing to having countries being open and honest with each other and you and Cho Ming stopped us."

"I'm not going to stand here and argue the political ramifications of each of our approaches. Your approach assumes everyone plays nice. Look how good that works at the UN," Lawson angrily responded. "The United States is still a sovereign country and it intends to remain so."

"As you wish," Dietrich countered as he was being led away by US Marshals. "We are too embedded in your government to stop us. Your efforts are futile."

"That may be true as we're only seeing the tip of the iceberg," Lawson shouted as Dietrich was being led across the parking area. "I'm sorry it had to end for you this way as we are both in the same business. By the way, you've been in Washington a lot and we haven't. What's a good place to get seafood?

"Why don't you try Marku's? They have great fried scallops. I hope you choke on them!" Dietrich snapped back.

"Thanks, Mark," Lawson spoke as he smiled.

"Why are you treating the guy so nice? He was trying to kill us!" Gunny exclaimed.

"Just stop and watch Dietrich," was Lawson's response. Lawson and Gunny watched the police move Dietrich toward their van. Suddenly, Dietrich looked back with a look of fearful realization. "You see, Gunny, Dietrich just made a fatal mistake. In messages from 'Peacock', we were able to determine that the Deep State people were meeting at a fish place in Washington, DC. He just gave me the name of the fish place and he just realized it. You see, he was so used to talking freely among his own people about the fish place that, in the stress of the moment, he let the name out to someone not in his circle. Feel like some seafood?"

"Sometimes, Lawson, you really scare me," Gunny replied. "Sounds like we're going to have some fish."

"I'll let Roedl know what's going on," Lawson informed the rest of those remaining as he took Norman's arm and headed for the car she came in. "You take our car back to the Warfare Center. We'll meet you there," he said while throwing the other car keys to Gunny.

Chapter 18

Reality is not Necessarily Real

"How come is it that it always seems the more complex something is the less likely it is to be the truth and, with that observation, the simplest things are not necessarily that simple? I look at how easy someone does their job but when I try to do what they are doing, it's much more difficult than it appears. Maybe things appear simple because we've never had to do them ourselves." – Lieutenant James Lawson, US Navy CAT205 Special Operations Group Commander, ONI

Before coming back to Roedl's office, everyone had changed back into casual civilian clothes but had their weapons strapped to their bodies. Admiral Roedl sat watching the reaction of both Commander Norman and Lieutenant Lawson while Gunny and Myers tried to keep from laughing.

"Well, are you going to get married or not," Roedl demanded once again as they sat looking at him.

"We're thinking about it," Norman answered.

"You both obviously have some morals about your relationship," Roedl continued. "You don't live together and my guess is that you haven't had a sexual encounter but yet you seem so much in love with each other, what's stopping you?"

"Stopping us from what?" Lawson questioned as Gunny and Myers broke out in subdued laughter while Roedl gave them a disgusted look.

"From getting married!" Roedl shouted. Lawson just smiled as Norman started blushing at Roedl's outburst. "Lawson, for a smart guy you sure can be dumb sometimes!"

"What's so new about that?" Norman inquired. "We all know that he is exceptional when it comes to dealing with life and death situations but he's dumb as a rock when it comes to dealing with intimacy. When it comes to that type of relationship, women are the ones that have to make the moves and he'll come around to setting the date when he knows I'm ready."

"So what's stopping you?" Roedl asked again as he stared at Norman. She grabbed Lawson's hand in an attempt to irritate Admiral Roedl and it was working.

"It's simple, Admiral," Lawson explained. "Once we get married we will be separated from each other with one of us having to leave the team, that's Naval policy. It's not something you can circumvent. So we decided that, as long as we have something to offer to our team, we won't get married and break up this fine unit."

"Fair enough," Roedl acquiesced. "It's your lives and it's your decision. Now let's get down to business. We know the name of the fish place the Deep State people seem to meet in or frequent is called Marku's Seafood," Roedl observed.

"We do," Norman admitted, "and we are all going there this evening."

"I wouldn't expect anything less. Now, you all know there were a lot of things that caught you by surprise in your mission in Osh," Roedl admonished. "The two biggest ones being the drone attack on the people viewing the demonstration along with those also attacked inside the facility and the realization that Colonel Zhu was actually working to stop the plot. However, I have to give credit to you both for taking the time to listen to Zhu before you acted on the impulse to take him out."

"Thank you, Sir," Norman responded. "Lawson was the one that determined that Zhu was hiding something important. He gave Zhu the chance to explain himself plus Lawson said he got a text from you ordering him not to kill Zhu."

"True," Roedl agreed. "I also commend you, Beth, for having the foresight to remove Benson's firing pin from her pistol. That being said, how were you sure she had the same weapon that you removed the pin from?"

"It was the one without the silencer," Norman replied. "All of the rest of us had silencers on our weapons. It's the first thing I observed when we got into Zhu's office."

"Well done," Roedl complimented as he reached out his hand to Norman. "So, as you guys are going out to that seafood place after we're done here, I hope you all will ratchet your emotions down a little. We don't need an incident in the restaurant, just information on who's there. Here, use my credit card for the meals. If you see someone that might be able to identify you, leave immediately. We don't want to nullify the results we got from Operation Chaos. By the way, you all have a psychological debriefing of the mission on Monday morning. Don't miss it. One other note, the information we got on the chip that was in the silver hat band and the data on the jump drives you brought back to us gives us a clearer picture of what was going on and the depth of the conspiracy that was not only present in our agencies but in governments of other countries around the world. It was significant and global. It was a real effort to destroy international boundaries and turn us into a one-world government. We've arrested 117 people from within our own government and more arrests are coming. Now Lawson, Gunny and Myers, go ahead and get to the restaurant. Norman, I want you to stay for some last items then you can go."

The others left while Lawson and Norman remained sitting as a thought was forming Lawson's mind. Roedl stared at Lawson for a moment at which point Lawson got up from the chair, gave Norman a passionate kiss, which Roedl recognized was meant to send a message, then proceeded to walk toward the door of the office. As he stepped to the door he paused and turned toward the Admiral and Norman.

Lawson stood looking at the ceiling for a moment then spoke. "What…if…the whole thing was a ruse?" Lawson queried while looking at Roedl and Norman. "Zhu's got over 900 drones in China and he is there as well. What if Zhu's plan all along was to do the simultaneous drone attack against world leaders and the act of Zhu's taking out his people in Osh was just a cleaning up of unneeded personnel. That's what he did with Lavlery, isn't it? Zhu has proven that he is brutal and life has little value to him. After all, hasn't this whole operation been a series of diversions with Zhu in the middle of them. Just a thought." With that comment, Lawson left the office, went out through the reception area, then through the vault and down the corridor to the exit of the Warfare facility. He met Gunny in the portico outside the building and took off his weapon.

After he left the Admiral's office, Roedl and Norman looked at each other, realizing Lawson's comment was an obvious observation that no one had been considering or, if they had, it wasn't at the forefront of concerns.

"Oh my!" Roedl exclaimed as Lawson's comment set in. "We've been so focused on the results of the mission and all of the complexity involved in getting to a resolution, we never considered the possibility that Zhu could still be playing us."

"It fits," Norman added. "He had us believing he was our enemy then comes out as our friend. He played us well in that regard. What if Lawson is right? What if he is still playing us?"

Roedl picked up the phone and dialed a number. Moments later he said into the phone, "Codeword: Maximillian. Get me the President!"

"Where's Norman?" Gunny asked while Lawson put his weapon into his briefcase.

"She's got more business with Roedl but she will be joining us shortly at the restaurant," Lawson answered. "Where's Myers?"

Gunny took Lawson's briefcase as he responded, "He's already left for the seafood place. Remember that he's a Bostonian and has to get his seafood fix." They both laughed as they started walking toward the car.

"What was your first reaction to the overall impression of our mission?" Lawson posed as they walked.

"My feeling on this whole thing," Gunny replied, "is what Beth usually says when we are working these missions. Her concern always is where does the truth end and the lies begin." Lawson thought about Gunny's observation as they got to the car. The truth was very fuzzy in this most recent mission and the boundaries of reality seemed to escape logic. The psychological briefing on Monday should be interesting for all of them. As they walked to the car, the thought kept rolling around in Lawson's mind:

"What…if…?"

About The Author

Mr. T. James LeDoux is a U.S. Navy Vietnam veteran, having worked on river operations on the upper Mekong River with the Mobile Riverine Force and, at times, supporting the Office of Naval Intelligence in Vietnam in 1969 and 1970. His military experience extends from years 1968 to 2000, in both active and reserve service in the Navy, Army, Air Force and Coast Guard. In Coast Guard Reserves, he was part of the Coast Guard security team for former President Nixon's ocean-side residence at the Western Whitehouse (called La Casa Pacifica) at San Mateo Point in California.

During his life, as a design engineer and manager, he has designed numerous defense and commercial systems and products in both the high-tech hardware and software disciplines as well as managed many product development projects. His last 10 years were dedicated to training, mentoring and aiding technical leaders in managing high-tech development projects and people.

He also spent time as a technical investigator, investigating patent infringement claims and acting as an expert witness in court cases involving development processes in both hardware and software development projects. Along with Warren Yates, he developed the 'Control-Feedback-Abort Loop' concept for problem solution analysis being used in a number of high-tech companies to aid in determining how people will use products to solve problems.

He and his wife presently live in Colorado Springs, Colorado writing books, doing research on high-tech development and historical events, analyzing present international events and providing consulting assistance to up and coming design engineers in managing their teams.

He is author of several books on business management and historical subjects such as 'The Barbarians Guide to Management' (2012), 'Amateurs With Egos' (2013), and 'Trouble on the Grand Canal' (2013).

His novels include 'The First Real Christmas' (2012), 'Unsanctioned Protocol' (2017) and 'Breaking Protocol' (2018).

For other offerings of books written by 'T. James LeDoux', go to: www.ag3publishing.com.

www.ingramcontent.com/pod-product-compliance
Lightning Source LLC
Chambersburg PA
CBHW061942170626
46813CB00006B/2508